JEFF
LYNNE

JEFF LYNNE

THE **ELECTRIC LIGHT ORCHESTRA**

BEFORE AND AFTER

JOHN VAN DER KISTE

FONTHILL

First published in Great Britain in 2015 by Fonthill
Reprinted in 2026 by Fonthill
An imprint of
Pen & Sword Books Ltd
Yorkshire – Philadelphia

Copyright © John Van der Kiste 2015, 2016, 2020, 2026

ISBN 978-1-78155-492-0

The right of John Van der Kiste to be identified as Author of this work has been asserted by him in accordance with the Copyright, Designs and Patents Act 1988.

A CIP catalogue record for this book is available from the British Library.

All rights reserved. No part of this book may be reproduced, transmitted, downloaded, decompiled or reverse engineered in any form or by any means, electronic or mechanical including photocopying, recording or by any information storage and retrieval system, without permission from the Publisher in writing. NO AI TRAINING: Without in any way limiting the Author's and Publisher's exclusive rights under copyright, any use of this publication to "train" generative artificial intelligence (AI) technologies to generate text is expressly prohibited. The Author and Publisher reserve all rights to license uses of this work for generative AI training and development of machine learning language models.

The Publisher's authorised representative in the EU for product safety is
Authorised Rep Compliance Ltd., Ground Floor, 71 Lower Baggot Street, Dublin D02 P593, Ireland.
www.arccompliance.com

For a complete list of Pen & Sword titles please contact

PEN & SWORD BOOKS LIMITED
47 Church Street, Barnsley, South Yorkshire, S70 2AS, England
E-mail: enquiries@pen-and-sword.co.uk
Website: www.pen-and-sword.co.uk
or
PEN AND SWORD BOOKS
1950 Lawrence Road, Havertown, PA 19083, USA
E-mail: uspen-and-sword@casematepublishers.com
Website: www.penandswordbooks.com

Contents

	Introduction	7
1	'Come With Me'	11
2	'What?'	26
3	'Mr Radio'	39
4	'Roll Over Beethoven'	50
5	'Daybreaker'	66
6	'Mr Blue Sky'	80
7	'Don't Bring Me Down'	89
8	'Secret Messages'	98
9	'Handle With Care'	108
10	'Free As A Bird'	123
11	'A Long Time Gone'	138
	Personnel	159
	Discography	161
	Endnotes	177
	Bibliography	182
	Index	185

Introduction

On 14 September 2014, several hours of live music at the annual BBC Proms in the Park, Hyde Park, London, came to an end with a ninety-five-minute set by Jeff Lynne's Electric Light Orchestra. It was the first major concert Jeff had played in Britain since 1986, since the group he had helped to form in 1970 and led for most of their existence had quietly ceased to exist. Not only did a spectacular performance of hit after hit have punters and journalists clutching for superlatives throughout the next few days, but it also seemed as if the occasion had united the British music-loving public like nothing else. To call it the triumphant return of a British musical icon who had been anything but fashionable for several years would be an understatement. The general verdict was unanimous; the music of Jeff Lynne and ELO was cool once again.

Having already written at length on ELO's co-founder, Roy Wood, it seemed only logical for me to accord Jeff Lynne the same treatment. My admiration for the man and his music stretches back to the late 1960s, when I caught an all-too-rare playing of the odd single by the strangely underrated Idle Race on Radio 1, and through to the early '70s, when he joined The Move to assist in the birth of this fascinating new combo, the Electric Light Orchestra. Here is one fan's chronicle of that remarkable career.

For my sources I have trawled through much print and online archive material, and been helped by fans whose extensive knowledge often puts mine to shame. Particular thanks must go to two old friends, Martin Kinch of the invaluable Cherry Blossom Clinic website, and Gill at Magic

Arts, for their regular advice, encouragement, suggestions, and generous provision of illustrations and archive material above and beyond the call of duty. A big thank you also goes to everyone from *Face The Music*, particularly Andrew Whiteside, Rob Caiger, Neil Frost, Serena Torz, and others who were involved in what began as an A4 fanzine in 1986 devoted to ELO, Roy Wood, The Move, and associated acts, and some ten years and twenty-four issues later made the transition to an online information resource. In its print days (and years), I was happy to be a regular contributor and reviewer.

This is a totally unauthorised and, I hope, suitably impartial work, written with enthusiasm and as much objectivity as possible. I owe a considerable debt to the pioneering interviews of others, as well as to friends who have shared their anecdotes and knowledge. At the same time, I have not sought the co-operation of any of the musicians mentioned, although it has been my pleasure to catch ELO—both the Lynne-led combo and the later Part Two—live on occasion, meeting and chatting to some of them and even collecting autographs after the shows.

The majority of quotations are taken from a wealth of interview sources from the music press, fanzines, miscellaneous press cuttings, internet sites, and transcriptions from radio and TV interviews. Several of these are complementary and overlap each other, and it has not been practicable to cite the full original provenance. General sources are listed in the bibliography.

My thanks also go to Helen Macdonald of the Carl Wayne website; Paul Carless, Chris Charlesworth, Ilka Heun, Lynn Hoskins, Steve Mathieson, Keith John Sinclair, and Hans-Henrik Steensborg for their help in supplying of additional pictures and the benefit of their knowledge, and in generally spreading the word around Facebook and elsewhere online; to my old musical friend Miles Tredinnick, whose idea it was in the first place that I should write this book; and to Nikki Geary for reading through the final pre-publication draft. I would like to thank Alan Sutton and Steve Lambe, too, for their faith in the project throughout its transition to book form and to my editor Connie Long. Last but not least, as ever, I am grateful to my wife Kim—a professional musician who was at music school with ELO cellist Hugh McDowell, and whose ever-hardworking string quartet's eclectic repertoire includes 'Mr Blue Sky'—for reading through and advising me on various musical issues, putting up with an endless diet of ELO-related conversation, music, and endless re-runs on television and DVD at home.

N.B. Unless otherwise stated, all chart positions refer to the official British and album chart listings.

Introduction

1
'Come With Me'

When British historians come to assess the major events of 1947, two or three events stand out above all. It was the year in which much of the country endured what would prove to be the harshest winter of the twentieth century, with freezing temperatures and exceptionally heavy snow for the first few weeks if not months. In retrospect, although nothing to do with the weather, it would mark the start of the Cold War between East and West. Towards the end of the year, the general post-war gloom would be lifted to some extent, if briefly, by the spectacle of a royal wedding at Westminster Abbey—that of the future Queen Elizabeth II and the Duke of Edinburgh. Musically, it was a time of gramophone records which played at 78 rpm, with singles (before the term was in common usage) 10 inches in diameter. Within a couple of years, choice would be extended with the advent of the 12-inch, 33-rpm long-player and the 7-inch 45-rpm single. In 1952 there appeared for the first time the weekly singles chart (initially just a 'top twelve').

No less significant would be the births of several individuals who were destined to help shape the British popular music scene some two decades later and beyond. The roll call of 1947 included David Jones, Reginald Dwight, Mark Feld, and Colin Flooks, later known to their fans as David Bowie, Elton John, Marc Bolan, and Cozy Powell respectively. Those who as pioneering musicians and performers would retain the names with which they were born included Sandy Denny of Fairport Convention, Steve Marriott of the Small Faces, Dave Davies of The Kinks, Ronnie Wood of The Faces and later The Rolling Stones, Ian Anderson of Jethro

Tull, Mick Fleetwood of Fleetwood Mac, Maddy Prior of Steeleye Span, Greg Lake of Emerson, Lake and Palmer, and Brian May of Queen. Finally, at the tail-end of the year, there was also Jeff Lynne.

Jeff was born to Philip and Nancy Lynne in Birmingham, on 30 December 1947. It was, coincidentally, also the thirteenth birthday of the man who would become one of his idols and long after that his friend, American rock'n'roll pioneer Del Shannon. Jeff, his brother, and two sisters grew up in Shard End. At first, he showed no real passion for music, although he was briefly a member of a school choir and had a few piano lessons at his father's insistence. If any youngster growing up in the early 1950s was exposed to music, it would almost certainly be the classics, and young Jeff soon came to share his father's devotion. 'What first got me interested in music was my Dad, really,' he recalled in retrospect; 'he used to have a great record collection, but all of classical music—and a lot of these great writers.' Philip Lynne knew not only all the great composers, but could also name every bit of music, every movement, and so on. While he did not really play an instrument properly, he could work out melodies on the piano with one finger, and sing harmonies to songs on the radio. One piece of music from his childhood which always stuck in Jeff's mind was Dmitri Tiomkin's theme music from *The Quick And The Dead*, one of the major movies of 1954, which his parents took him to see when he was about six years old—'I remember being knocked out by it.'

1954 was also the year that rock'n'roll began to sweep all before it, the year that Bill Haley & His Comets recorded 'Rock Around The Clock' and Elvis Presley began his career in the studio by laying down 'That's All Right'. Within the next few years, several more names had joined the musical revolution, ranging from Chuck Berry, Little Richard, and Jerry Lee Lewis to Buddy Holly, Roy Orbison, Del Shannon, and the Everly Brothers. Some thirty years on, Jeff would contribute to the latter stages of the recording careers of three of these names.

I've always loved Del, he was my first hero when I was young. When 'Runaway' came out I was only 13 or 14. I had to have my own rock star. Well, they weren't called 'rock stars' then—they were all pop stars. But my sisters had had Elvis, and I loved Elvis of course, but you had to have your own hero. So Del Shannon was my one.

Del Shannon was also top of the bill at the first gig Jeff saw, at Birmingham Town Hall. But within two years Britain had The Beatles. Jeff was one of thousands of teenagers on whom the debut album, *Please Please Me*, released in the spring of 1963, had an indelible impact.

> I love the opening drumbeat and the bleed with all the drums leaking onto the guitar mics and sometimes onto the vocals if they did the whole track live. The sound of it, to me, was real, raw excitement. From their days in Hamburg they were so tight, and on that record it really shows how brilliant they were.

As for the opening track, 'I Saw Her Standing There', for Jeff it was

> [...] probably the greatest ever English rock'n'roll song ... as good as any old American rock'n'roll song, like the real thing. As good as a Chuck Berry tune or something. It was as solid as anything I'd ever heard or better. With the rock'n'roll records, I'd started playing a bit by then—not bad, but a bit—and this song was nice and simple, but don't let that simplicity fool you. Some of the hardest stuff to do is the simple stuff, to make it effective and make it real and make it worthwhile. I thought it was unbelievable and I still do. It was like giving it back to the Americans: 'ere y'are—we can do this as well!

Another major influence among the major British groups was The Who.

> They had something about them. It was like magic, the sound. And just watching Pete Townshend, he was always amazing. Did I ever catch them back in the day? Not half! The loudest bloody thing I've ever heard in my life!

At the time Jeff was attending Alderlea Boys' Secondary School, where some of his friends were equally besotted. His father bought him his first guitar, an acoustic, for £2, and when he was fifteen he formed a group with two contemporaries, Robert Reader and David Walsh. With their acoustic guitars and cheap amplification, The Rockin' Hellcats, then The Handicaps, and later The Andicaps practised at Shard End Community Centre, playing local gigs each week. For a while their drummer was Kex

Gorin, who later went on to play with Magnum and also Roy Wood's Helicopters. About two years later, Jeff left to replace Mick Adkins of local band The Chads.

Jeff was playing with Jeff Silvas and The Four Strangers at a church hall in Shard End in December 1963. It was here that guitarist Dave Morgan, whose path would cross with that of many a noted Birmingham musician over the years, met him for the first time. Jeff came up to him while they were taking a break during their gig, to ask if he could have a go on his guitar. Dave watched him strumming the chords to 'Glad All Over', the hit of the day by the Dave Clark Five, which was to break The Beatles' stranglehold on the top of the singles chart a few weeks later. He did not even know the lad's name, but recognised him just over a year later when he was playing in another group, The Chantelles; this same boy, now seventeen, turned up to an audition to answer an advert for a guitarist.

The group spent more time rehearsing in the drummer's garage than going out and playing actual gigs. They did, however, pride themselves on their vocal harmonies. During one of their rare gigs, Dave thought the harmonies sounded a little sparse, and when he looked round he saw that Jeff was deliberately standing well back from the mic. When he was tackled about it afterwards, he said that singing was for wimps, and he just wanted to play the guitar.

It was around this time that his fascination with the recording process began, and he bought a stereo reel-to-reel tape recorder, a Bang & Olufsen Beocord 2000 De Luxe. As far as domestic equipment in those days went, this was comparatively state-of-the-art, and he was one of the first people in the area to own one. The sound-on-sound facility, enabling its owner to overdub additional instruments and vocals to his or her heart's content, meant that Jeff was in seventh heaven experimenting with it, even 'until there's so much hiss you can't hear anything.' If the guitar he wrote all his first songs on taught him how to be a songwriter, he said, the tape recorder taught him how to be a producer. The front room of the Lynne family home at Shard End had been completely taken over by the aspiring teenage rock star. As another of his contemporaries also fired with musical ambitions noted, the room was a veritable Aladdin's Cave, filled with tape recorders, guitars, amps, records, wires and leads, and various assorted gadgets.

Meanwhile, Jeff went from group to group, playing small gigs on a regular basis. At least one member of the Lynne family could not believe the financial power of rock'n'roll, as Jeff mused in later life.

> My Mum one day said, 'Where the hell did that money come from in that drawer?' She thought I'd nicked it or something. I said I'd earnt it playing music. 'Don't be ridiculous. Where did you get that from?'

One of the most notable of the early Birmingham outfits was Mike Sheridan and the Nightriders, who released four singles on Columbia between 1963 and 1965, and two more on which they were billed as Mike Sheridan's Lot. None of them quite made it into the national top fifty, and in 1965 their teenage lead guitarist Roy Wood left to link up with other local musicians and break into the big time with a new group who were going to be called The Move. Mike, on the other hand, decided to put his musical career on a more casual footing.

The remaining members of the group—rhythm guitarist Dave Pritchard, bassist Greg Masters, and drummer Roger Spencer—then recruited lead guitarist Johnny Mann. Now simply called The Nightriders, they went into Pye Studios at Marble Arch with producer Claire Francis, and recorded several tracks with a view to selecting the best two for a single. But Mann's tenure with the group was short-lived—by the summer of 1966, he had moved on. It was time for them to place an advert in the *Birmingham Mail*: 'Keen new guitarist wanted'.

Having seen them at Shard End Community Centre several times, Jeff was thrilled at the opportunity.

> I just flipped! I couldn't believe it because they were my favourite group.

Throughout his career, he acknowledged that this was the event which helped more than anything else to launch his musical career.

> I'd been doing all these horrible little menial jobs, because I didn't really want to go to work—I wanted to play the guitar!

He passed the audition, the other members being impressed with his enthusiasm and ability as a singer and harmoniser, and ability to pick things up very quickly.

A further session took place at Hollick and Taylor Studios, closer to home this time at Handsworth, again with Claire Francis as producer. 'It's Only The Dog', written by Artie Wayne and Hugh McCracken and previously recorded by American garage band The Kingsmen, featured Roger on vocals. It sounded like a cross between The Troggs' 'Wild Thing' and The Rolling Stones' 'Get Off Of My Cloud'. Dave sang on the ballad 'Your Friend', which appeared on the B-side. Jeff's lead guitar on both owed something to the violin-like sound which Johnny had been developing before he left.

The contract with Columbia had expired by now, and they took the single to Polydor for release. It failed to create much interest, and fared no better than the previous 45-rpm singles. At this point a general rethink was called for. By common consent, it was agreed that Jeff was developing into a good frontman as vocalist and lead guitarist. They would start again under a new name, The Idyll Race (as in perfection), and somehow this developed into The Idle Race. Jeff recalled that they were indeed 'a lazy bunch', and legend has it that this handle was given to them sarcastically by his grandmother Evelyn Lynne, who thought that playing pop music was not a proper job. Dave Morgan's mother once asked Jeff why his group had such a stupid name. He thought for a second, then quipped, 'I can't be bothered to answer that!'

Much later on in his career, Jeff would say that one of the great things about being in the music business was no longer having to get out of bed at an unearthly hour. His mother would run upstairs at around 7.30 or 8.00 a.m. with admonitions of 'Get up, you lazy bugger.' 'I'm not getting up today—or ever again, Mum,' he retorted, 'I'm a professional musician!' All things considered, Idle Race was perhaps not an inappropriate name.

But being a member of the group was definitely hard work, and they soon had a busy date sheet. Once they had rehearsed a repertoire and got their foot on the ladder, they were taking bookings to go and play in a different pub or club in Birmingham nearly every night. Looking back on it over forty years later, Jeff recalled that these gigs were 'the best apprenticeship, if you like, that musicians could ever have.'

On the local scene, everybody knew everybody else. The Move, the group which Roy Wood and four others had formed at the end of 1965, had already paid their dues on the live circuit and released their first single on the new Deram label in December 1966. 'Night Of Fear' peaked at

No. 2 in the first few weeks of 1967 and put the city firmly on the map. They had been recording at Advision Studios, West London, and on Roy's advice engineers Eddie Offord and Gerald Chevin went to the Cedar Club in Birmingham to see The Idle Race live on stage. Suitably impressed, they offered to record the group and invited them to come and lay down some tracks at Advision, where they would act as producers while allowing the group plenty of artistic freedom.

One of the first tracks they recorded was 'Here We Go Round The Lemon Tree', a song which Roy Wood had written and offered them. He joined them in the studio, playing guitar on the session. Offord and Chevin were pleased with the results and, given Roy's success as a songwriter after he had penned both sides of The Move's first two singles, both top five hits, suggested that it should be The Idle Race's first single under their new deal. The American label Liberty had just opened a British office in London and was beginning to sign a few select British acts, the first being The Idle Race, The Bonzo Dog Doo-Dah Band (prior to shedding the two hyphenated words), and The Aynsley Dunbar Retaliation. By September 1967 it was all set for release as a 45, and the group obligingly posed for a promotional photograph around a real lemon tree with the song title displayed in large letters on a placard in front.

Only then did they learn that The Move had also recorded it, that their own version was also on the B-side of their new single 'Flowers In The Rain', and that both sides were receiving heavy airplay on Radio 1. Unwilling to be seen as a cover outfit, they prevailed upon Liberty to cancel the British release. It was issued in the USA and Europe, but without chart success. Meanwhile, The Move's record soared to No. 2, although their delight at healthy sales and having the first record played in full when BBC Radio 1 began broadcasting on 30 September was tempered when a promotional postcard featuring a suggestive drawing of Harold Wilson, the Prime Minister, led to a charge of libel and a court case. They lost and not only had to pay all costs, but also forfeit all royalties from 'Flowers In The Rain' to charities of Wilson's choice in perpetuity.

The Idle Race's sessions continued apace, with Jeff proving a prolific songwriter as well as accomplished guitarist and vocalist. All four members were also learning a good deal from the experimentation of their two producers, who spent hours in the studio trying to create new sounds all the time. Offord was fascinated with the idea of cutting up bits of tape with a razor blade and swapping them around, running them backwards, or splicing them into different sections of tape. The Beatles had thrown down the gauntlet on *Revolver* and *Sergeant Pepper's Lonely Hearts Club Band*, while The Rolling Stones and Pink Floyd were following them in venturing where rock groups had never gone before on record. The challenge was eagerly embraced by others, not least Messrs Lynne, Pritchard, Masters, Spencer, and their producers.

A few weeks later their first single arrived in the shops, both sides written by Jeff. 'Impostors Of Life's Magazine' boasted an oddly abstract lyric and quirky instrumental effects. 'Sitting In My Tree' was more of a music hall sound redolent of The Kinks, the story of an eccentric character who would sit alone in a tree, 'waving to the ones that wave at me,' while he recorded the numbers in a little book, asking for nothing more than for them to walk more slowly to be counted as they passed below. Its black humour and childlike naivety proved an accurate foretaste of the spirit of many other songs by Jeff which would be immortalised on vinyl during the next two years.

'Liberty's First British Produced Single,' the press release was proudly headed, as it announced the release date of 29 September. It informed the reader that the group had

> [...] a high reputation for originality [...] technically and artistically this record bristles with ideas and unusual sounds.... Double-speeded guitars in harmony impart a quaint and novel sonority to the instrument, a wah-wah pedal produces weirdly fascinating vocal-type sounds, and a device whereby the group utilise one cello note on a piece of tape—played at different speeds—produces a cello passage as if played by a *live* musician. A ghost cellist, in fact! Then there is a double-speeded piano passage, with a most peculiar echo effect, and a guitar tracked five times.

As for the lyrics, they made it

> [...] a song which tells the truth about people. We are all actors on life's stage—putting up a brave façade.

The effort expended in putting the carefully typed information on a single side of paper, underneath an imposing pictorial masthead, 'The

Liberty Bell', was not matched by attention to detail on the dark blue and turquoise record label itself. A production credit to 'Peanut Chevin' and 'Metric Offord' was fair enough, but the writer was very disappointed when he saw his name had been rendered as 'G. Lynn'. Having been looking forward to the arrival in the post of his new creation with his name on it, he opened the package with dismay.

> This thing comes, and I go, 'What the hell is that?'

Though it did not sell enough to reach the top fifty, there was some media interest all the same. An invitation from Radio 1 producer Bernie Andrews arrived to record the first of several Radio 1 sessions. Going from Birmingham to London to record for the BBC was a major event. As they had not had much experience of a recording studio, Jeff said, they were relieved to find it quite easy-going: 'You got to record and got paid for doing it. I think the fee just about covered the petrol from Birmingham.' As he aspired to be a producer himself, he learnt much from the experience, not least in the sartorial department.

> I even got some blue corduroy trousers just like Bernie's and wore them for my first attempt as a record producer, the second Idle Race album. From then on, corduroy trousers were always called 'Producer's Trousers'!

Over the next two years, the group recorded several sessions for John Peel's *Top Gear*, and *Top of the Pops*, a radio programme hosted weekly by Brian Matthew which also featured selections from BBC recording sessions assembled for syndication and export outside the United Kingdom. Despite the name, it had no connection with the better-remembered, long-running television show, which would remain beyond the group's reach.

Interest but poor sales continued to greet the group's subsequent singles. Like the first, both sides of the next two were written by Jeff. In March 1968 'The Skeleton and The Roundabout' was released. As the accompanying press release said, it was definitely different;

> Fast-moving and with a fairground atmosphere—which tells the tale of the Roundabout Man. Because business is poor, he gets rather

undernourished and transfers to the Ghost Train, where business is very good. Consequently he becomes rather obese and is transferred back to the Roundabout. No doubt there is a moral here somewhere, but the whole record is tuneful and amusing and with a rollicking tempo.

Singles were invariably issued in mono at the time, and the panning of the fairground organ-like intro from one channel to the other would be lost on listeners unless they acquired the album in stereo. The B-side, 'Knocking Nails Into My House', featured a lead vocal from Dave Pritchard, and the song was covered by fellow Midlands group Ambrose Slade (later Slade) on their debut album *Beginnings*, issued in May 1969 and later released in the US as *Ballzy*.

Radio 1 presenters John Peel and Kenny Everett were by now among Idle Race's staunchest cheerleaders in the broadcasting world, with the latter becoming Honorary President of the group's fan club. For the next two years, the group continued to aspire to the big time with the usual round of live gigs, including appearances at the London Speakeasy and Marquee Club, recordings, BBC sessions, and further releases. In June 'End Of The Road' was released, backed with 'Morning Sunshine', and three months later came the quirky 'I Like My Toys', coupled with 'Happy Birthday/The Birthday'. The latter A-side was one of the finest examples of its writer's black humour. It tells the story in the first person of an eccentric man of nearly thirty-one who has a train set, a garage, and a car, and of a soldier with a gun. At his time of life, his mother admonishes the former, he should have more responsibility. Joking aside, one can argue that people like this in the late 1960s were regarded as harmless oddballs and figures of fun. Only from a more enlightened perspective some four or five decades later might one consider that they were not merely eccentrics, but probably had a disorder somewhere on the autistic spectrum and were genuinely in need of help.

The B-side was an equally individual song, opening with the time-honoured 'Happy Birthday' singalong on cello, segueing into the mournful tale of a girl who had sent invitations to friends for her birthday the previous day. Nobody came, so she cried, took down the decorations, and fell off the ladder. Was this disturbing pairing of mini-epics the stuff of mass appeal for teenage buyers? Evidently not. A markedly inferior version of 'I Like My Toys' credited to Stewpot and the Save The Children Fund

Choir followed a few weeks later. Stewpot was Ed Stewart, a BBC radio and television presenter best known at the time for hosting the Radio 1 weekend morning request show *Junior Choice*.

While The Idle Race were in the recording studios later that year, working on their first album, they had an experience they would never forget. One day an engineer suddenly appeared to ask if any of them wanted to go down to Abbey Road Studios, where they could watch The Beatles at work on the sessions for *The White Album*. Aspiring to be a producer himself, Jeff for one did not need asking twice, and they were on their way immediately. The memory of it never left him, he said. Although they were 'chucked out' after about ten minutes, seeing his idols working together gave him a surreal thrill: 'To be in the same room as the four of them caused me not to sleep for, like, three days.' Less than thirty years later he would be in the same studio as three of them, doing much more than simply watching them at work.

In October the group's first long player was released. Following the theme of the preceding single, *Birthday Party* was in effect partly a concept album. Its thirteen tracks included the previous three A-sides and the B-sides of the last two singles. Jeff's imagination as a songwriter fully flourished in a clutch of other, out-of-the-ordinary tracks. The deceptively jolly 'Lucky Man', which belied its title as a tale of bad luck, included speeded-up and scrambled voices and tape effects, while 'Mrs Ward' was a light-hearted anti-military song. 'Don't put your boys in the Army, Mrs Ward,' the singer warned to a mock music-hall tune, presumably inspired by Noel Coward's 'Don't Put Your Daughter On The Stage, Mrs Worthington'. With disaffected youth and some of the more unashamedly radicals of the music scene openly speaking out against the Vietnam War—if not supporting and even joining peace demonstrations—it was timely fare indeed.

As if to underline the fact that Jeff did not have a monopoly on songwriting talent, Dave Pritchard wrote and sang 'Pie In The Sky', which clearly owed something to The Kinks, The Beatles, and significantly The Move. And to add to the album's conceptual flavour, the B-side opened with 'On With The Show', a song preceded by a fifteen-second montage of sound effects including snippets from the first two A-sides and brass fanfare presumably borrowed from the closing credits of a vintage children's cartoon film.

The packaging for the British release was also quite remarkable. Gatefold sleeves for single albums were expensive to produce and had not yet become the norm, except for The Beatles and The Rolling Stones, who were always guaranteed to recoup the costs. But a gatefold sleeve for The Idle Race it would be, with the group on the front holding a large invitation in fancy script, in which 'The Directors of Liberty Records' cordially invited everyone to 'The Birthday Party of The Idle Race'. On the inside was a black-and-white photomontage showing the guests all seated at large tables, an assortment including not only members of the group as small boys and adults, but also Radio 1 disc jockeys, The Beatles, Brian Jones, actor Warren Mitchell (in his most famous role as Alf Garnett of the controversial comedy *Till Death Do Us Part*), television games show host Hughie Green, and the Duke of Windsor. On the back was a key identifying them all. It was certainly an extremely arresting sleeve when viewed in the browser racks on the high street, and John Peel and Kenny Everett rallied to the cause, as ever, in playing tracks from the album on Radio 1. But once again, the public failed to respond in droves.

Although the group were beginning to become disillusioned by their lack of commercial success, they were still convinced, or at least hoping, that perseverance would bring its just reward. The friendship between Jeff and Roy Wood was still firm, and they met from time to time at the Pack Horse in Shard End for a friendly chat, or visiting each others' homes to raid record collections and make demo recordings. Like Jeff, Roy also enjoyed experimenting with two tape recorders, transferring from one to the other and building up the sound a little each time. They could actually multi-track on it, and 'used to get to a point where you'd multi-track so much that you could see through the tape!'

It was at Jeff's house that they worked on a demo of what would be one of Roy's most successful songs ever, 'Blackberry Way', beginning work one afternoon and working on arrangements until about 1.00 a.m., by which time the rest of the family were fast asleep. Roy had to kneel on the floor holding the mic and singing while Jeff and Dave Pritchard were holding a pillow around his face so that Jeff's parents would not be woken upstairs—but by that stage they were all giggling so much that nothing but laughter could be heard throughout the last verse of the song. Laughter apart, the final recording turned out very like the demo. It was the single that really changed The Move's style, as it was the first of Roy's own demos (instead of him going into the studio and explaining what he wanted). It featured mellotron and keyboards from Richard Tandy, a member of Birmingham group The Ugly's, who had played gigs with them on keyboards and bass guitar while their usual bassist Trevor Burton was nursing a broken arm. Released just before Christmas 1968, in February 1969 it made No. 1 for one week, becoming the group's only chart-topper.

The Move had already undergone a personnel change earlier in the year, when bassist Ace Kefford left and rhythm guitarist Trevor Burton took over the role. Within a few months, Trevor was increasingly at odds with the group's ever-more commercial direction, as personified by 'Blackberry Way', a make-or-break single following the complete failure of their previous 45, 'Wild Tiger Woman'. Trevor had thought this last record was heading for No. 1, while the rest of the group considered it nowhere near commercial enough, if not a major *faux pas*. At one gig he had an altercation with drummer Bev Bevan, slung his bass on the floor, and stormed off the stage, declaring he had had enough and was quitting. Now they were briefly down to a trio, The Move initially asked Roy's childhood hero Hank Marvin of the recently disbanded Shadows to join, but he declined. Next they invited Dave Morgan, but without success, and then Jeff. He still had faith in The Idle Race's eventual success and so likewise said no, and the vacancy finally went to another musician on the local music scene, Rick Price.

With a brace of critically-approved singles and a much-lauded album, all of which had failed to dent the charts, The Idle Race were becoming ever more restive. In the spring of 1969 they began recording their eponymous second album at Trident Studios, where they had the use of an eight-track machine for the first time. A regular visitor there was Marc Bolan, who as one half of the Tyrannosaurus Rex duo was enjoying modest chart success with singles and albums, but was likewise still looking for that elusive big break. One night on stage not long before, The Idle Race had broken almost spontaneously into 'Debora', Tyrannosaurus Rex's first single and a top thirty hit the previous year. Marc had been in the audience, and this was reportedly one of the factors which led him to reconsider his position and think about changing the line-up of his outfit from an acoustic duo to a full group, with him playing electric guitar. He was a devoted Idle Race fan and an admirer of Jeff's songs in particular. Now he would come and drop in on them in the studio, arriving at three o'clock in the morning while they were at work, sitting quietly in the corner barely saying a word.

Wearing the corduroy trousers to which he had once aspired, Jeff was now not only lead guitarist, lead vocalist, and main songwriter, but for the first time in his life also the producer, admittedly with help on some tracks from Noel Walker. He had had no experience, said Roger Spencer, but 'he just bluffed his way through it!' His fascination with the process and enthusiasm carried him through. Some years later, Jeff said that for him it was

> [...] the most thrilling thing in the world to go into a recording studio, see a blank reel of tape, fill it up with all these things, mix it down, and it comes out on a bit of vinyl. It's magic! It's the same feeling every time I look at it!

As more than enough tracks for the album were put down on tape, two were extracted for release as a stand-alone single in April. The curse of the record label typo struck again when the B-side, 'Worn Red Carpet', a Dave Pritchard song, was originally mistitled 'Warm Red Carpet'. The A-side, 'Days Of The Broken Arrows', was and would remain arguably the best song in their entire catalogue. Lyrically it was another dark number, with mysterious references to a little girl and a pretty teddy bear, birds falling from the trees, lines like 'don't be too sad when you're waiting for death,' and a message on the garden wall saying that 'Mickey Mouse is bad.' Musically, it was chock-full of hooks, starting off deceptively slow then picking up speed after the first verse, with at one point a melody line which for a few seconds sounded uncannily like The Move's 'Wild Tiger Woman'. Yet glowing reviews and a few plays on Radio 1 still failed to bring it the success it deserved.

The word was spreading, and Ray Coleman, editor of the pop and rock weekly *Disc*, described them after a gig at the London Speakeasy as 'the most exciting British group since The Beatles.' Glowing praise indeed, not least as The Beatles had long since turned their back on live performances, that famous and more or less spontaneous rooftop show on a freezing day in January 1969 being their last. In July, yet another Idle Race offering reached the shops in the form of 'Come With Me', coupled with another Pritchard-penned and -sung number, 'Reminds Me Of You'. The A-side was another very melodic number, with none of the dark overtones of the preceding single, and might have been tipped to appeal to would-be buyers who had found 'Broken Arrows' a little too chilling. It was not to be.

Idle Race, the second album, was released in November 1969, in stereo only, a few months after nearly all record companies had ceased to issue long-playing records in old-fashioned mono. It was a solid set of songs, arguably less eccentric than the first album. This time around, music hall influences were subdued in favour of a more standard pop sound. Distinctive touches persisted, however, particularly in the melancholy 'Please No More Sad Songs' with its ethereal harmony vocals, and the slower, string-laden 'Going Home'. 'The Girl At The Window' tipped its hat to the group they had seen at work the previous year with the line 'John and Paul and George and Ringo were playing lovely tunes, from the window of her room,' while 'Hurry Up John' married bagpipe-sounding guitar with harmonies reminiscent of groups like The Marmalade.

The vaudeville aspects had not gone completely. 'Mr Crow And Sir Norman', a mock-vaudeville number telling the story of a ventriloquist and his dummy—including overdubbed applause among other effects—would not have sounded out of place on an album by label-mates The Bonzo Dog Band (who had by now abbreviated their original name somewhat), while 'Big Chief Woolly Bosher', a kind of 'Running Bear' brought up to date, was a tale of Red Indians 'fighting for love and glory.'

However, to quote the title of the last track from their first album, it was the end of the road. For Jeff Lynne, two years with The Idle Race, a batch of distinctive singles, two lovingly-crafted albums, and regular Radio 1 sessions, had brought critical acclaim but no commensurate chart success. They were earning well on their live dates, including £200 a night on the college circuit for gigs such as a freshers' disco at York University in autumn 1969, supporting King Crimson. It was a good fee for a so far 'hitless' act, but even so, a new career path was beckoning for their ambitious frontman.

2
'What?'

While Jeff Lynne and The Idle Race were striving for the commercial success which should have been theirs from the beginning, something else was stirring nearby in Birmingham. Ever since The Move had recorded their first album, released in April 1968, their lead guitarist and songwriter Roy Wood had been increasingly frustrated by the limitations of a standard rock group line-up. He had taken to recording songs on his own, overdubbing all vocals and instruments, on what would later come to fruition in his first solo album. At the same time, he wanted to form another group which would be capable of using additional instruments like violin, cello, and French horn, and playing more experimental, classically-orientated music on stage. The Beatles were using an eclectic range of sounds on their records, but they were now a totally studio-bound creation. There was no reason why another group could not pick up the gauntlet and incorporate these instruments into their stage performances—or, in effect, continue from where The Beatles had begun with the cello-driven 'I Am The Walrus'. But to realise such a project would require far more cash than they as a group, record company, or management could afford.

Some of The Move's early songs had relied partly on string and woodwind arrangements from Tony Visconti, who had been assistant to their producer Denny Cordell. Roy had had the ideas for the string parts, but as he was unable to write them out in musical notation, he had to rely on Visconti to do them instead. When he went to the studio to hear and watch Visconti conducting the orchestra and hearing them playing his song, he was totally captivated. That, he said, was what started him 'off on the road to get ideas for ELO.' It occurred to him that there must be other young musicians playing classical instruments, such as cellos, violins, French horns, yet who would like to play in a rock band instead of an orchestra. Once the more ambitious tracks had been recorded with Visconti's orchestral arrangements, 'that's when I started to get bored with The Move, with the band, because I thought there was something more to it than that.'

The alternatives were either to develop the sound of The Move by adding these instruments and additional players, or else to plan a new group under a new name, and use The Move as a vehicle, hopefully making enough out of hit singles and gigs to finance the brainchild until the latter was big enough to take off under its own steam. His fellow members did not share his enthusiasm. When he drew pictures of how his ideal orchestra would look—including one with a cello section at the front and a picture of vocalist Carl Wayne playing timpani—the rest of them thought he had lost his marbles. Bev likewise felt it was too much of a risk to give up an established hit-making group in pursuit of this ambitious venture which could not be guaranteed to succeed.

Fortunately, there was at least one other like-minded musician and friend in Birmingham who could see the potential. Jeff had been invited to join The Move early in 1969 after Trevor Burton's exit but he refused, still hoping The Idle Race would make it one day. Several months later, realisation that they never would be really successful, combined with Carl's departure and Roy's interest in starting something new and more interesting, brought Jeff into The Move. During the last few days of February he completed his live commitments with The Idle Race, and then jumped ship.

The rest of the band thought that Jeff was the spark that they in general, and Roy in particular, had needed all along. The latter now had a new creative foil to throw down a friendly challenge as regards writing original material. Rick Price was convinced that Jeff's joining 'sent Roy in a completely new direction.' Roy agreed, welcoming the fact that they had two songwriters instead of one, and somebody whom he really rated as a writer. In Britain The Move were regarded as an out-and-out *pop* group. But on a short tour of America in the autumn of 1969, despite total lack of support from their US record label, they had been able to make a fresh start as a *rock* group, playing to audiences which had no preconceptions of them as a hit single factory.

The new project needed a name. During one of their initial conversations, the three members discussed the possibility of having a large light show along the lines of the one that Pink Floyd were using. That night as he went home, Roy thought about the BBC Light Orchestra, 'light' in this case describing the style of music. If they were to include a light show—and they were using electric instruments as well as electric lights—why not call themselves the Electric Light Orchestra?

Meanwhile, The Move still had a schedule of college and university gigs to fulfil. Now their frontman was gone, but in practice they had begun to assume something of a dual identity, as the shortly-to-be-released second album *Shazam* would demonstrate. Carl had taken lead vocals on the cover versions which were increasingly dominating the stage set, while, as the sole writer among them, Roy was doing the same on more and more of the original material. He was the obvious choice as lead vocalist, but he had been used to standing in the background playing guitar and adding backing vocals on stage. As one who disliked the idea of pushing himself, or even being pushed, into the spotlight, such a role suited him. Basically, he was shy and self-effacing, ready to admit that he was not great at conversation and found small-talk difficult. Yet as the obvious singer as well as the lead guitarist, he could hardly have had it otherwise.

The new Move's first gig with the new line-up, in Dublin, would prove a memorable affair—but for the wrong reasons. As they came on the MC gave them the customary big build-up on stage. Preparing to launch into the opening number, Jeff casually walked to the front of the stage, and as a safety test gently touched the neck of his guitar against the microphone. The resulting blue flash and bang sent him reeling. To his horror, when he looked at his guitar, he saw that all six strings had completely blown off, and the neck of the instrument was charred black. Showing Roy what had happened, he left the stage somewhat shaken to restring his guitar, leaving the now three-piece group to start the show without him. Had he touched the mic with his lips, he would not have lived to tell the tale.[1]

Yet within a few weeks Jeff would be in the charts. The first recording by the newly-reconstituted group, 'Brontosaurus', was released in March. A kind of heavy metal dance song with tongue-in-cheek lyrics, it was built around an engaging guitar riff and ended up as a frantic rock'n'roll duel between slide guitar and Jeff's boogie piano. For some weeks it seemed destined to disappear quietly, especially after unenthusiastic reviews from journalists who preferred The Move's more poppy sound. But an appearance on *Top Of The Pops* and plays on Radio 1's contemporary show *Sounds Of The 70s* helped boost it to No. 7 in the charts. The B-side, 'Lightnin' Never Strikes Twice', written by Rick Price and Mike Tyler (the real name of Mike Sheridan) and with Rick on lead vocal, had been recorded shortly before Jeff joined.

But regular interviews which Roy, Jeff, and Bev were giving to the music papers about the launch of ELO made it obvious where their interest lay, with talk of a nationwide tour as soon as the right musicians to augment them could be found. It eventually reached the point where a *New Musical Express* reader, claiming to be tired of reading about it, wrote a letter which was published in the paper urging Roy as the public face of The Move to put an advert in the small columns for the right musicians and give everyone else a break.

The aim of the project, Roy said, was to break down the barrier between classical music and rock, by bringing them together for the first time. It had recently been tried by The Nice, who had disbanded early in 1970 and left keyboard player Keith Emerson free to form the classically-influenced trio Emerson, Lake and Palmer, and also by Deep Purple, whose classically-trained keyboard player Jon Lord had composed a 'Concerto For Group And Orchestra', first performed at the Royal Albert Hall in 1969. Both outfits had to acknowledge that the fusion of classical and rock musicians had only been achieved in part.

During their brief cabaret days the previous year, The Move had been managed by Peter Walsh; in 1970, they acquired a new manager in Don Arden. While Don initially shared Bev Bevan's misgivings about the viability of this eccentric new project so eagerly embraced by Roy and Jeff, after a meeting with the group and representatives of EMI Records, he opened negotiations for an advance against any future sales. EMI likewise had their reservations. The Move had been a consistently successful name with a good track record on the singles charts, and they insisted that the group should keep going. Only then would they accept an experimental album by the untested new project as well.

With his uncertainty about the ELO concept, and having just launched a record shop, Heavyhead Records, in Birmingham, Bev was regarded as the best businessman of the three, and he encouraged them to carry on with The Move in order to finance the new group. While Roy and Jeff were full of musical ideas, he thought they were reluctant to give sufficient thought to more mundane, practical considerations. On his shoulders fell the task of trying to organise the recruitment of other musicians and rehearsals, as well as getting the funds together to make it all possible.

In September The Move signed a deal with EMI as 'The Move performing under the name Electric Light Orchestra'. This made provision for three albums plus singles over the next three years, which would be released on the Harvest label, launched the previous year as a new outlet for EMI's more 'progressive' and experimental acts, including Deep Purple, Barclay James Harvest, the Edgar Broughton Band, and Tea & Symphony.

A few weeks earlier, they had begun recording in the studio. '10538 Overture', a song about an escaped prisoner with a number instead of a name—and with something of a resemblance in the opening chord sequence to The Beatles' 'Dear Prudence'—had been written by Jeff. It was originally intended as a The Move B-side, but soon it took on a life of its own and was now talked about as being the forthcoming first ELO single. As soon as they started working on it, Jeff immediately thought they had something special. As well as writing it he played the big guitar riffs, while Roy experimented with adding phrases from the brand new Chinese cello he had just bought for £30. 'We started overdubbing that onto this track we'd just done,' he said, 'and it started sounding like this orchestra we'd had in mind for all these months.'

After bass and drums had been added, Roy took it into the control room while they listened to the playback, scraping away on the cello in 'I Am The Walrus' fashion. Jeff was so enthusiastic with what he was hearing that he insisted they add it to the track there and then, and Roy ended up putting about ten cello parts, maybe more, on the track. Meanwhile, Bev and Rick, who had had enough of the song for the moment, had gone home. They left Roy and Jeff to run riot in overdub paradise until, in their words, it sounded 'like some monster heavy metal orchestra.' Roy later erased Rick's bass tracks and overdubbed his own.

When they came to record the vocals between them, Jeff was looking for a title. After staring into space for a while, they noticed the serial number on the modules of the recording console, 1053. An extra digit was needed to make it scan, and it ended up as 10538. They did a rough mix of the track, and both took a cassette home which they played non-stop for a while. While travelling to gigs to fulfil the last few bookings they had been contracted to play as The Move, Roy and Jeff were demoted to the back seat, out of reach of the cassette player in order to try and prevent them from putting the track on yet again. They circumvented this by bringing their own portable cassette player with two speakers in the back, and played it again and again, 'to the point where it got up everybody's nose.'

Had Roy and Jeff had their way, The Move would have been consigned to history forthwith so they could concentrate full-time on ELO. But when the EMI contract was signed, there were one more Move single and one more LP to fulfil the deal with Fly Records, as the Regal Zonophone label (their label from 'Flowers In The Rain' onwards) had effectively become. The track chosen for the A-side of the new single was another heavy rock'n'roll epic, 'When Alice Comes Back To The Farm', featuring similar instrumentation to 'Brontosaurus', with the addition of Roy's multi-tracked cello, and an interesting tempo change or two. Despite a new release slot on *Top Of The Pops*, it failed to chart.

Both of the 1970 Move singles appeared on the subsequent LP *Looking On*. Packaged for the British—though not the European—market in a sleeve with a picture of bald heads and no photograph of the band anywhere (the band were certainly not the baldies on the front), made up of completely original material, and recorded between May and August 1970, it was quite democratic in terms of writing credits. Four of the eight tracks were Roy's, two were Jeff's, a final short one was written by both, and for the first time there was one by Bev.

Some thought that *Looking On* was The Move's lamest LP of all, a grim exercise in heavy metal bandwagon-jumping, unrelieved by the spontaneous if corny humour of *Shazam*. In Bev's words, it was 'a bit ploddy.' But it was a more colourful work than its predecessor, arguably self-indulgent in places but lightened by Roy's inventive use of oboe and sitar in places as well as Jeff's two songs, the melodic 'What?' (also the B-side of *Alice* and an early forerunner of ELO balladry) and the semi-jazzy 'Open Up Said The World At The Door'. Bev's 'Turkish Tram Conductor Blues' was a riff-orientated rocker in the 'Brontosaurus' mould, complete with saxes, described by him as 'the sort of thing the Wild Angels might like to play.'[2] Perhaps strangest of all, the opening title track was based on heavy guitar riffs and solos, broken up by sweeping piano interludes and a vocal more like Black Sabbath's Ozzy Osbourne than Roy Wood, and then turned into an instrumental with jazzy guitar, sitar, and oboe.[3] The effect was of a song and instrumental merged together, both with different tempos.

The album's longest track, 'Feel Too Good', a nine-minute marathon, started out as a studio jam with Jeff instead of Bev on drums. P. P. Arnold, a former singer with Ike and Tina Turner who had enjoyed some success as a soloist in the '60s, and Doris Troy appeared on backing vocals. It was followed by a short hidden track, 'The Duke Of Edinburgh's Lettuce', a charmingly absurd snatch of doo-wop which then went into a singalong around the pub piano, credited to Roy and Jeff as co-writers. A further song written by Jeff, 'Falling Forever', was recorded around this time and broadcast as part of a BBC radio session but never made it to official release.

Bev thought the record suffered from their not having enough songs to start with, and from their having to contend with 'Roy's never ending line of weird and wonderful instruments,' which rather tested his patience. The drummer would go out for a break to the cinema, and when he came back Roy was still experimenting with a part on cello. With some tracks, which he admitted to find downright embarrassing, he would put the drums on afterwards, and had to play out of time to keep in with them properly. When it came to promoting the record, he had to do all the interviews with the music press. Having been less involved in the recording than Roy and Jeff, he freely admitted that he sometimes had little idea what he was talking about.

Again, *Looking On* never sold in sufficient quantities to make the album chart. The second single's failure might have been a contributory factor, coupled with lack of promotion by Fly Records. The Move had announced they were leaving the label, and Fly's interest was in any case fully taken up with its flagship act, T. Rex. As Tyrannosaurus Rex the duo had been something of an underground cult act, and having shortened their name they were about to become the biggest band in British pop since the recently disbanded Beatles.

During the closing months of 1970, The Move were still playing live regularly up and down the country, with Rick doing most of the talking between songs. The set list generally contained five tracks from *Looking On*, all but 'Open Up' and 'Feel Too Good', The Beatles' 'She's A Woman',

'Lightnin' Never Strikes Twice', and 'I Can Hear The Grass Grow'. Calls from audiences for 'Flowers In The Rain' and 'Blackberry Way', evidently now seen as part of the pop heritage they were trying to shake off, went unheeded. At one gig in September, the audience were asked to pause for a moment in memory of Jimi Hendrix, who had died the previous day.

Rick left The Move shortly after their final gig. The Electric Light Orchestra was now obviously their priority, with Roy and Jeff co-producing the album, and Jeff, he said, 'was never the underdog in any shape or form.' Jeff was writing a large number of songs and Roy was adding finishing touches to them, and Rick realised there was no longer any place for him. As he had a family to support, he could not afford to give up live work and make a living off his modest share of Move royalties. So by early 1971 the group were reduced to a trio, existing almost completely on record and television only. Even at this early stage Jeff was not keen on touring, and much happier once they were more fully studio-bound, especially as he was finding live work a distraction from creating and recording new songs. With him, it was a state of affairs which would never really alter.

The last months of 1970 and the first of 1971 saw the creation of two new albums by one group operating under two different names. For Jeff, the main concern was completing sessions for the debut Electric Light Orchestra album, recorded at Philips Studios, Marble Arch, at various times between July 1970 and June 1971. Once '10538 Overture' was finished, more tracks awaited their attention.

Roy and Jeff were in seventh heaven with their new creation. But as time went on, Bev became increasingly frustrated with what seemed like excessively slow progress, wondering whether they would ever come to the end of a full album, let alone be ready to perform on stage. He would wander into the studio, an environment which he did not enjoy for its own sake, disliking the claustrophobic atmosphere and 24-hour darkness. Jeff was in the control box and Roy was there with his cello, both urging him to have a listen to what they had just done. Next day he would return to find them in the same places—still overdubbing cello and still working on the same song. Recording costs were escalating to a horrendous degree as they worked till 3.00 or 4.00 a.m., then grabbed some sleep and began the next working day around midday in the King and Queen on Edgware Road, where they stayed there until 3.00 p.m.—Roy clutching a couple of bottles of vodka and Jeff a crate or two of beer.

Of the remaining eight tracks which were eventually done and dusted and made it onto the album, four were by Jeff and four (including two instrumentals) by Roy. Their intention to carry on where the Fab Four had left off was self-evident, in songs evoking parallels with The Beatles' more adventurous phase from the *Revolver* album onwards. The second song of Jeff's (following '10538 Overture') was 'Nellie Takes Her Bow', about a girl seeking fame and fortune on Broadway. It started off quietly, with mainly cello behind echo-soaked vocal, before almost turning into a different piece altogether with a brisk drum roll and some striking, almost oriental violin work, harking back to a 1930s Palm Court ensemble, at which point the horns and cello began playing variations on a theme of 'God Rest Ye Merry Gentlemen'. On the other side of the original album were three more of his compositions. 'Mr Radio', which Jeff called 'a quirky one made to sound like a 1920s recording, deliberately having no bass part,' appropriately started with a few seconds of sound effects from a radio being tuned in on the dial, before the writer's piano and Lennon-like vocal delivered a song about a man who has just his radio for company now his wife has left him. It was supplemented by more inventive strings, sounding in part as if played on a reversed tape, yet in the same breath reminiscent of one of Beethoven's string quartets. 'Queen of the Hours' was another of his dreamy songs, featuring mysterious poetic lyrics, crunchy sawing cellos and horns, and a faint but very pretty acoustic guitar in one channel. A third instrumental, 'Manhattan Rumble (49th Street Massacre)', sounded at the start like a rather martial piece of film music—mostly piano with cello and drums providing a kind of stately rhythm, woodwinds plus horns producing a brass effect. Then a tempo change, and the piano suddenly plays a tune from an old music box, after which more Jazz Age tunes takes over. As a fusion of jazz, pop, and the classics, it was arguably the most ambitious piece on the album.

As for Roy's two songs, 'Look At Me Now' recalls The Beatles' 'Eleanor Rigby', with its multi-tracked cello, woodwind, and horns sounding like a medieval crumhorn, and acoustic guitar intervening shortly before the end. The closer, 'Whisper in the Night', opened with a lightly-picked acoustic guitar and church bell chime, introducing a hymn-like song with choral vocals joining in softly a little later. Of his two instrumentals, 'First Movement (Jumping Biz)' was unashamedly influenced by Mason Williams's 1968 hit 'Classical Gas', a glorious mix of melody, acoustic guitar, drums, strings and woodwind. 'The Battle of Marston Moor (July 2nd, 1644)' opened with a speech from Roy 'Oliver' Wood berating King Charles I as a prelude to a piece featuring mainly cello, horns, multi-tracked recorders—adding a slightly Jethro Tull flavour—and drums, which Roy played as Bev refused to do so because he disliked it so much. To this day it remains probably their most *un*loved track of all time.

The credits on the sleeve made it clear that the record was very much a studio creation. In addition to the two main creators sharing vocals, Roy was responsible for cello, oboe, acoustic and slide guitars, string bass, bassoon, clarinet, and recorders, while Jeff provided piano and electric guitar, and both played percussion. Bev provided drums and additional percussion, with the only other two musicians involved at this early stage being Bill Hunt on French and hunting horn, and Steve Woolam on violin.[4] An interesting selection of black-and-white photos appeared on the inside spread of the gatefold sleeve, while the front and back pictures were both taken at the Banqueting House, Whitehall, to emphasise the baroque and classical theme. One showed a huge lightbulb in the middle of the floor in an empty room, while the other was a bird's-eye view of the three principal musicians in eighteenth-century court costume; Jeff with violin, Roy with cello, and Bev, sporting a tricorn hat, with flute.

When the album was released in November 1971, reaction from the music press was positive on the whole. Roy Hollingworth of *Melody Maker* hailed it as 'magnificent' and 'a fascinating album,' calling it 'the most relevant release on Harvest since Pink Floyd's 'Ummagumma', as it invited listeners to imagine a combination of *Sergeant Pepper*, 'Strawberry Fields Forever', 'I Am The Walrus', The Move, Ray Davies, and The Idle Race gigging together. He also congratulated Roy effusively twice in the first five sentences without mentioning Jeff at all, an ominous sign of things to come. Despite a generally favourable reaction, yet again sales were modest, and for its first nine months on sale the album failed to dent the charts any more than the last three Move or Idle Race albums ever did.

One of the most enduring misunderstandings in music history came after a deal was signed to release the album in America on the United Artists label. Somebody in the office asked a secretary to phone Don Arden for the title of the record, but she could not reach him so she left a message on the pad saying, 'No answer'. When the company boss saw it, he thought that was the title, and it stuck.

In retrospect, ELO's first album—in which they were clearly experimenting and finding their feet—underlined the musical differences between the two joint leaders, and the pushing and pulling between the different dynamics. On balance, Jeff's songs leaned closer towards commercial pop, albeit with an imaginative or even progressive twist, and with an undeniable nod to The Beatles' latter phase. Roy's often quirky songs and instrumentals were a long way from the early '70s pop/rock-based material he had been writing for Move singles and albums, with nods to the English folk tradition, a hint of medievalism, and a contemporary strain of classical music.

Recorded in parallel was the fourth and what they knew would probably be the final Move album. It had been preceded by two non-album singles. 'Ella James' was originally scheduled as the first, and promotional copies were pressed but withdrawn when they came up with the more commercial 'Tonight', in May 1971. 'Chinatown' followed at the beginning of October. All three titles were written by Roy, although Jeff sang lead vocal on one verse of 'Tonight' and 'Chinatown'. He also wrote and sang the B-side to the latter, 'Down On The Bay', a gritty rock'n'roll number which sounded more like Chuck Berry and Elvis Presley jamming with the new denim-clad Status Quo than anyone else. More appearances on *Top Of The Pops* and generous airplay greeted both singles: 'Tonight' peaked at No. 12 in the charts and 'Chinatown' at No. 23.

Message From The Country was also released in October 1971, once again to positive reviews but, as ever, modest sales. Of the ten tracks, four were written by Jeff, four by Roy, one by both, and one by Bev. The whole set was a genuine collaboration from start to finish, with the front cover painting by Roy based on an idea from Jeff. Yet again, Jeff's songs showed a marked Beatles influence for the most part. 'No Time', a semi-acoustic folksy ballad, was swathed in recorders and bore something of a Paul McCartney imprint, while the complex, percussion-heavy 'Words Of Aaron' immediately called the coda of 'Strawberry Fields Forever' to mind. Notwithstanding some inventive woodwind towards the end, 'The Minister' had more than faint echoes of 'Paperback Writer'. As for the title track, this bore similarities with '10538 Overture', minus cellos. Two of Roy's songs, the near-single 'Ella James' and 'Until Your Moma's Gone', were clearly in the rock'n'roll tradition, while 'It Wasn't My Idea To Dance' was closer to sophisticated jazz-rock, and 'Ben Crawley Steel Company' was a spoof country number with Bev on vocals. The drummer's song, 'Don't Mess Me Up', sung by Roy in an ersatz Elvis and the Jordanaires fashion, was a rock'n'roll tune that leant heavily on Presley's 'Mess Of Blues'. To complete the album was a song credited to Roy and Jeff, a light-hearted, music hall singalong, 'My Marge'.

The band knew it would probably be their swan song, and so in Roy's words they just decided to enjoy themselves. Jeff said it was 'all about experimentation, weird stuff and being silly.' Bev called it 'eclectic,' and named it as probably his least favourite Move album, although he conceded that it did exude a sense of fun, 'which was rare at that time, with many other bands taking themselves far too seriously.'

Most of the bass guitar was played by Roy, in addition to the sax and woodwind instruments. As with the cello, which was not used on the album, he had lately developed a keen interest in the oboe so he could play it onstage when ELO began gigging. He was increasingly bored with playing guitar, and Jeff had now more or less taken over as their lead guitarist. As to where in 1971 did The Move finish and ELO start, Roy emphasised that they were trying to keep both as far apart as possible. He wrote in two totally different ways for both, always conscious of not putting strings on a Move record in case it came out like ELO, and keeping saxes out of the latter. Although Jeff was contributing Move B-sides and album tracks on which he sang lead vocal, as the new member he seemed content to let Roy remain the kingpin. With ELO, he doubtless saw it as more of an equal partnership.

Also in October 1971, The Move played what was their first gig in about a year, and what would also be their last. A testimonial for long-serving Birmingham City footballer Ray Martin, it took place in the Swan pub, with The Idle Race and Raymond Froggatt also on the bill. Augmenting them on rhythm guitar was Richard Tandy, who had virtually become a member of The Move in their final phase in all but name. A former schoolmate of Bev, he had been a guitarist with The Chantelles, one of the most hardworking names on the Birmingham live circuit, before joining The Ugly's. He also worked as an occasional guest musician with The Move, and then after Trevor Burton's departure forming a new, short-lived group, Balls with him. On this farewell gig they played a set including 'I Can Hear The Grass Grow', 'Fire Brigade', and 'Tonight', Jeff's 'Down On The Bay', plus covers of 'Great Balls Of Fire' and The Beatles' 'She

Came In Through The Bathroom Window'. At around that time they also appeared on the German television show *Beat Club*, playing 'Ella James' joined by Bill Hunt on piano, 'The Old Grey Whistle Test', and 'Words Of Aaron' with Roy on bass.

What turned out to be the final Move release was recorded in December 1971 and hit the shops four months later. This farewell maxi-single was one of their best and most successful, putting them back in the top ten for the first time since 'Brontosaurus'. The A-side, 'California Man', was a glorious Jerry Lee Lewis inspired rocker with multi-tracked sax, pounding piano, and Roy and Jeff sharing lead vocals on different verses. On the B-side were 'Ella James', and another brand new track, Jeff's 'Do Ya', which became The Move's only US Billboard Top 100 hit when released as a single in October, climbing to a modest No. 93. When Jeff incorporated it into ELO's stage act some time later—the only Move track to be thus honoured—the reaction was so favourable that they re-recorded it on the *A New World Record* LP in 1976.

3
'Mr Radio'

The first ELO session for BBC Radio 1 was recorded for Bob Harris's *Sounds of the 70s* at BBC Radio Birmingham on 4 February 1972 and broadcast ten days later. At around this time Richard Tandy joined them initially on bass guitar, thus relieving Roy of the necessity of playing it so he could concentrate on his other instruments. He also played a part in helping them to oversee the project, and they gradually began recruiting additional musicians. They had started putting out feelers for extra players, particularly more cellists and violinists, so they could start that all-important first tour. Cellist Andy Craig was the first to come on board, although he did not stay for long.

Rehearsals were held at Roy's house, punctuated by regular calls on the telephone from Don Arden to ask when they would be ready for that long-awaited first tour. Under pressure, after several such requests they agreed with some reluctance to go out on the road in March. A large sum was spent on advertisements in the press for gigs that month in Birmingham, Liverpool, and Wolverhampton, but all were cancelled as they did not yet have the right sound, let alone the necessary musicians to reproduce the album adequately in concert. At length they recruited violinist Wilf Gibson, soon to be known as Wilf-VAT-Gibson, as his terms were £15 a day for rehearsing, plus expenses and VAT, and cellists Mike Edwards and Hugh McDowell. The venue for rehearsals was then moved to East Birmingham Working Men's Club, where they apparently spent much of their time playing snooker.

After endless assurances given to Don and David Arden that everything was coming on fine, that all-important live debut could not be postponed any longer. ELO took the stage for the first time on 16 April at the Greyhound, Croydon, which had a policy of featuring live progressive music once a week. Accompanying Roy, Jeff, and Bev were Bill Hunt on piano, Richard Tandy on bass, Wilf Gibson on violin, Hugh McDowell, Mike Edwards, and Andy Craig on cellos. Sympathetic critics who had been eagerly awaiting the show acknowledged that this was indeed very innovative, but admitted that, to an impartial observer, the sound left much to be desired. The group's three main members could not have agreed more.

In spite of optimistic interviews with Roy, Jeff, and Bev, and praise from some of the more partisan music journalists who had always loved The Move and were keen to give them the best possible heads-up, the show at Croydon and the other early gigs were less than spectacular. Five dates scheduled and advertised throughout the second half of April, including venues at Bangor, Hemel Hempstead, and Hanley, were cancelled, and they did not return to live work until the beginning of May. Jeff played guitar at every one, while Roy alternated between cello, bassoon, and oboe in addition to sharing lead vocals with him, and as he was playing different instruments on stage, his leads invariably became entangled. The audiences were not quite sure what to make of this intriguingly unorthodox outfit.

Now in his mid-forties, Don Arden's interests in the group were strictly entrepreneurial. Whether the album was regularly—or ever—on his hi-fi at home in the evenings, nobody was to know. But he was clearly not their biggest fan. On the contrary, at this stage he was dismissing them, or at least their performances on stage, as 'a classical orchestra gone mad, with this awful, distorted heavy-rock guitar thrown over it.' His son David, who was part of the management team and also of the same generation as the group, was often in attendance at their shows but seemed too embarrassed to make it obvious to anyone else that he was responsible for what his father's generation would have called 'that racket'. After the show he came backstage, trying to smile and telling them rather unconvincingly that it had been 'nice'. It was not the word any of them would have chosen. Jeff admitted that he 'was probably too drunk to notice' how bad the sound had been, and was doubtless not the only one. Before the earliest gigs they would be found at the nearest pub, anaesthetising themselves generously with lager (Jeff), vodka (Roy), or brandy and dry ginger (Bev), followed by a curry to mop the alcohol up, and arriving on stage in a state of what they called 'bloated bliss.'

A British music press advertisement for ELO's first dates, March-May 1972, some of which were subsequently cancelled

Pioneers generally have a rough ride when it comes to technology. In those days, ground-breaking rock musicians blazing a path for electric orchestras were some way ahead of what the amplification world could muster for them. It proved impossible to reproduce the album properly on stage with such a small number of string players. They had no proper way of amplifying the instruments effectively, and the best they could do was to buy contact mics and jam them down the bridge of the cellos. The rhythm section had been used to playing loudly, and the string instruments were completely drowned out on stage as they could not match the guitars and drums for volume. When the contact mics were turned up, horrendous feedback resulted. Instead of having the cellos at adequate volume, the players had to wear headphones so they could hear through one earpiece and catch the rest of the group as well. To make a bad situation worse, there were times when gaps between numbers to change instruments were almost as long as the numbers themselves. Then there were arguments as to the volume of Jeff's guitar or the artistic merits of Roy's assorted collection.

Part of the problem, they were sure, was in playing too many large venues before they were really ready for them. If they had concentrated on small clubs at first, they would have had time to get the sound together. But in the bigger halls everyone turned up the electric instruments, and nobody could hear properly what the string players were playing. The sound mixers had an unenviable job trying to hold it all together for them on stage.

By now the dual identity of The Electric Light Orchestra and The Move was at its height. Roy, Jeff, and Bev would be dashing from the TV studio where they had been promoting 'California Man' as The Move, miming usually with a few assorted friends and roadies in tow, to play live as ELO, sometimes on the same evening. On stage their repertoire included some songs from the first album, notably '10538 Overture', 'Queen Of The Hours', and 'Whisper In The Night', alongside two lengthy epics written by Jeff the second they had begun recording, both going under the working titles of 'Jeff's Boogies'—'From The Sun To The World' and 'In Old England Town'—Roy's wistful 'Dear Elaine' (which had been recorded as part of his as-yet-unreleased solo album), and a new arrangement of 'Great Balls Of Fire', with additional cello embellishments.[1]

A session was recorded on 9 May for Granada TV's *Set At Six* in Manchester, and broadcast within the Granada region on 20 June. Thought to be the only surviving film of the first ELO line-up performing live for TV, it included Jeff's 'Boogie No. 2' ('In Old England Town'), 'Whisper In The Night', 'Queen Of The Hours', 'Mr Radio', and 'Great Balls Of Fire'. In addition, long before such practice became commonplace, a video featuring them miming to '10538 Overture' was made largely to promote the group overseas. It featured Jeff wearing a black patch over one eye and a frock coat, alongside Roy in black glasses and his Old Father Time garb.

The sixteen dates they played in Britain that May suggested that, for some of them at least, the group was not really going to work. For a gig at The Dome, Brighton, where they planned to land by helicopter from Battersea, they arrived late as the pilot could not find the racecourse on which to land, leading them to circle above Brighton for more than an hour. The road crew, who were travelling by car, arrived long before they did. By the time they got in they found that, although The Dome had a capacity of 2,000, less than 150 had paid to come and see them. It was even worse at the Sunderland Locarno, where the audience numbered just seven; Bev commented grimly afterwards that the group felt like applauding them. Nevertheless, footage shot by a member of the audience of the performance at Guildford Civic Hall, thought to be the only in-concert film of the first line-up to survive to this day, suggests that they had their good nights as well.

At a gig at Fairfield Hall, Croydon, on 14 May, they topped a bill including Fishbaugh, Fishbaugh & Zorn, and Colin Blunstone, and left several who were present in two minds. According to Robert Ellis in *Sounds*, the material they played (mostly from the album) sounded interesting but seemed to lack cohesion. 'When they steamed into Chuck Berry rock'n'roll, with Wood on sax, and the string ensemble sawing away for all they were worth—well I almost gave up and went home, except it was all so intriguing.' But he added that a group of Americans were much more enthusiastic, one telling him that they were 'just great.'

But things could have been worse. A film director called John Elton, inevitably dubbed 'Dwight Reg', invited them to star in a picture to be shot in around two weeks in the Barbican area of London. With the working title *Freedom City*, it was intended to be a science fiction epic with vaguely political overtones set sometime in the future. It was Elton's idea to use their album as a soundtrack and the three frontmen as the main stars, despite their total lack of acting experience. To their relief, what might have been the ultimate cinematic disaster of all time was started but never finished. No script had been prepared, and the costumes they were given to wear were bus conductors' uniforms from London Transport—except for Roy, who had to make do with a long black coat with black and white flaps which he had worn on *Top Of The Pops*. Ever the lucky one, Roy's main role was to carry a voluptuous blonde up to the top of a flight of steps while she was supposed to be dead. She was wearing a very flimsy dress, which failed to preserve her modesty. As she was too heavy for him to carry with ease, they had to do repeated takes until he was unable to lift her any more.

Jeff's sole line of dialogue came when he was meant to drink a glass of wine, glance to his right, and say, 'Time to go.' He ended up getting the dialogue right, but then on camera turned his head and poured the wine down his ear. Perhaps Laurel and Hardy could have done it better.

After the first week they were invited to an office in Denmark Street, Soho, to look at the rushes, and fell off their chairs laughing because it was all so dreadful. It would all come clear in the end, Elton assured them, and that was the last they—or apparently anybody else—ever saw of it. Rumour has it that Jeff, Roy, and Bev each have copies, and are more than keen not to share them with anybody else. Some three decades later, archivists and others engaged in working on re-mastering and compiling early ELO material for reissue on CD were asked not to search too hard for the great lost ELO movie.

Despite these unpromising beginnings, the group were eagerly looking forward to crossing the Atlantic. Bev admitted that ELO were aiming primarily at the American market, where The Move had been regarded as an underground or progressive act rather than the hit singles pop group which they were to British audiences. Unlike Roy and Bev, Jeff had never been to America before, and could not wait to go. He was particularly excited at the talk of themed goodies being marketed to promote them, such as giveaway ELO light bulbs. To Keith Altham in *New Musical Express*, he joked about how they were waiting for a call from Osram, the leading multinational lighting manufacturer, to do a commercial for them. 'I've always used Osram. Used to eat them as a kid for breakfast. Once I got one I saved up for the set.'

At the time 'California Man', a record by a now non-existent group, was firmly in the top ten, spending three weeks at its peak position of No 7. The

Move were still very much in the public eye as regulars on *Top Of The Pops* on Thursday nights, and the single was being played regularly on Radio 1. Meanwhile, it was increasingly clear that the main factor holding back the promising but highly flawed band was having two leaders. Jeff suffered from the problem that the better-known Roy was getting nearly all the media attention and interviews. Roy Hollingworth's review of the album in *Melody Maker*, which appeared to give Roy the main credit for it, was typical of the unbalanced general appraisal. As soon as they came off stage, the cameras would click in Roy's direction. A performance of '10538 Overture' on BBC-2 TV's *The Old Grey Whistle Test*, a late-night show focusing on album-orientated artists rather than singles-based acts, was followed by presenter Richard Williams's enthusiastic but woefully misinformed 'Great song, Roy.'

Moreover, musical differences were beginning to emerge. Roy spoke in at least one interview of adding a brass section, or at least a row of saxophonists, which seemed somewhat at odds with his and Jeff's ambitions for perfecting the fusion of pop and classical music. It was also ironic, given the view of Nigel Reeve, Director of Repertoire at EMI Records, that at the time Roy's ideas were almost completely orchestral, outside the rock'n'roll spectrum, unlike those of Jeff. In an interview some twenty years later, Bev said that Roy did not do much for ELO, once he had had the idea to start it and thought up the name. In his view, there had been nothing of real substance on the debut album apart from '10538 Overture'. Significantly, many punters who would buy ELO albums in their thousands towards the end of the 1970s when they were among the bestselling British acts around would always find this first album a very acquired taste, if not downright unlistenable in places. Conversely, said Bev, Jeff never really did anything for The Move.

It was clear that sooner or later somebody had to go. Bev had assumed that when Roy and Jeff got together, they would collaborate on writing songs as a team. As the first album showed, that did not happen. Rick Price, who had remained a close observer as well as friend, knew that while Jeff's encouragement had been vital for Roy in their getting the group together, ego and musical rivalry between two accomplished songwriters and multi-instrumentalists persisted. The fact that their songs were so very different only emphasised the gulf between them.

To Mike Sheridan, it was like witnessing 'two egos on a stick.' At the start of an ELO gig at Selly Oak Town Hall, he saw what almost seemed like a fight for who was coming on stage last. The impasse was resolved, or so they thought, when David Arden suggested that they should both walk out together, in step, once the rest of the group were already on stage.

An additional difficulty was that journalists only wanted to interview Roy. Although he explained that the band was a team effort and he was not the sole leader, the frustration was getting to him and Jeff, and the atmosphere between them was not merely deteriorating, but also impacting on the performance and morale of the rest of the band. Moreover the main members had been under considerable strain to get the band together in the first place and to try and represent the sound of the album properly on stage, something they were still a long way from achieving. It all made for a rather fractious environment.

In order to resolve the issue amicably, the band decided to go to Europe for a while, and undertake a short and none-too-happy tour of Italy. Shortly before one sold-out show was due to begin, according to Don Arden, an announcement was made that the group were unable to perform that night. Fearing that something terrible had happened to one of them, he went backstage and found that Roy and Jeff were refusing to go on until it was mutually agreed which one would walk out first. He grabbed them both by the hair, shoved them out of the door and marched them on stage, threatening to beat the hell out of them if they didn't get on with it. They accordingly obeyed and the audience were ecstatic, but he noticed that neither of the two main men would even look at each other during the show. Afterwards they both went to see him separately in his hotel room and told him that they could no longer work together. Don thought that Roy was the talented one, the one who had been coming up with the hits for years and would doubtless continue to do so, and that Jeff, who 'had always been just the other guy,' could easily be replaced.

Instead of taking a few days away to cool off, they were under pressure to return to the studios to work on the second album, on which Roy was playing bass more than anything else. Fuses were short, and when Jeff insisted he was playing it wrongly on one number, Roy snapped at Jeff to play it himself, put the instrument away, and walked out.

For a few days there was no communication between them. Then Bev received a phone call from Don Arden to say that Roy had decided to leave the band and was taking Bill Hunt and Hugh McDowell with him. An astonished Bev was left wondering why on earth his old friend Roy had not broken the news to him in person. As Jeff had just moved into a flat in Sutton Coldfield and was not on the phone, Bev drove over to see him. He was equally amazed, and to make matters worse, they heard later that night that it was common knowledge among several of their friends that Roy had been rehearsing with a new band.

Roy later opined that the management should have stepped in, taken him and Jeff aside, and advised them to take a break. Instead, it seemed that they were encouraging and exacerbating the situation for their own ends. Unwilling to socialise with anyone else, on the Italian tour Roy had stayed in his hotel room much of the time and written mainly the lyrics for songs that would appear on the debut album of the next band he was beginning to visualise.

As for Jeff and Bev, they wondered whether Roy, still the best-known name of the three, was planning to take the name ELO and leave them to continue as The Move. Only thirty-five years afterwards, following the death of Don Arden aged eighty-one, did Roy reveal all in an interview with *The Daily Telegraph*. He stated categorically that Don had deliberately fomented discord between him and Jeff, with the objective of putting pressure on him to leave ELO and form his own band, thus creating another money-spinning venture from which Don would benefit as manager.

To resolve the situation, Arden made a special journey to Birmingham to see Jeff and tell him that the group had never been any good, so this was the best thing that could have happened. 'You can get out there and show us what you can do.'

As far as fans were concerned, after several weeks of rumour and uncertainty, the outcome was revealed at a press conference organised by EMI and Don Arden in July 1972. Jeff, Don said, was not receiving the recognition he deserved, and would be taking over the leadership of ELO with immediate effect, as the new compositions for them had been mainly his responsibility anyway. The group would also include Bev Bevan, Richard Tandy, and other musicians whose names would shortly be revealed. Roy was no longer involved and would be working on a completely separate project, full details of which would soon follow. Meanwhile, The Move would continue as they had for the last three years, a recording-only unit comprising Roy, Jeff, and Bev.

Bill Hunt realised that problems were inevitable with two very talented and ambitious musicians, and it came to a head on the Italian tour. He

THE MOVE HAVE A NEW SINGLE OUT BY THE ELECTRIC LIGHT ORCHESTRA

entitled
"10538 Overture"
It is the official follow-up to their Top Ten Hit "California Man"

Musically it maybe somewhat different, and that's why it is released under the name of ELO instead of the Move. But it's still basically Roy Wood, Jeff Lynne, and Bev Bevan, rocking on with the assistance of some 'heavy' string players plus Bill Hunt on French Horn–he's the one who recently played tenor sax on their outrageous Top Of The Pops appearances. And if you thought those TV performances of "California Man" were

hilarious, wait till you see them do "10538 Overture" as a bizarre 9-piece mini orchestra!

If that turns you on, you'll probably want the album from which it is taken: simply entitled "The Electric Light Orchestra" (already in the U.S. album charts).

For those who can do without the cellos, there's the Move album "Message From The Country" which includes "Ella James" (also to be heard on the "California Man" maxi).

Electric Light Orchestra
Harvest
SHUL797
Including their new single '10538-Overture'
HAR 5053

The Move
Message from the Country
Harvest
SHSP 5013
Including 'Ella James' from their hit maxi single 'California Man'

A British music press advertisement for '10538 Overture', ELO, plus the current ELO and Move albums, 1972

had had his misgivings about the viability of ELO and was considering leaving anyway. Hugh McDowell thought Roy was being elbowed out of the group, especially in the recording studio, where he believed he was not having enough say in the production. All this resulted in Roy's asking both musicians in confidence during the Italian tour whether they would be interested in a completely new band. Despite the rumours and dramatic music headlines, Roy was never pushed. It was his own decision to leave in favour of a more rock'n'roll path with his new outfit, Wizzard.

From those uncertain beginnings and with Jeff in charge, within a few years ELO would be unquestionably one of Britain's top groups, with a run of global successes on a scale not far removed from the Liverpool group whose influence they had acknowledged so freely.

A glance at the letters page of *New Musical Express* in the 5 August 1972 issue showed that at least one person had anticipated the shape of things to come. Signed 'Beatle Fan, Warwickshire,' it came from a buyer who wrote that the group's first LP contained

> [...] the most refreshing music you've ever heard since The Beatles. Now that Wood has left it does not alter the fact that ELO led by Jeff Lynne are to become the second biggest happening in pop history.

4

'Roll Over Beethoven'

Now that Jeff Lynne was fully in charge of ELO, the immediate priority was for them to recruit the right musicians for a successful live line-up. Out went Andy Craig, while in came former session player Colin Walker on cello. Richard Tandy, always a versatile multi-instrumentalist, agreed to relinquish his bass in favour of concentrating on keyboards and learning the synthesiser.

The next rehearsals were held at The Boggery in Solihull, in a room belonging to the East Birmingham Working Men's Club. One day they had a phone call from David Arden, who had just managed to fill their most pressing vacancy. He had found a bass guitarist who could also do backing vocals, by the name of Michael d'Albuquerque. Within minutes a bright red and white Austin Metropolitan pulled up outside and an extremely well-spoken young man in a tweed jacket and pressed cavalry twills stepped out and introduced himself, saying he had been sent by the Ardens to see whether he could 'get a jolly old gig with you chaps.' Although they were somewhat taken aback at first, feeling that he was not exactly your typical rock musician, they invited him to jam on some Chuck Berry numbers. It was immediately evident that in spite of an accent that would have put a BBC newsreader to shame, the man whom they would come to nickname 'Albert Turkey' was an excellent bass guitarist and singer, and would fit in perfectly.[1]

With this new line-up came a small but major aural innovation. Don Arden had also acquired some Barcus Berry pick-ups, which were custom-made for the string instruments. At last everybody could hear properly on stage what everybody else was playing. The time was now right for a single, and an edited version of '10538 Overture' which faded out shortly after the final verse and at four minutes long was about ninety seconds shorter than the full album version was released on 23 June. 'The Move have a new single out by the Electric Light Orchestra' read a strapline in the music press ads. Radio 1 presenter John Peel, who also reviewed the new singles every week in *Disc And Music Echo*, was unsparing in his praise of 'this lovely single and the fine LP from which it is taken,' remarking that it had 'the same dense, swirling, unreal feel' as 'I Am The Walrus'.

An appearance by the group to promote it on *Top Of The Pops* increased everyone's confidence, with Bill Hunt brought back temporarily into the line-up to join in the miming. After steady airplay it entered the charts at the end of July at No. 45, and rose to No. 9 during an eight-week run. Towards the end of the year 'No Answer' became a very minor American hit, never reaching any higher than No. 196. At around the same time 'Do Ya' gave The Move their sole American single success, albeit at a modest No. 93.

During this period the new line-up of ELO played their first gig together on 12 August at the 12th National Jazz, Blues, and Rock Festival at Reading. It was a bill which they shared with Wizzard, who had made their debut to a very mixed reception at the London Rock'n'Roll Show at Wembley Stadium the previous weekend. Other acts taking part included Status Quo, Mungo Jerry, Focus, Vinegar Joe, Ten Years After, and The Faces. A review in *New Musical Express* commented approvingly that it was good to see the ELO concept working so well; 'with immensely strong, sweeping sounds, the whole outfit got through some really remarkable sounds.' It confirmed Jeff's assessment that the old group had been 'wrong from the beginning—I knew we should never have done any gigs in the first place.'

That same week, after having been in the shops for around nine months, the album entered the charts at last. Like the single it debuted at the position of No. 45, reaching a peak of No. 32 the following week during a four-week run.

But there were still difficult times ahead. On a nationwide tour in the autumn, taking in venues in Bradford, Leeds, Manchester, Glasgow, Dunstable, Margate, Torquay, and Southampton among others, audiences were sometimes still disappointingly if not insultingly small. To the group, it was as if they were turning up to crowds numbering thirty people or less, and not always even listening once they appeared on stage. It seemed like a poor reception for a group who had had the benefit of so much music press coverage, airplay on Radio 1, appearances on *Top Of The Pops*, and a debut top-ten single under their belt.

At one particularly badly attended show on 7 October at City Hall, St Albans, there were only seventeen punters. Afterwards a furious Jeff, increasingly convinced that the home market was a sheer waste of their time, called Don Arden. He said they were not being promoted properly, he did not want to play in England any more, and he wanted to take ELO to America. Don then went to United Artists Records all barrels blazing: he demanded first-class treatment and proper publicity for his group, and paved the way for them to undertake a stateside tour the following year. It was a bold move which would pay handsome dividends. Moreover, it was his and the group's good fortune that Mike Stewart, head of United Artists at the time, agreed with him that the band had the potential to be a major concert attraction. He was prepared to finance them on both sides of the Atlantic, especially as support for them in Britain was initially nowhere near as strong as it might have been.

Recording sessions for the second album had begun at Air Studios in May, in the final weeks before Roy Wood's departure. It was a great place to record, according to Jeff:

> [...] you felt you were at the centre of things, on the top floor right in the middle of Oxford Circus. Watching all the crowds battle their way across the streets down below made you feel sort of privileged.

Roy had played bass guitar and cello on two tracks and his contributions remained on the record, though they were uncredited on the album sleeve by mutual consent. Completed in October and featuring the rest of the new line-up, the album was originally to be named *The Lost Planet*, but by the time of release in January 1973 it bore the title *ELO 2*.

With five tracks all between six and twelve minutes long, it would always remain their most 'progressive rock' opus and, possibly barring the debut, the least commercial album in their catalogue. 'In Old England Town (Boogie No. 2)' and 'From The Sun To The World (Boogie No. 1)'—the two which featured the playing of their former co-leader—had been part of the live set. Like 'Momma' and the marathon 'Kuiama', which stretched to nearly twelve minutes and had a subtle anti-war message, they all alternated verses with musical passages of different time signatures, incorporating elements of the classics with their sawing cellos and violin, tinkling piano and synthesiser, bursts of rock guitar, occasional hints of strings-led jazz, and even boogie-woogie piano. According to Jeff, 'Kuiama' was probably the best track, and generally named by fans as their favourite. In his words, it told the story

> [...] of a soldier in the sort of place where they're actually having a war at the moment—it could be anywhere—and he kills this little girl's Mum and Dad. The little girl's wandering around the streets, all she sees is terror, and he tries to explain that it was him who killed her Mum and Dad, because he was ordered to.

If much of their music demanded repeated listening and was far too long for daytime airplay on the radio, ELO did make one concession to radio-friendly commerciality. During rehearsals the group realised they were rather short of material and needed something for an *encore*, so somebody suggested that like many a group before them in time-honoured fashion they should play something from the Chuck Berry songbook. There was one obvious Berry title which seemed tailor-made for an outfit that prided itself on mixing rock and the classics—'Roll Over Beethoven'. This and 'Great Balls of Fire' had been in the live set almost from the beginning, as the group's way of defining themselves as a rock group with classical instruments, with the former's title being particularly appropriate. Initially they tried it with a few bars of Beethoven's Ninth Symphony, until they realised that the opening bars of the Fifth would fit far better.

While they were recording it in September, as Jeff fondly recalled many years later, Paul McCartney and Wings were in the studio next door recording 'Live And Let Die', with George Martin producing them as he had done in the days of The Beatles. George came to have a listen to the new version of the rock'n'roll standard which he had overseen as a cover version on the second album by his most famous clients nine years before, and he gave a nod of approval.[2]

The full album version lasted seven minutes, but a four-and-a-half-minute edit was released as a single in January 1973. The press ads showed a drawing of Beethoven with his fingers in his ears, above the strapline 'The follow-up to "California Man".' Copies with the initial B-side, 'Manhattan Rumble', were withdrawn and re-pressed with 'Queen Of The Hours' instead. Music press, radio, and TV reactions were overwhelmingly positive, and it entered the chart at No. 28, peaking at No. 6. As Jeff said, it was unbeatable as a live number, and 'you can't help but tap your foot to it.' What the writer would have made of it, he never knew. A while later he saw Chuck in a coffee shop, 'but I didn't fancy going up to him in case he said, "You messed up my song."'

Of course, Chuck would have been justified in pointing out that the lyrics were incorrect. When the backing track had been completed, Jeff realised that he did not know the words properly, so they rang Bev's record shop, Heavyhead. The assistant obligingly played the record, a bit at a time, and read the words to him over the phone. It took about an hour to get all the words, 'and they were wrong anyway!' History does not tell us whether Jeff actually bought the record as well and duly sent the receipt to his accountant or not. In America, interest was building in the group, and the single reached No. 42 on the billboard charts.

A particularly interesting session took place at Air Studios in February with Carl Wayne. The original Move vocalist whose exit had paved the way three years earlier for Jeff to join was looking for new material to record as a single, preferably something more soulful than the middle-of-the-road fare which had so far failed to provide him with a hit.[3] Don Arden, who was Carl's manager as well at the time, suggested approaching Jeff with this purpose in mind. Jeff provided two new songs, 'Your World' and 'Get A Hold Of Myself', and also a new version of 'Mama'. These were recorded with himself, Richard, Bev, and Michael as a slimmed-down, non-orchestral ELO. The backing was never completed and the session multi-track was considered lost for almost thirty years. Even so, Carl was full of admiration for the group and their leader, whom he praised as a brilliant producer.

The second ELO album was released in Britain in March, and despite its lack of commerciality, was greeted enthusiastically by some sections of the media. Roy Hollingworth, who remained their main cheerleader in *Melody Maker*, admitted that he had thought the group would fall apart with Roy's departure—'but, nay, it got better!' ELO, he said, were 'conceivably the most original band about.' Some less partisan journalists admitted that they found the tracks too long and pretentious. Ultimately this album proved less successful than the first, charting for only one week at No. 35. At that time, Yes and other prog-rock bands thought nothing of issuing albums with two or three lengthy tracks per side, before fashions changed in the mid-1970s. Jeff conceded with hindsight three years later that when they were recording the album, he thought they had to do long numbers, 'otherwise people would think there was something wrong with us.' Now he found the record 'really boring' and 'impossible to listen to.'

At the same time, Wizzard were enjoying success in their homeland with their first single, 'Ball Park Incident', which had been released in November 1972 and was also peaking at No. 6 early in the New Year. As the press conference in July had stipulated, The Move's recording contract with EMI technically still had another two years to run. But as Wizzard and ELO had both begun their recording careers with a top-ten single, EMI allowed it to lapse, thus allowing the musicians concerned to concentrate properly on two potentially very successful new bands. There would therefore be no new Move singles or albums, only compilations.

By this time, any cultural bridges between the classically-trained string players and the rest of the group had been broken down. Jeff remarked at the time that, when the second album was released,

> [...] when they first joined, we had to tell them what to write down so that they could read it, but now they all play by ear, same as us. And so, when we learn anything, they get at it the same as we do. I usually bring along a tape or something, and we'll go through it basically until we know it, and then we put the arrangements in.

The important thing was that everyone was gelling together as a group, no matter what their background. They had an ideal rhythm section, Jeff thought;

> [...] the cello players and violin player are really interested in the rhythm of it as well, playing all the funky stuff—off beats and quarter notes—it's good, really tight now all over the place.

The tone variations were getting them a much fuller sound than they had before. Richard, a naturally gifted multi-instrumentalist, was coming on well with the Moog which he had only recently taken up, Michael was 'laying down a really deep, rumbling sound' on bass, and Bev was 'playing ten times better than he ever used to. It feels like a group now, when we go on stage.'

The group were also generally getting a better reaction live. On 17 March they played the first of many sell-out dates, at Malvern Winter Gardens, at which sixty fans were caught trying to enter with forged tickets. Six days there followed another triumphant gig at the Rainbow Theatre, London, where they used stage scenery for the first time, combined with back projections from the album cover artwork. Although it cost them £3,000, it paid off in the reviews, and the whole concert was recorded for a planned live album to be released in the US, later cancelled, as well as filmed for TV and cinema broadcast. Successes like these helped to compensate for inevitable disappointments such as what was meant to be a prestigious affair in Brussels which would be inked to a live Radio Luxembourg broadcast, where, after a white-knuckle ride by car with the promoter to the venue, there were about a hundred disinterested punters and no broadcast technicians or crew to be seen.

All the same, Jeff was more than happy with the new general direction. Talking to Steve Peacock of *Sounds*, he explained that this was only the beginning;

> Really we're still learning and we haven't explored the combinations we've got yet. We've got so much more scope we haven't even touched yet.

Any doubts that Jeff might be unable to handle his role as frontman were soon dispelled. Don Arden was among those who had initially had reservations. In the early 1970s, the British music scene was dominated by male performers, soloists and leaders of groups who all had a very strong visual image in print and on television. Beside the likes of Marc Bolan of T. Rex, Noddy Holder of Slade, Ian Hunter of Mott The Hoople, Bryan Ferry of Roxy Music, Rod Stewart, David Bowie, and Elton John—to say nothing of his former comrade in arms Roy Wood—the modest-looking Jeff seemed at first glance to offer little competition, even if he did briefly resort to a glittery silver wig when they appeared on *Top Of The Pops* to promote 'Roll Over Beethoven'. Something similar happened to Genesis a few years later, when the flamboyant Peter Gabriel left, to be replaced front of stage by their anonymous-looking drummer Phil Collins. The latter, as Don Arden pointed out, was a musician with no obvious charm or powers of showmanship, but one who when given the chance to prove himself revealed a powerful voice and an uncanny knack of delivering hit after hit.

But everyone, not least Jeff himself, knew his strengths as a singer, guitarist, and in fact all-round musician and songwriter who could come up with the goods time and time again. Moreover, as he would remark modestly many years later, he knew exactly what he wanted. During that era, 'it was all big long guitar solos, that lasted seven or eight minutes, even longer sometimes.' He wanted to do something entirely different, as it would stand out from all the rest. In his words, 'You got your rock'n'roll, harmonies, classical bits—stick them all together, what have you got? ELO!' And the manager who had initially called them 'deep and meaningless,' and likened them to a classical orchestra gone mad with awful distorted heavy metal guitar, now conceded that Jeff had done the right thing in scaling down his musical ambitions until they were basically a pop group augmented by a classical string section. It was rather like what George Martin had once done for a certain very successful quartet from Liverpool, in fact.

Jeff also had an invaluable asset in Richard Tandy, the man who had effectively become and would remain his right-hand man in the group, or No. 2 in the ELO hierarchy. 'People know him as the ELO keyboard player, and he is a great keyboard player,' said Jeff, 'but not many people know he is also an accomplished jazz guitarist. He knows all the naughty chords!' Although Richard never co-wrote any of the material, it went without saying that while Jeff created the songs, he helped to record them. During the next decade-and-a-half of the group's career, his role varied according to the different stages they went through. When he later came to analyse it, he divided it into three separate periods: pre-orchestral, orchestral, and post-orchestral. In the early days they would rehearse a song together and get an idea of how to begin recording it, normally with Jeff, Bev, Michael d'Albuquerque, and himself as the four core members. The strings would be added later. These being the early days of electronic keyboards and synthesisers, all they had was a mini-Moog, which would be dubbed on later by Jeff or himself.

Once they began using a full orchestra with the fourth album, the pattern altered. Now the first stage was to produce arrangements for the orchestral players. Richard would play the tunes on the piano, while Jeff suggested riffs, and Louis Clark, who worked with them as arranger from 1974 onwards, would write them down. Richard and Louis would make further suggestions until the string arrangements were complete, and they would hear them for the first time in the studio when the orchestra was running through them. Meanwhile, the rhythm tracks were laid down but with the emphasis on simplicity, in order to leave enough space for the orchestral parts. For Bev, this involved him double-tracking his drums in a suitably ambient space, more often than not the lavatories. Once the orchestra had been recorded, additional keyboard parts were overdubbed.

By ELO's post-orchestral stage, the onward march of technology had greatly broadened the sound texture and sequencing possibilities. Richard's contributions could be anything from laying down a basic string pad to working out sequences on an Oberheim Sequencer, twiddling the knobs on whatever they had, and 'saving sounds, loading sounds, sitting down with calculators working out the milliseconds,' in addition to playing keyboards.

However, it was evident that within a few months of Roy Wood's departure, ELO was to some extent a two-man group. Engineer Dick Plant would later confirm, 'Jeff pretty much knew exactly what he wanted and worked towards the idea he had in his head, and he guided and instructed his musicians to that end,' Richard more than anyone.   But he was always very keen 'to let an engineer go his own way about achieving something just as long as the end result was how he envisaged it.'

Dick gave the example of how Jeff approached the recording of drums, at least on the sessions which he was engineering. They would close-mic Bev's kit and he would play the part as instructed by Jeff, who would tell him where to put the fills and keep the part strong but simple. Next they would set up ambient mics at some distance from the kit and re-record the complete drum part, double-tracked, then balance both tracks together, thus obtaining a very powerful drum sound on record. As Jeff had also been playing drums himself for several years, he always had an exact idea in his head of how he wanted the finished work to sound.

Another interesting point about Jeff's methods in the studio was that, not being one of those songwriters who always had a batch of lyrics awaiting music, he would frequently put down a guide vocal on a song before he had completed writing the words. Once he had a tune but no words, he would sing phonetic noises to sit comfortably on the melody and later write a lyric that sounded close to the noises. Once he was so happy with a garbled guide vocal on tape that he did not want to re-do it. When Roy Wood, who was working next door on one of his own projects, happened to walk into the studio, Jeff asked him for a helping hand, suggesting that bits could be changed into something sensible with no more than a small overdub. The end result largely remained as initially recorded, with only minor changes. When they mixed it, they added sound effects to the vocal so that it was pretty indistinct and the new lyric worked well in relation to what had gone on tape.

Jeff, Dick Plant said, 'was more regimented than Roy Wood.' Although just as musically driven and full of ideas, the latter had a more easy-going attitude and preferred 'to enjoy himself, probably a little too much sometimes, in the studio.' By comparison, Jeff had a stronger work ethic, and his principle was more a heads-down one—simply getting on with the job.

In April the group began recording what they called the Elizabeth Lister Observatory sessions (the clue, dear reader, is in the initials) at Air Studios for what would be their third album, featuring uncredited appearances from one of the hottest properties in the British music scene. Jeff had been friends with Marc Bolan since The Idle Race days, and since the acoustic duo that was Tyrannosaurus Rex had morphed into the fully electric group T. Rex in 1970. Their first hit at the end of 1970 under the new shortened name, 'Ride A White Swan', had been one of the first two singles on the new Fly label, alongside The Move's non-charting 'When Alice Comes Back To The Farm'. Since then T. Rex had topped the singles chart four times. Now, during a break between sessions at Air Studios working on his own material, Marc would come next door and look in on Jeff and his group again. But this time he did more than just take his place as a silent bystander. He contributed guitar parts to the sessions on two songs which would appear on the album, and on a new song, 'Everyone's Born To Die', which would remain in the can for thirty years.[4]

While he was there, Marc asked if the group were doing any local gigs in the near future. As a result, when they played Watford Town Hall a few days later, he came on stage and joined them at the end of the show for 'Roll

Over Beethoven'. 'Right from the beginning, the girls at the front spotted him at the side of the stage and they were screaming all through the set,' Jeff recalled. 'It was an experience for us just to see it really happening, but he must get choked off by the fact that he can't hear himself play because he really is a good guitar player!' It was no less an experience for the audience, who roared their approval, and the song lasted for around fifteen minutes.

Early that summer came the long-awaited first visit to America. ELO took a plane to Los Angeles (where United Artists had their headquarters), were greeted at the airport, and taken in limousines along Sunset Boulevard, where they were treated to a sight of a huge billboard advertisement welcoming them to the USA. A similar red-carpet reception was extended to them on their arrival at the Continental Hyatt House Hotel. At last they were being treated like stars, whereas, as Jeff commented wryly, they could barely even get arrested at home. They made their transatlantic debut on stage at San Diego Stadium on 2 June. The promotional groundwork had been done thoroughly and 'the English guys with the big fiddles' were getting an amazing reaction wherever they went, suddenly playing to enthusiastic crowds of thousands. Among the acts who played on the same bill were Procol Harum, the Climax Blues Band (whose guitarist Pete Haycock would become part of the post-Jeff group almost twenty years later), the Edgar Winter Group, Joe Walsh (for whom Jeff would later produce some recordings), and Mr 'Roll Over Beethoven' himself, Chuck Berry.

'America is like the dream I've always had, a dream come true,' said Jeff. According to Bev, they loved everything about the country, be it the weather, the TV, the music, or simply the atmosphere. 'It was as if the Promised Land was there for the taking.' Reaction to the second album was good, and it reached No. 62 in the album chart, while 'Roll Over Beethoven' peaked at No. 42 as a single.

With TV appearances on Dick Clark's *American Bandstand*, an in-concert special filmed at the Los Angeles Palladium, and *Midnight Special*, the word soon spread. One of ELO's most memorable gigs was a sold-out show at the Celebrity Theatre, Phoenix, Arizona. The audience reaction to the first-ever live performance of the new concept piece 'On The Third Day' in its entirety as the stage revolved around 360 degrees could not have been better, and they ran out of encores at the end. When

An American music press advertisement announcing the dates for ELO's first American tour, summer 1973

they arrived in the dressing room from a sweltering 105 degrees in the shade, they found a brass tap on the wall with no indication of what it was. Jeff turned it on and found it was ice-cold beer. At another date on the tour, at the Academy of Music, New York, they were part of an all-British show, with Savoy Brown headlining, followed by Manfred Mann's Earth Band, Status Quo, and ELO in that order. One review afterwards stated that ELO were the killer act which stole the show. By the end of the tour, they knew that they were on the point of breaking really big stateside.

But the group were still too well-behaved for one member of the entourage, namely Don's daughter Sharon, who would one day meet her match by managing and then marrying the West Midlands' wild man of rock, former Black Sabbath vocalist Ozzy Osbourne. Either bored out of her mind or fed up with the group, or a combination of both, she decided things needed livening up. In true Keith Moon style, she threw a television out of the hotel window. She also instigated one or two drunken post-gig parties in hotels which left the furniture, wallpaper, light fittings, and everything else in a sorry state—but when asked by the management, would without question promptly write a cheque to cover the cost of the damage.

The downside of ELO's American success was returning to Britain, where it was hard not to feel that they had still not really been accepted. Despite ready chart success for singles if not albums, as-good-as-guaranteed appearances on *Top Of The Pops*, and open arms on the Radio 1 playlist for each new single, they were still playing to half-empty houses on the town halls, guildhalls, and polytechnics circuit, where they generally had to take their place with the punters and queue for drinks from the public bar.

That autumn, the first results of their spring sessions appeared on record. A six-minute mini-classical epic, an adaptation of Grieg's 'In The Hall Of The Mountain King', referred to during recording sessions as 'In The Hole Of The Mounted Parrot', was for a while the most obvious candidate for their third single, until they realised that to release two cover versions in a row would not help to create the right impression.

Instead, 'Showdown'—their last to appear on the Harvest label—was released in September and reached No. 12. Probably nobody outside the group and those closest to them could have foreseen the change in direction on a song which owed less to rock and classics than to Motown and Philly soul, not least in Richard's funky synths and its echoes of Stevie Wonder's recent hit 'Superstition', to say nothing of a guitar solo played on a Gibson 1953 Firebird guitar which Jeff borrowed from Marc Bolan. Not long before, the group had been rehearsing 'I Heard It Through The Grapevine' for fun at the cricket club, and Michael thought it sounded so good that he thought Jeff might have 'filed' it with the intention of writing something similar. There was certainly the intention of fusing soul rhythms and classical strings, which might on paper have seemed an incongruous clash of cultures but actually worked to perfection. 'I'd got this thing going in my mind, which didn't sound like ELO at all,' Jeff said. 'But eventually it grew into 'Showdown', which sounded more like a black American record.' Engineer Dick Plant had pleasant memories of the session, though not necessarily for musical reasons. Three girls who were regular session singers appeared on the record. At the time they were wearing very fashionable floaty, transparent dresses, and the men discovered that by turning off the main studio lights and putting a single light low down at the back of the studio, they could see right through. The girls knew exactly what they were doing, but took it in good part.

Praise for the single would come from one of the group's greatest heroes. On 28 September 1974, John Lennon was a guest of Dennis Elsas on WNEW-FM, New York City radio station. On air he said that if The Beatles had stayed together, they would be sounding like ELO, whom he called the 'Son of Beatles', as they did on 'Showdown'. He remembered their comment that when they first formed they intended to carry on from where The Beatles left off with 'I Am The Walrus', 'and they certainly did.' As for 'Showdown', he remarked, it was 'a beautiful combination' of 'I Heard It Through The Grapevine' and Lou Christie's 'Lightning Strikes', 'with a little "Walrus" underneath.'

On a subsequent tour of the States, Jeff had lost his voice, and one afternoon he asked Michael d'Albuquerque croakily if he would mind singing some the songs that night. Michael was happy to oblige, as long as he was given the words to anything he did not know. Jeff asked him if he would do 'Showdown', and went away to write the lyrics down. The bassist was mildly dismayed to realise that towards the end, one of the lines read, 'It's unreal, the suffering.' He admitted that he had always thought Jeff was singing, 'It's surreal, this submarine.' 'I wish I'd thought of that!' was the temporarily voiceless Jeff's reaction.

One place where support was not forthcoming was their old home in the heart of London, namely the headquarters at EMI. Don and David Arden were adamant that the group's third album, recorded during the spring and due for release towards the end of 1973, had to be promoted adequately as a make-or-break record. A meeting with a hesitant Roy Featherstone, managing director of the company, turned into an ill-tempered disaster and ended with a furious Don giving him a piece of his mind, turning the air blue as he told him he could say goodbye to ELO. Off he went to Mo Ostin at Warner Brothers, where another contract was arranged with more enthusiasm.

Further line-up changes were on the way. The other members found 'Wilf + VAT Gibson' increasingly difficult to work with, as well as demanding too much money, and he had to go. Colin Walker had just got engaged, and realised that his role as a husband-to-be was incompatible with that of a touring rock musician. Several violinists were auditioned, among them a middle-aged gentleman immaculately attired in evening dress who treated them to an elegant rendition of 'Fly Me To The Moon', someone 'who could play at 1,000 miles an hour and was full of flash,' and Mik Kaminski, who was so shy at first that he had to be persuaded to attend but was a very nice guy with a superb ear for music. He soon made it clear that he would fit in perfectly on a social and musical level.

Meanwhile, Hugh McDowell, who had just left Wizzard, returned to fill the cello vacancy. During his year with Roy Wood and Wizzard he had contributed the B-side to their first No. 1, 'See My Baby Jive', an instrumental 'Bend Over Beethoven'. The obvious mickey-take was not really appreciated by Jeff or the rest of the group, but his musical skills as well as his suitability meant that he got the job. In any case, although his name went in brackets after the title on the record label, Hugh had probably been less responsible for the composition or title of the piece than the King Wizzard himself.

Recruiting musicians whom the group already knew was generally safer than auditioning complete unknowns, who sometimes did not know what they were letting themselves in for. After the departure of one of the cello players, auditions were held for his replacement at the cricket club. One, who had formerly been a member of a major orchestra, duly arrived with his instrument. The group told him that they would run through some of their material, and that they did not write parts down, so it would be up to him to play along by ear. Jeff immediately let rip on his Les Paul with the intro to 'Roll Over Beethoven', which as Michael d'Albuquerque later recalled was so loud that it almost unglued their new hopeful's instrument; 'you could see the whole thing creak!'

His eyebrows shot up, he put his hand in the air, and implored them all to stop. Once they had done so, he turned to Jeff and said politely, 'Would you mind turning that guitar down a bit?' Jeff did not merely turn his guitar down, but took it off, put it down, and walked out of the room. As he did not return for a while, the others went to look for him, and found him sitting in the kitchen. 'Are you coming back in now or what?' they asked. He shook his head, insisting that he would not do so until the cello player had left. Brian Jones, the roadie, offered to run him back to the station, a distance of about 8 miles. 'You're not running him back,' Jeff said firmly. 'He can walk!'

5

'Daybreaker'

The third album, the appropriately-named *On The Third Day*, hit the shops in November 1973. The soul music feel of 'Showdown', the stand-alone single which initially appeared on the American pressing of the album, and only on British CD reissues more than thirty years later, had not been a harbinger of things to come. Most of the sound on the album reverted to cello-dominated rock, although this time all tracks were kept to a reasonable length, with only one exceeding six minutes. In his own words, Jeff was aiming 'to make music that was melodic and different.'

The interlinked tracks on one side were a tentative concept, based around biblical themes connected with the formation of the land and the seas in the Old Testament, and Jesus arising from the dead in the New Testament. Side Two featured separate, self-contained tracks, from the rousing synth and strings instrumental 'Daybreaker', which Jeff wrote particularly for Birmingham Town Hall—as he felt that when the group returned there they needed a really powerful new tune—to 'In The Hall Of The Mountain King'. The album's most commercial moment was 'Ma-Ma-Ma Belle'. This was and always would remain one of the most powerful rockers in the entire ELO catalogue, and a regular favourite in the set list on stage. Musically it was close to classic Rolling Stones territory, although some suggested that it had more than a passing resemblance to Mott the Hoople's 'Jerkin' Crocus'.

Both violinists, the departing Wilf Gibson and the newly-recruited Mik Kaminski, played on the album. Mike Edwards was the only cello player used, although the sleeve on the original release credited a certain Ted

Blight as the other cellist. During the hiatus when Mike had been the only cello player, the group's sound engineer Rick Pannell, who had previously played guitar in a couple of groups, stood in with them on *Top Of The Pops* for 'Showdown', miming cello because 'as a guitar player I could make it look convincing.' He also appeared in a few group photos, as well as in the very blurred individual mugshots used on the album sleeve. When curious fans later asked, 'who on earth was Ted Blight,' Rick's response was, 'I guess that was me!' According to Bev Bevan, the name was no more than a figment of Jeff's imagination.

Towards the end of 1973, Britain was in the throes of a bleak economic crisis, with petrol rationing, regular power blackouts caused by industrial action, and a three-day working week. It was the perfect cue for adverts in the music press headed 'Let there be light!' However, the album marked something of a downturn in fortunes on ELO's home territory, being the first of three which failed to chart on initial release.[1] 'Ma-Ma-Ma Belle' was released as a single in March, and despite an active touring schedule as well as another appearance on *Top Of The Pops*, it never rose higher than No. 22. In America, enthusiasm for the group on their tour was reflected in healthy sales, as the album made No. 52 on the album chart and went silver. On the singles chart, 'Showdown' reached No. 53. 'Daybreaker' was included on the American B-side of 'Ma-Ma-Ma Belle' but attracted more airplay and was listed as the A-side on the charts, in which it made No. 87.

Around then came a taste of things to come in Jeff's later career. Del Shannon had always been one of his greatest musical heroes; but by the mid-1960s, his hits had dried up on both sides of the Atlantic, and he was only recording and performing sporadically. Although he was without a contract at the time, Jeff and other members of the group played on three tracks with him, which were begun at Air London and completed at Cherokee Ranch Studios, California, when Jeff went to stay with him and his family. Also acting as producer, Jeff was delighted that Del was resuming his musical career, and even more so to be the catalyst for his doing so. Two of the tracks, 'Alive But Dead' and 'Deadly Game', remained unreleased, but 'Distant Ghost' appeared on the B-side of a single, 'Cheap Love', which appeared ten years later.

From February to August 1974 at the De Lane Lea Studios, ELO recorded a fourth studio album. Shortly after sessions began, Michael d'Albuquerque left the group for family reasons. His wife was expecting their first child, and life as a musician touring the world was not compatible with a stable family life. Jeff overdubbed the remainder of the bass work himself. While Hugh and Mik continued to perform on recordings, Jeff hired an orchestra for the first time, with Louis Clark co-arranging and conducting the strings as well as a choir.

This led to new troubles, and *Eldorado* was the last album that ELO ever recorded in Britain. At one of the sessions, the orchestral musicians packed up before the track had been completed. As Dick Plant recalled, it was Louis Clark's first London session. Because he was relatively young and inexperienced at the time, and as none of them recognised him, 'they gave him a particularly hard time, larking about and taking the mickey.' Moreover, the parts were unusually complicated, and the players gave the impression that they felt they were being put upon, so the session over-ran and the last track was not quite done when time was up. At this point the players at the back—mainly cellists—began putting their coats on and playing with their gloves on. Some of them took even more drastic action. A very careful listen to 'Nobody's Child' will reveal the sound of working-to-rule musicians as they slammed their cases and packed their instruments away during the piano part in the middle. It was easy enough to conceal on vinyl in those days, although the CD and digital age can be less forgiving.

On one occasion, a furious Jeff stopped the session and let them all go. However, they had not heard the last of it. Two days later they were all back in the studio, and Jeff told them all that Don Smith of the Musicians' Union was coming in to discuss the situation with him. Once the intercom rang to announce his impending arrival, Jeff told everyone present not to say anything to him when he turned up. Smith came in and sat down while everyone else continued with overdubs for about twenty minutes. Jeff then stopped, turned to Smith, told him that his members had behaved appallingly the other day, and the only reason they overran was because they were so incompetent that they were unable to play the parts and had to go over them so many times to get them right. (Was this the same Jeff whose method of dealing with difficult cellists at auditions was to walk out in angry silence?) A thoroughly chastened Smith immediately told Jeff that he could have the musicians back to finish the work at no additional cost, and that the union would pay for the additional studio time required. In future, Louis Clark was accorded more respect.

During this period the group continued their busy live schedule in the United States. While they were playing gigs in towns that he had never heard of before, Jeff was thrilled that,

> [...] in somewhere really obscure, some small town in the middle of the desert, there would be people singing along. They knew the words to the songs—it was a great feeling.

On 12 May 1974 they recorded a live album at Long Beach, California. The truck carrying their equipment was delayed as it had broken down en route, and they had no time for a sound check before going on stage. But the show and the album must go on, and they delivered a storming set including every track from *On The Third Day*, though for technical and timing reasons most of these tracks were omitted from the record. However the rest of the set was included, with extended versions of 'Showdown' and '10538 Overture', the latter briefly interpolating the intro from 'Do Ya'.

The Night The Light Went On In Long Beach was initially released in Germany and other overseas territories, though not in Britain or America, partly as it was intended mainly as a promotional tool to be used in countries as yet unfamiliar with the group. Another reason for withholding release in their two prime markets was that only an unfinished, rough mix was available and they were not too happy with the sound. In 1985, a better quality mix was discovered in the record company vaults and it was given a long-overdue British release but deleted soon afterwards. In 1998 a re-mastered version was made available on CD. For technical reasons, only two tracks from *On The Third Day* appeared on the live album. Also included were extended versions of 'Showdown' and '10538 Overture', with a few seconds of the chord sequence from 'Do Ya'. Most remarkable of all was the six-minute tour de force 'Day Tripper', in which themes from Mozart's 'Piano Sonata in C Major' and Handel's 'Arrival of the Queen of Sheba' and a few seconds of the opening riff from '(I Can't Get No) Satisfaction' were integrated into the old Beatles' hit. The album was rounded off with a segue of 'In The Hall Of The Mountain King' and 'Great Balls of Fire', and a rip-roaring version of 'Roll Over Beethoven' to finish. 'Day Tripper' was also released as a single in Germany and Holland.

By the time *Eldorado* was completed, Jeff revealed in an interview with

Colin Irwin of *Sounds* in September 1974 his growing disillusionment with Britain, from problems with the Musicians' Union and poor record sales to the lack of enthusiasm and friendliness on the part of audiences and promoters respectively. On a British tour early that year they had full houses at some venues, but plenty of empty spaces at others. 'We might sell out in Birmingham one night, and do nothing in Grimsby the next,' he said doggedly. 'Why should we play here when we can earn fortunes in America?'

Although he would evidently have a major change of heart only a few years later, Jeff said they would be perfectly happy if they could get away with not having to issue any more 45s, at least not in Britain. At the time, there was something of a stigma associated with names who were concentrating their efforts thus and were dismissed as appealing mainly to the more fickle early-teen market.

> We don't want singles out, it ain't our scene. It's against our principles. I suppose we've been lucky that every record we've had out has been a hit, but it's not part of our scene. We're not a singles band but if you have a hit single there's always people who think you're a singles group. Over here for the majority of people if you haven't got a record in the charts it means you're not doing anything, but that's a pathetic attitude. But if the record company say they're going to release a single what can you do about it? You can't argue. I could write horrible hit singles. I'm sure I could but I don't want to do it. I like to get my teeth into something serious, something with a bit to it. You do whatever you like, and I like something a bit deeper than pop clichés.

The anything-but-horrible single from *Eldorado*, 'Can't Get It Out Of My Head', was written in part as a response to his father Phil's criticism of his song-writing. 'The trouble with your tunes, it's got no bloody tune,' remarked Mr Lynne Senior. 'I said, "I'll show you a tune"' was his son's response. Everyone loves a challenge, and Jeff was thus spurred on to prove that he could write a beautiful classically-influenced song, which he promptly did in the front room of the family home in Shard End. Released in America in November 1974 and in Britain two months later, ironically it was their first to miss the top fifty in their home territory altogether, but on the other side of the Atlantic, it would at last give them a top-ten hit, peaking at No. 9.

[It] was just like a go at a real serial kind of orchestral work. And I'd never done one of those before and I was really thrilled with the way it came out.

The plot of *Eldorado* followed a Walter-Mitty-like character dreaming that he was high on a hill in this mythical land, journeying into fantasy worlds to escape the disillusionment of mundane reality. Subtitled 'A Symphony by the Electric Light Orchestra', this record with its forty-piece orchestra and choir was their most classical-sounding ever.

Shortly before it was due for release, Jeff and Bev had a phone call from a very excited Sharon Arden, telling them how thrilled she was with the cover and that she was certain it would win awards. When they were sent a copy a few days later and found themselves staring at a pair of red shoes with a golden flash and a pair of green hands, they were appalled. Jeff's initial reaction was that it was 'a load of crap' and had to be stopped immediately. They were only pacified when she told them that it was based on a scene from *The Wizard of Oz*, which was one of America's all-time biggest cult movies.

Although it might be a little too far-fetched to suggest that the sleeve design alone sold the record, it became their first American top-twenty album, released stateside in the autumn of 1974, peaking at No. 16, and their first gold disc for sales of 500,000. In a comparatively indifferent Britain, it hit the stores shortly after Christmas. British reviews were unfailingly good, with Bob Edmands in *New Musical Express* calling it 'an astonishing album,' while an unrestrainedly enthusiastic Roy Wood pronounced it the finest thing he had heard since *Sergeant Pepper*. Regrettably, in terms of chart positions, sales in Britain did not match this reception.

The album was loaded with excellent songs, from the single, the infectious 'Boy Blue' (also a single in America, which failed to chart), and 'Mister Kingdom', which likewise had something of an 'Across The Universe' feel to it, to the almost jazzy shuffle of 'Laredo Tornado' and the exhilarating mix of rock'n'roll and strings in 'Illusions in G Major'. Throughout each song the rock instrumentation was embellished to great effect by the orchestra, punctuated with occasional variations on a theme from 'The Prince of Denmark's March', composed about 1700 by Jeremiah Clarke and for some years mistakenly attributed to his contemporary

Henry Purcell. It proved to be one of those albums which was only fully appreciated a while later. In July 2010 *Classic Rock Magazine* named it as one of '50 albums that built prog rock.'

But after two albums which had refused to sell enough to register in the British charts, something had to give. Don Arden told Mo Ostin in no uncertain terms that he wanted ELO off the Warner Brothers label. After initial resistance because the group were hot property stateside, they were eventually released by the company at a price which Don was happy to pay.

For the Ardens had just launched their own record label, Jet. It got off to a promising start with its first single, 'No Honestly' by Lynsey de Paul, the theme tune to an ITV situation comedy of the same title and a top-ten hit in the closing weeks of 1974.[3] Now ELO would be free to become part of the Jet roster, and in fact would prove the only act to chalk up a consistent record of hit singles and albums. Several other artists were signed at various times to the label, among them Roy Wood (inevitably), veteran rock'n'roll legend Carl Perkins, Alan Price, Britt Ekland, Raymond Froggatt, Magnum, and Trickster, a group who would support ELO on tour a few years down the line, but with no more than fleeting moderate success. Those who jokingly called Jet Records 'Jeff Records' had a point. Mik Kaminski's splinter group Violinski, which would also include Michael d'Albuquerque, enjoyed a top-twenty hit on the label in 1979 with the instrumental 'Clog Dance', although a follow-up single and two albums never managed to capitalise on its success.

Jet Records did, however, provide a better track record for the group than Bev Bevan with his solo single, a revival of Sandy Nelson's 'Let There Be Drums' released in May 1976. Jeff, who produced, new bassist Kelly Groucutt, and Richard Tandy all helped out on their respective instruments and backing vocals. The B-side, 'Heavyhead', taken from a jam session named after Bev's record shop, also included Roy Wood on saxophone—his first collaboration with them since the parting of the ways in 1972. But Bev was not able to match fellow drummer Cozy Powell's run of hits, and according to him it only sold about half a dozen copies.

In November 1974 the group began a tour in support of *Eldorado*. An extensive schedule of dates was drawn up, covering North America in November and December with Deep Purple as headline act on some dates, Britain in February 1975, then Europe in March and April. A break from live work was planned for May and June, which were set aside for recording the next album; concerts were resumed in North America during the summer, finishing off in Australia and New Zealand in September. After having been seen playing bass guitar with a band called Barefoot in a Birmingham nightclub, Michael Groucutt was recruited to fill the vacancy left by Michael d'Albuquerque's departure. His role would also include backing and occasionally lead vocals on stage. As the group had already had more than one Michael and also a Mik, he was asked to adopt another forename to avoid confusion. He came up with Kelly, which had been his nickname at school.

After the last date of the first leg of the American and Canadian tour, Mike Edwards announced that he too was leaving. He had become the clown of the group with his party piece, during which he would mime Camille Saint-Saëns's 'The Swan' from *Carnival of the Animals*, played by Hugh in the background, running pieces of citrus fruit up and down the cello. He would then press a switch and the instrument would explode. Like much switch-operated modern technology, it sometimes worked—occasionally with such sheer force that it would topple him from his chair—and sometimes refused to function at all. But two-and-a-half years of life as a rock musician had been enough for him. He was replaced by Melvyn Gale, an old friend of Hugh.

Once the British dates were completed in February 1975, ELO left for Germany, where the next part of the tour proved a troubled one. Barclay James Harvest were the support act for some of the German dates, but they already had a huge fan base there, and at some gigs much of the audience left after seeing their heroes. Several dates were cancelled, and the group returned to Britain for a few days.

While back at home, some of ELO went into the studio to do some recording with their old friend, comedian Jasper Carrott. A double A-side, 'Funky Moped' and 'Magic Roundabout', was the result, with Jeff producing both sides while he, Bev, and Richard all played on it. 'Roundabout' was an adults-only, rather *risqué* send-up of the children's TV series deemed unsuitable for airplay; but on release as a single that summer, 'Funky Moped' reached No. 5 in Britain, in effect giving ELO (or the core of it) a top-five single at last. Later in March the tour resumed in Spain and Holland with different support acts, one of them being Michael Nesmith, formerly of the Monkees.

The group had discussed their problems while recording *Eldorado* with members of Deep Purple, and the latter recommended that next time Jeff give some thought to recording in Musicland Studios, Munich. They accordingly went there to lay down the fifth album. *Face The Music*, recorded in May and June and completed in New York in August during another break in the tour, was released in the United States in September 1975, where it reached No. 8 status—their first top-ten album—and in Britain two months later.

Although it would be the third album in a row not to chart on their home ground, it would see the start of a gentle turnaround in their British fortunes for the better. It opened with an instrumental 'Fire On High', in which at least one reviewer detected little nods to Schoenberg and Handel, containing a reversed message at the start, 'The music is reversible, but time is not—turn back—turn back—turn back—turn back,' spoken by Bev. This was a tongue-in-cheek response to ridiculous satanic allegations which had been made about *Eldorado* by Fundamentalist Christianity members. They claimed that the line 'Here it comes, another lonely day, playing the game, I'll sail away, on a voyage of no return to see' actually said something along the lines of 'He is the nasty one—Christ you're infernal—It is said we're dead men—Everyone who has the mark will live' when played backwards. People who believed that would believe anything, and Jeff rightly dismissed the accusation as utter nonsense. Two tracks, the breakneck-paced rocker 'Poker' and the more country-ish 'Down Home Town', featured Kelly Groucutt on lead vocal.

The image on the front of the sleeve showed the execution of a body in an electric chair in progress, admittedly in suitably subtle dark tones to make it look less obvious and not give nightmares to would-be purchasers browsing on the high street. On the back was a picture of the group with all but one of their faces pressed against a glass panel, apparently watching the grim spectacle. The exception was Richard Tandy, shown looking away from the camera, as he thought the concept was in questionable taste.

The most successful song on the album was the one written the most quickly of all. Jeff reportedly took about six minutes to pen 'Evil Woman', in which case it must have been the most lucrative six minutes of his career altogether. It was also a song which showed a slight musical concession to disco, and the verse 'there's a hole in my head where the rain comes in' pays homage to a line from The Beatles' 'Fixing A Hole' from *Sergeant*

Pepper. Thanks to heavy exposure on TV and radio, it restored the group to favour in Britain by peaking at No. 10 in January. In America it reached the same position shortly afterwards, finding similar success in several other countries.

Two more tracks were subsequently released as singles in Britain. Another slot on *Top Of The Pops* for the appearance in March of 'Nightrider' failed to chalk them up another hit, although the follow-up, 'Strange Magic', reached No. 38 in Britain during the summer, having climbed to No. 14 in America. Alert to the fact that Jeff was once again hot property—or at least closer to it than he had been for three or four years—United Artists reissued The Idle Race's *Birthday Party* album on their budget-price Sunset label, with an inferior non-gatefold sleeve, and 'The Skeleton And The Roundabout' as a single.[4]

By that time ELO had been touring extensively on both sides of the Atlantic. Following five dates at Glasgow, Edinburgh, London, Birmingham and Manchester between November 1975 and January 1976, they went to America, where they worked from 3 February to 13 April, playing sixty-five shows in seventy-six days, with several different acts opening as support, including Roxy Music, Journey, Little Feat, and Bachman-Turner Overdrive. They made use of coloured lasers for the first time, concentrating on songs from the new album, and on a new arrangement of 'Do Ya' from The Move's final days. In another interesting fusion of classic rock and genuine classical music, at some shows they featured a segue of The Rolling Stones' 'Let's Spend The Night Together', Grieg's 'Piano Concerto in A Minor', and, to finish, a section from The Beatles' 'The End' from *Abbey Road*. At a performance on St Valentine's Day at the Winterland Ballroom, San Francisco, after playing 'Strange Magic' they temporarily stopped the show so they could hand out red roses to the audience. That summer, a reissued 'Showdown' made the American charts at No. 59, while a compilation album, *Olé ELO*, reached No. 32.

In Bev's words, the tour had been 'a real ball-breaker,' and ten British dates planned for May were cancelled because they were suffering from exhaustion. The tour was rescheduled for June, with fellow Brummies the Steve Gibbons Band in the opening slot. The climax of this British leg of the tour came on 20 June 1976, when in a long hot summer in the capital, a performance at the New Victoria Theatre sold out. The show was filmed for television and subsequently released on video and DVD.

Just as Jeff and the rest of the group had been becoming increasingly disenchanted with being largely neglected in their home country, a change came for the better. During their breaks from touring, he had been working on new material at his Worcestershire home. He was coming up with new songs written on an old upright piano under the stairs, then laying down ideas on his trusty, time-honoured B&O tape recorder.

In July they went to Musicland Studios in Munich to record what would be their sixth album. Eight new songs were laid down, plus a new arrangement of 'Do Ya', as it had been greeted so rapturously on stage as part of a segue with '10538 Overture' during the tour. As Bev remarked, everybody else seemed to be doing it at the time,

> [...] so we figured we should give it a go—it *is* Jeff's song, after all. We always said that we'd never do any Move material onstage because we really had no connection to it anymore, but we've found that it's immensely popular onstage. We just hit the opening chords and people go crazy. We kept the arrangement pretty much intact from the original, but I think it's more powerful, especially with the strings, the middle part is really something with the strings undercutting.

During the sessions they were augmented by backing vocalists Patti Quatro (sister of Suzi), Brie Brandt, and on 'Rockaria!' by opera singer Mary Thomas, singing 'far, far away the music is playing' in German— with a momentary false start which remained on the record. On what would become one of their most-loved songs, 'Telephone Line', the sound of a phone ringing was played on a synthesiser. From England Jeff dialled an American number which he knew would remain unanswered, while Richard tuned the oscillators to the same two notes on the ringing phone.

It had been an easy album for Jeff to write;

> The songs started to flow and most of them came quickly. [For Jeff] it was amazing really, going from OK for probably three or four years to suddenly being in the big time. It was a strange but great thing. The touring was the only bit I could have done without but even then it was good most of the time.

During breaks in recording, they watched the Montreal Olympics on television. Frequent references to 'a new world record', coupled with the group's continuing success in the New World, provided them with an obvious title for the album. Once it was recorded and mixed, in August and September they played a further thirty dates across North America. One was the Freedom Festival at Nelson Ledges Road Course, Youngstown, Ohio, on 6 September, where they shared a bill with headliners Heart, the Steve Miller Band, Elvin Bishop, Roy Buchanan, and Widowmaker. The latter were a British group formed by ex-Mott the Hoople and Spooky Tooth guitarist Luther Grosvenor (alias Ariel Bender), onetime Love Affair vocalist Steve Ellis, former Chicken Shack and Mungo Jerry bass guitarist Bob Daisley, and Lindisfarne drummer Paul Nicholls. They were one of several acts signed by Jet Records who never managed to find chart success.

On the American dates the group used a new, more sophisticated laser light show, in which lasers were bounced off of their instruments to dazzle the audience. At the end of each show, a large black balloon with the new ELO spaceship logo emblazoned on it and carrying a mirrored disco ball rose up behind the stage, and lasers were shot off that as well. After one of the shows in August at the Universal Amphitheater, large numbers of city residents panicked at what they thought was a UFO sighting, and over a thousand phone calls were made to the police department. The balloon had been floating across the city and up behind the stage while lasers reflected off the disco ball, and the result was visible some miles away.

Final mixing sessions for the album took place at Los Angeles in October. When the first single from the new album, 'Livin' Thing', was released in Britain at the end of October, it immediately went on to national radio playlists and quickly rose to No. 4—ELO's best chart performance at home to date and a considerable improvement on the peak American position of No. 13. Jeff was amused by the speculation as to what the lyrics were about, whales and orgasms being suggested among other things. He put an end to the speculation when he said that they were actually about love, nothing more and nothing less.

More importantly, a few weeks later *A New World Record* shot into the British charts at No. 10 in its first week. Kept alive by two subsequent top-ten singles, it stayed there for 100 weeks and peaked at No. 6 the following summer, one place lower than its American best of No. 5. It was ironic that the man who had derided 'horrible hit singles' only a couple of years previously should be fronting a group who for the next four or five years would rarely be far from the British top forty.

In Britain, 'Rockaria!', which Jeff said was his attempt 'to make a 12-bar with different chords,' was edited of its false start and issued as the second single, reaching No. 9. A few weeks later the ballad 'Telephone Line' followed to No. 8, as well as becoming ELO's first gold single in America, where it reached No. 7. 'Do Ya' also found release as a 45 in America and reached No. 24, probably thanks in part to long-time fan Todd Rundgren performing it in concert. And there had been further potential hit singles if required, in the form of the almost dancefloor-orientated 'So Fine' and the lively 'Tightrope', which was lyrically 'a song about being in trouble and trying to get help.'

Three years earlier, bands like Genesis, Emerson, Lake & Palmer, and Yes had rarely bothered to release singles in Britain, putting their energies into the more lucrative album market. But by the end of 1976, fashions were changing—The Sex Pistols, The Stranglers, The Clash, and others were all over the front pages of the music press (if not sometimes the tabloids as well), and the humble 7-inch 45 was respectable once more. Each Thursday night around this time, viewers who sat down to watch *Top Of The Pops* could normally expect a diet of punk or new wave, disco, prog rock, and out-and-out pop, generally within the same thirty-minute slot. One memorably eclectic show in July ran the full gamut with a line-up of Supertramp, The Real Thing, the current No. 1 by Hot Chocolate, a new release from Cilla Black, and a filmed slot featuring the Sex Pistols—the latter much to the horror of middle Britain.

A New World Record was not only the first of an unbroken long run of top-ten studio albums in Britain, but also a major global success which consolidated ELO's position as one of the biggest selling rock bands in the world—five million units worldwide within its first year of release alone. It was also notable for the sleeve design, which featured the first use of the group logo designed by John Kosh, based on a 1946 Wurlitzer jukebox-model 4008 speaker. Music press ads proclaimed proudly that 'Soon, millions will hold A New World Record.'

Despite a busy recording and touring schedule with the group, Jeff found time to make a couple of appearances on record under his own name as a soloist. In November 1976 he was one of several artists, including Roy Wood, the Bee Gees, Elton John, Leo Sayer, Rod Stewart, Bryan Ferry, and the Four Seasons, to appear on the soundtrack album of *All This And World War II*—an album of covers of Lennon-McCartney compositions, mostly with accompaniment from the London Symphony Orchestra. His contribution was a segue of 'With A Little Help From My Friends' and 'Nowhere Man'.

In the summer of 1977 Jeff wrote, recorded, and released his own contribution to the disco market, the single 'Doin' That Crazy Thing'. Despite the group's high profile at that time, the public were evidently not ready to accept Jeff as a solo performer as well, for the record received little airplay and did not chart. But as far as the group were concerned, things could hardly have been better—and there would be more new world records to follow.

6
'Mr Blue Sky'

By early 1977, Jeff was making no secret of the fact that every time he finished an album, he just wanted to get back into the studio and start another one for the sheer joy of the creative process. The next time he did so would result in what was surely the height of his and the group's career. After the *A New World Record* tour was completed in April 1977, the next project would be what he called 'probably the hardest work' he had ever done, but also the most satisfying. 'It was a time of total music for me,' he recalled of those heady months in 1977, 'and once I'd got rolling, the songs just kept on coming.' For several weeks, it was a time of total music, the very welcome distraction of beer gardens in Munich, and plenty of soccer to clear the head. What else could a rock musician want?

In the case of someone as creative as Jeff, maybe it was a simple matter of not having to talk to the press too much. Journalists were now wise to the fact that he was sometimes reluctant to open up, and could be obscure if not downright curt when confronted by interviewers. Being more outgoing by nature, Bev Bevan was the natural public relations man, always happy to offer the press a friendly word or two and explain the division of labour at the top of the group. Talking to Billy Altman of *Circus* at around this time, he explained that Jeff was the one who liked to be totally involved in everything from the musical point of view, an ever time-consuming process.

> On other things, he's not that interested, so when it comes to interviews, or organising the band, I take care of things, because after all we are

partners in this, and have been since the beginning. When you're in a group, there's usually one person who's the musical leader, the one who has the ability to create things, and there's one who looks after the business side of things, and I've always been that way.

The period stretching from May to August 1977 saw the group involved in creating the next album. Jeff wrote all the songs on *Out Of The Blue* in three-and-a-half weeks, after a sudden burst of inspiration while he was hidden away in a rented chalet in the village of Bassins in the Swiss Alps, just beyond Lake Geneva. Armed with his guitar and a Revox tape recorder, he just sat there trying to write. For two weeks, the dreaded musical equivalent of writer's block thwarted him, and with a deadline of four weeks to write the material, the situation was less than ideal. Added to this, the weather had been really dispiriting. Then one day he got up to see the mists had lifted; the sun was shining and the mountains were all lit up. This change was well worth celebrating in music, and 'Mr Blue Sky' was the result. Perhaps, to quote another evergreen, good-weather song from about five years earlier, he could see clearly now the rain had gone. From that moment, the songs poured forth, and he came up with about fourteen in the next two weeks. Another number, 'Starlight', was inspired by the night skies he watched over the Swiss mountains. He busied himself with recording demos, sorted through orchestral and choral arrangements with Richard Tandy and Louis Clark, held rehearsals with the other band members, before scheduling recording sessions at Munich.

When interviewed by Roger Scott on Capital Radio a couple of years later, Jeff was at a loss as to say where all these songs came from. Songwriters often find it difficult to analyse the nuts and bolts of such an individual craft, and he was no exception. He did, however, reveal that he generally started with a chorus, sometimes a verse, or perhaps with just four or five notes 'with a chord that sounds really nice.' Sometimes he was able to complete the basis of a song in about ten minutes and return to it the following day. If it failed to make sense on first listening, it was probably a bad idea in the first place and he would throw it away. 'But if you play it back, and you've forgotten about all what you did, and you can suddenly pick it up again, it means it's pretty good.' Words were always left to last, until the point before it was time to add the vocals. When asked if he could hear the arrangements in his head while writing the song, he admitted that was true about 75 per cent of the time, and that he had a good idea of how he wanted it to sound when he took it into the studio.

Apart from the better sound, another virtue of Musicland Studios at Munich was the football pitch that lay just outside. The general idea was for the group to spend four or five hours working at a stretch, go out and have a good game of football to clear the mind, and then carry on working into the early hours. Heavy rain sometimes interrupted the football during what turned out to be one of the wettest German summers on record, and also gave him the idea for 'Concerto For A Rainy Day', which occupied Side Three of the album and of which 'Mr Blue Sky' comprised the fourth and final segment.

Have songs, will travel—although there was one minor setback at the early stages. They had been booked into a large and very grand studio to record the strings. As soon as they started, Jeff knew they had to get out of there. The strings sounded weak and thin, the room was far too large, and there was a reverb time of about twenty seconds. He was looking for a tough, dry sound, and he imagined that forty musicians might not like the idea of moving elsewhere. Fortunately they proved amenable, and all of them returned to the relatively small but more suitable Musicland. As he had never tried recording a large orchestra there, he initially had his doubts. But he was reassured when the musicians arrived there, each bringing their own chair as well as their instrument. They condensed the strings into two three-hour sessions on two days running, and got the crisp dry clean sound he had been looking for. And the attitude of everybody involved could hardly have been more refreshing, as they would complete a take and most of them would try and squeeze into the control room straight afterwards, keen to listen to the results.

After the final mixing sessions, Jeff personally delivered the master tapes to Jet Records and left for a holiday in Barbados. But once a songwriter, always a songwriter, and it was hardly surprising that he returned refreshed from a few days off with another three new songs in the bag. At the time, 'Telephone Line' was still in the charts worldwide, most inconsiderately delaying the release of the new track they had chosen as the first single.

As with the previous album, Richard was responsible for christening the epic double album. *Out Of This World* was considered, until they decided it sounded too much like its predecessor. However, Birmingham City Football Club, the Blues, 'Mr Blue Sky', and another track, 'Birmingham Blues', soon led to something colour-themed—*Out Of The Blue*.

The end result was packed with quality songs, twenty-one tracks in all—over four sides of vinyl. Kicking off Side One was the brisk opener 'Turn To Stone', featuring Jeff on Moog as well as guitar. The crisp, irresistibly commercial 'Sweet Talkin' Woman', which had initially been named 'Dead End Street' after a phrase from the first line, opened with a nifty mock-classical violin intro. Making a contrast were the yearning ballads 'Steppin' Out' and 'Wild West Hero', the latter including a couple of remarkable, totally out-of-character blues-based breaks on piano, played—unusually—by Melvyn Gale.

The album's undoubted high point came on Side Three, with 'Concerto for a Rainy Day', a four track musical suite based on the weather, culminating in the gloriously uplifting 'Mr Blue Sky'. In just five minutes it was part catchy song, part classical bombast in the best possible way, and according to some, yet again with a definite nod to The Beatles. As a journalist from *Mojo* some years later would have it, 'counterfeit confections were never more obvious, nor delicious, than this imitation of 'A Day In The Life''s middle section.' It also benefited from state-of-the-art technology. A brand new vocoder was coming onto the market, and they got hold of the prototype. The electric voice, Jeff joked, 'sounded like it had asthma!'

Although 'Mr Blue Sky' was not destined to be their biggest-selling or highest-charting single, it would become probably the best-loved song in the entire ELO canon, with a timeless appeal which crossed all generations and all tastes.

> It was one of the first songs I ever wrote with really posh chords and a very simple melody, and I think it's the simplicity of the song and the tune. And the words are quite simple. It's like a nursery rhyme kind of thing, that's how I meant it to be.

The large spaceship which adorned the album's cover was designed by John Kosh with art by Shusei Nagaoka, while the packaging included an insert of a cardboard cut-out of the space station and a fold-out poster of the group members. When the time came to take the record on tour, this space theme was extended onto the stage in the form of a vast glowing flying saucer set in which they performed.

Jeff clearly dominated the group as producer, songwriter, arranger, lead singer and guitarist, and at the end of the year he received his first Ivor

Novello award for Outstanding Contributions to British music. But in 1977, they were far from a one-man band. The contributions of others were vital, particularly the co-arranging skills of Louis Clark and Richard Tandy, and the powerful drumming of Bev Bevan. Richard's integration of Moog, harmonium and mellotron, with the more novel keyboard technology gradually becoming available, helped to give the music a more symphonic sound. Ironically, in a sense *Out Of The Blue* was not a full group album. Mik Kaminski only played on 'Sweet Talkin' Woman', 'Across the Border', and 'Wild West Hero', the latter being the sole track on the collection to feature Melvyn Gale (on piano, rather than his usual instrument, the cello). Hugh McDowell played on none at all, although all three were still credited on the sleeve as full members.

The record set several records of its own, with four million advance orders worldwide. It went multi-platinum on release in October, spawned five hit singles in various countries, and became the first double album in Britain to generate four top-twenty singles. Originally issued on Jet/United Artists, this was to change after American copies found to be defective were seen being offered at discounted prices in American and Canadian record shops not long after release, with an obvious impact on new record sales. Jet sued United Artists and early the following year switched their distribution to CBS and Columbia Records on a worldwide basis, including the rights to all past and future ELO albums.

As for the album's singles in Britain, 'Turn To Stone' was the first to be released. It fell short of the top ten by some way, rising no higher than No. 18 in November, and No. 13 in America. However, the following year 'Mr Blue Sky', followed in turn by 'Wild West Hero' and then 'Sweet Talkin' Woman', all reached No. 6, the last three all being issued on coloured as well as black vinyl.[1] The album itself, which was appropriately treated to a limited edition pressing on blue vinyl as well as the standard black, peaked at No. 4 on both sides of the Atlantic and spent a healthy 108 weeks on the British chart.[2]

By then Jeff could look back with considerable satisfaction on his latest achievements. As he told *Melody Maker*, on the last two albums he was finally doing what he had always really looked for. 'All I ever wanted to do was write pop songs. It took me ages to get that violin out of my arse!'

Another round of busy live work ensued with the nine-month *Out Of The Blue* 92-date world tour. After rehearsals in Los Angeles, the Pacific leg of the tour from January to March 1978, comprised gigs in Australia, New Zealand, and Japan, followed by European dates in April and May. On 2 June the British tour started with a charity show at the Empire Pool, Wembley, in the presence of the Duke and Duchess of Gloucester.[3] It was followed by seven more dates, like the first all sold out in advance, at the same venue, and then a single show at Stafford. After one of the Wembley shows, Jeff went backstage and was startled to find that Bob Dylan, who was then in London playing several concerts at Earl's Court, had been in the audience that night. Fate would bring both performers together again on a more regular footing ten years later.

After a short break the group flew to North America for a further series of concerts, from 30 June to 29 September. Billed as 'The Big Night', these shows were their largest to date. The average attendance at each of the forty-four stadium and arena dates was over 20,000, with an audience of 80,000 at Cleveland Stadium. It ultimately became the highest-grossing American live concert tour to that date.

With the exception of those at the Stafford gig in June, most British and American audiences witnessed what was one of the most spectacular stage presentations of the age—for which Don Arden was quick to claim the credit. This comprised a giant hamburger-shaped spaceship, made out of fibreglass, emblazoned with a motif which had developed from the image seen on the front of the sleeve of *A New World Record* and had come to fruition as the flying saucer from space on *Out Of The Blue*. *Star Wars* was the cult movie that everybody was talking about at the time, and in Arden's words, his strategy was an unashamed cash-in on the phenomenon. Rock music was entering the stadium era, and the punters would pay good money for tickets, but they wanted something spectacular for their hard-earned cash in a 20,000-seater arena in the days before TV screens in every venue. Hence a real live spaceship, which would land, take off, and have the members of the group in it!

The result was a larger-than-life device that opened up at the beginning of the show with lasers, fog machines, and taped music from Benjamin Britten's 'Sinfonia da Requiem', performed by the London Symphony Orchestra. As it did so, the group appeared from out of the floor, standing on hydraulic risers and playing the entire show, at which point they walked off stage and it closed again with more laser and fog theatrics and a repeat of Britten's music.

In addition to housing all the lighting, the spaceship contained hydraulic lifts in the floor. At the beginning of the show, there was an almighty rumbling as the spaceship opened up and lasers shot forth. Jeff could not resist the opportunity to leave the stage most nights after they had finished performing, rushing out to join the audience so he could watch it close and get on one of the lifts. 'The noise and spectacle of it and the smoke, these great big whining engines—it was really good,' he recalled. 'It made our classical music feel like a science fiction movie, it was a big show for its time.' After they had held their first 'spaceship rehearsals' in May at The Who's Shepperton Studios, Pete Townshend was so impressed when he saw it that he declared he wanted one as well.

Nevertheless, it had its drawbacks. It was a cumbersome piece of equipment, which required thirteen 18-wheelers to transport it from one city to another. An army of technicians was needed to construct, operate, and dismantle it every time, and because of the additional work and expense involved it was generally used only at alternate shows, dubbed the A-shows as opposed to the spaceship-free B-shows. The hydraulic lifts were prone to malfunctioning, and when this happened the entire group were not on stage at the start of the show, including the taped song intros. There was also the problem that somebody would get stuck with just their head sticking out, saying, 'help, you bastards!' It was so funny that Jeff curled up with laughter, barely able to play or do anything else—'it was better than *Spinal Tap*!'

Moreover, it was incredibly hot inside the spaceship, with dire effects on the tuning of the violin and cellos, and the acoustics inside made it difficult for members of the group to hear each other properly. Even when the spaceship stage was not used, the laser light show with its 80-channel light console and four krypton and argon laser units, and two portable power units to generate 525,000 watts of light were always called into service. The combination of lights and lasers, which meant the whole spectacle was estimated as four times brighter than the average rock show at the time, generated an incredible amount of heat for the group and their heat-sensitive instruments to perform in.

Some of the difficulties could be circumvented by using a tape system as backup for certain parts that could not be played live because of the use of sound effects, including the intros to 'Night In The City', 'Standin' In The Rain', and 'Mr Blue Sky'. For the rest of the time, the music on tape was turned down low so it could be used as a guide for the group to keep in sync. When the instruments went out of tune in the heat, the tapes could accordingly be turned up to correct any errors. It was not the intention that they would be heard by the audience when the group was playing.

But the whole principle of using tapes created one or two unforeseen problems. After the group had played the Pontiac Silverdome, Michigan, on 12 and 13 August, the promoter filed a lawsuit against them on the grounds that he had paid for a live show, and the use of tapes did not constitute a live performance. This, it later emerged, was an attempt to help recoup some of his losses as a result of heavy costs from poor local production support and lower ticket sales than anticipated. A spokesman for the group countered with the statement that it was common knowledge in the music industry that many other groups used tapes as part of their show. Although the promoter's action failed, once news of the proceedings emerged it did not bode well for ELO's reputation that they were having to rely on tapes to some extent. Moreover, with the group so popular and high in profile, it was a gift to critics—particularly those who were championing punk and new wave rock, and regarded ELO and their ilk as rock dinosaurs—who were looking for any stick to beat them with and pull them down from their pedestal. Compounding the issue later was the television broadcast of the charity show at Wembley in which recordings were mixed over the live performance, so it appeared as if the group was miming, *Top Of The Pops* style.

Finally, the tour ended in something of an anti-climax. The last two shows on the North American leg that had been scheduled to take place in Montreal with the spaceship set were cancelled due to a tax disagreement with the Canadian Government.

In spite of this disappointing conclusion, *Out Of The Blue*, the album and tour, was always going to be a formidable achievement to surpass in terms of creativity as well as sheer numbers, or bums on seats. During the eight-month, ninety-two show trek, they had played to more than two million people. As a live attraction for one of the global top-selling groups, the (blue) sky was evidently the limit, and it marked the end of an era for ELO.

Moreover, at the beginning of 1979 the group created yet another record. On the week ending 13 January, as a four-track EP featuring 'Can't Get It Out Of My Head', 'Strange Magic', 'Ma-Ma-Ma Belle', and 'Evil

Woman' fell six places to No. 40 in the British singles chart, *Out Of The Blue* went back up eleven places to No. 23 and *A New World Record* re-entered at No. 63 in the album listings. Dropping five places to No. 71 was a new entry from the previous week, *Three Light Years*, a boxed set containing *On The Third Day*, *Eldorado*, and *Face The Music*—the three albums which had signally failed to make the album chart the first time around. For the rest of January and most of February, all of them remained in the charts, *Out Of The Blue* climbing back into the top twenty and *Three Light Years* reaching a peak position of No. 38 for the week ending 20 January.[4] This gave them the unprecedented achievement, for several consecutive weeks, of having a single, a double, and a triple album on the chart simultaneously. Moreover, 'Can't Get It Out Of My Head' at last saw fleeting chart action for the week ending 20 January as well. Jukeboxes were ill-adapted to 7-inch EPs with a total playing time of around seven or eight minutes per side, and Jet issued a small pressing for the jukebox trade with this track on one side and 'Evil Woman' on another. This little-publicised contribution to the discography sold sufficiently to make an appearance at No. 52.

With hindsight, Jeff later acknowledged that the group had peaked artistically if not commercially with the previous two albums, and there was really no way of following that. But there were contracts to fulfil,

> [...] so I was forced to do things I didn't want to do, just because of signing bits of paper when you don't know what you're doing. Sign that? Oh yeah, of course, thank you! You can have fifty quid and all the brown ale you can drink. You don't realise what you're getting into. So it turned out I had to do another 93 albums for ELO!

That could have been a slight exaggeration. Unlimited brown ale, memory, and the finer points of mathematics, to say nothing of show business, do not generally mix too well. Even so, where would ELO go once they had done everything? After six years on and off the road across much of the world, Jeff decided it was time to cut down on playing live. As a result, the string players were now virtually redundant: Mik, Melvyn, and Hugh were about to be released from the group, though Mik would re-join them on their subsequent but increasingly rare gigs, occasional studio contributions, and promotional appearances. It was the end of a chapter.

7
'Don't Bring Me Down'

After a short break, *Discovery*, the next album, was recorded like its predecessors at Musicland during March and April 1979, with Louis Clark again in charge of the string and choral arrangements. It marked something of a change of direction on two tracks. When the opening track 'Shine A Little Love' preceded it in May as the first single, becoming their fourth consecutive 45 to peak in Britain at No. 6, it was a sign of things to come. For in a music scene which had been dominated to some extent by The Bee Gees' 'Saturday Night Fever' soundtrack album and chart-topping dance singles from the likes of Blondie, the Village People, Gloria Gaynor, and Anita Ward, Jeff proved that ELO could go with the flow and adapt to the contemporary musical climate as well as anybody else. Released at the end of May, *Discovery* gave the group that long-coveted first No. 1 album in Britain, entering the charts at pole position and staying there for five weeks.

Yet again the title had been thought up by Richard Tandy, and punters immediately seized on the play on words—'disco-very', or 'very disco'. Those who thought that ELO had sold out to dance music were exaggerating, for apart from 'Shine a Little Love' and 'Last Train To London', none of the other tracks seemed to fit particularly into that genre. Yet Jeff was happy to admit that he appreciated 'the force' of disco;

> I love the freedom it gave me to make different rhythms across it. I enjoyed that really steady driving beat, just steady as a rock, I've always liked that simplicity in the bass drum.

The album's second track, 'Confusion', was allegedly written by Jeff halfway through a game of snooker with his friend, footballer Trevor Francis. As he was about to take a shot, he went into another room, wrote his ideas down before he could forget them, and returned for the rest of the game—although to this day we do not know who won. Even more than snooker, love seemed to be a definite inspiration for part of the album. No less than three tracks fell into the love song category: 'Need Her Love', 'Midnight Blue', and 'Wishing'. Perhaps it was significant that their writer, whose first marriage had ended in divorce two years earlier, was about to be married for the second time.

The hits kept on coming from the album in quick succession. 'The Diary Of Horace Wimp', 'a story about someone who's a bit of a twit and could ever get anything done,' was not a million miles removed in feel from 'Mr Blue Sky', and a few weeks later reached No. 8. Single No. 3, 'Don't Bring Me Down'—'a great big galloping ball of distortion' which Jeff wrote at the last minute because he 'felt there weren't enough loud ones on the album'—was in fact a completely solo recording. Built on a drum loop from a previous track on the album, 'On The Run', written on piano with guitars and bass added later, it also became the first ELO song thus far released not to feature any strings. According to Jeff, it contained not only the drum loop, but also 'eight grand pianos, a cement mixer, and two crates of Newcastle Brown Ale and that got the ball rolling.' (Every hit songwriter should have them all, perhaps.) His use of the word 'grooosss' in the chorus was the subject of some speculation, but was in fact made up on the spot because it fitted. Thinking it was actually 'Bruce', fans would sing it at live performances until Jeff eventually adopted it himself at later shows. The final sound to be heard in the closing seconds was a fire door at Musicland Studios being shut, apparently intended as a suitable ending to the track because it was the last song on the album, as if to signify that they had finished and were leaving the building. Ironically, if a future collaboration the following year is to be excluded, 'Don't Bring Me Down' also became their highest-charting 45 on both sides of the Atlantic. It reached No. 3 in Britain, No. 4 in America, and No. 1 in Canada.[1]

In some ways the song was the end of ELO. Using strings on the recordings had increasingly become something of a time-consuming chore. The *Discovery* sessions were the group's first in which the string players were not used in the studio. The fact that 'Don't Bring Me Down' turned out to be far and away their most successful single possibly had some bearing on Jeff's decision that strings, which were becoming surplus to requirements, would be scaled down on future recordings.

Towards the end of the year two more tracks from the album, 'Confusion' and 'Last Train To London'—the latter about 'the hours and hours we spent on trains going back and forth from Birmingham to London to make records'—were released as a double A-side in Britain and reached No. 8. This set yet another record in making the album the first to generate four top-ten singles, a successful new milestone in spite of the fact that this was the first which the group did not support with a tour. Instead they made videos for each song, in which Mik Kaminski, Hugh McDowell, and Melvyn Gale all appeared, and all of them miming on keyboards for 'Don't Bring Me Down'. It was an easier way of promoting the music, though as the group were at the head of their game, with the album and each single being very successful in their own right, promotion on a major scale was arguably not strictly necessary.

The spaceship tour of the previous year had been exceptionally hard work, and none of them were in a hurry to repeat the experience. As he had the responsibility of writing and producing, Jeff felt that touring, which he had come to enjoy less and less over the years, was becoming something they could do without. Studio time and the creative process was far more enjoyable 'than playing the same old songs every night on a tour.' The group were offered a chance to headline the bill at the Knebworth Music Festival in August, playing before a capacity crowd of 120,000. They turned it down and Led Zeppelin gratefully stepped into the breach, playing what would turn out to be their last major British show.

That same month Jeff was married to Sandi Kapelson, whom he had met in Los Angeles, and in December their first daughter Laura was born. The family had homes at Walsh Hall—a fifteenth-century mansion in Meriden, Warwickshire—and Beverly Hills, LA.

Soon Jeff had another major recording project to oversee, the soundtrack for a forthcoming movie, *Xanadu*. This was an American romantic musical fantasy starring Olivia Newton-John and Gene Kelly, Xanadu itself being a nightclub which took its name from the summer capital of Kubla Khan's Yuan dynasty. Jeff was asked to contribute some songs and five were recorded by ELO for the soundtrack. Of these, three—'I'm Alive', 'All Over The World', and 'Don't Walk Away'—were released as singles in Britain, though each one fell short of the top ten.

The title song, with Olivia Newton-John on vocals, credited to singer and group, was released on Olivia's then label MCA in America and on Jet throughout the rest of the world. It gave the group their first and last British chart-topping single, ironically at a time when there was no weekly *Top Of The Pops* on BBC television to hail them as 'this week's No. 1', for the show was missing from the schedules for several weeks that summer due to a Musicians' Union strike. Because Jeff had never produced anybody but himself until then—with the exception of a small amount of work on Del Shannon's sessions a few years earlier—he found it strange to say, '"Can you try that bit again," but she was such a nice person that everything I suggested she tried.' However, as Olivia added her vocals to the backing track in a different studio entirely, it is apparent that she and the songwriter were probably not working together much in person. Hot property since co-starring in and recording two years earlier in the musical *Grease*, Olivia had for sixteen weeks been at the chart summit in Britain in 1978 (with two duets with co-star John Travolta). She also appeared on the other songs in the soundtrack, none of which had any ELO involvement.

The film had mixed, mostly negative critical reviews, although the album was better received and made No. 2 in the UK charts. All the same, Jeff subsequently found it wise to play down his contribution to the project. Maybe it had been a mistake, but as he pointed out, the difficulty with film music was that a songwriter when asked to contribute never knew what the movie was like when he wrote the tunes, and there was no way of judging it. The world would have to wait for more than thirty years before even one of the ELO songs would ever be performed live by its creator. Even so, around twenty years later he re-recorded the title song with his lead vocal, for release in the 2000 box set *Flashback*.

Although the boundaries between critically respectable rock and apparently disposable pop were less clearly defined in 1980 than they had been about five years earlier, and the humble 45 was once more respectable again (did Jeff ever regret that comment from 1974 about 'horrible hit singles'?), some held the view that ELO had sold out to the pop and disco world. But Jeff was not bothered about hatchet jobs in the British music press, which in general was notorious for its build 'em up, knock 'em down attitude. He admitted that he did not read the music papers much by then.

They usually slag us off anyway! But I think since we've been successful, which is about two years, maybe three years success on the level that we appreciate now, it seems like whatever you do, the more a lot of people dislike you for it.

The important thing was that the public bought the records. After all, *Out Of The Blue* had sold five million copies. 'It's unbelievable, I still can't let it sink in really.'

When asked some years later how much the *Xanadu* project had contributed to the group's sudden decline or fall from grace in the press, Richard Tandy was non-committal. At the time, he said, he merely considered the group's work for the film as just another bunch of songs.

Working on a film was an educational experience, and Olivia Newton-John was great to work with, and a very fine singer. Since then, people have commented that this was a bad career move, maybe they are right, it's hard to say.

For the music world, the autumn of 1980 brought tragedy with the unexpected death of John Bonham in September. The hard-drinking Led Zeppelin drummer, who in the mid-1960s had been considered as a possible member of the new young Midlands band which became The Move, had been a musical hero to many musicians of his generation. Jeff and Bev were reunited with Roy Wood briefly once again at the funeral at St Michael's Church, Rushock, Worcestershire, on 10 October. All three were squeezed in at the back of the small church, a miserable occasion which Bev later described as the saddest, most horrible funeral he had ever attended. Even more devastating was the murder that December in New York of John Lennon, the man who had so influenced Jeff and countless others throughout the years, and whose praise for his music had been so deeply appreciated.

Towards the end of 1980, Bev Bevan published *The Electric Light Orchestra Story*. Based on the diaries and scrapbooks he had kept over so many years, the 174 profusely-illustrated pages started with his early days as a drums-loving schoolboy, through to his time with The Move and the group into which they had morphed. In the last chapter, after noting that ELO had just celebrated their tenth anniversary, he concluded by writing that while it was impossible to make predictions in such a precarious business as music, he saw no reason why they should not still be playing together in the '90s.

Early in 1981 the group returned to Musicland Studios to record the album *Time*, augmented by strings conducted by Rainer Pietsch. Some regarded it as a return to their prog rock roots; others saw it as a step into the electro-pop sound of the '80s, in which the likes of Gary Numan, Ultravox, The Human League, and Depeche Mode were making the running, with more emphasis on keyboards. In Richard's opinion, the album was a fusion of ELO strings and modern keyboard sounds.

Basically it was a concept album, telling the time-travel story of a man from the 1980s who found himself in the year 2095 and tried to come to terms with being unable to return as he adjusted to his new surroundings. Some might have observed a faint parallel between this and one of The Kinks' sadly-neglected concept albums of the mid-'70s, *Soap Opera*, in which an ordinary man and a star-maker briefly change places to see how the other one lives.

The lead-off single, 'Hold On Tight', including a verse in French which had been translated from English by the Lynnes' French nanny on the day before the session, was released in July 1981. Things looked good when it peaked at No. 4 in Britain. Arguably a superior number, the follow-up, 'Twilight', driven by some marvellously phased drums and a thoroughly infectious chorus and keyboard figure, performed less spectacularly a couple of months later and stalled at No. 30.[2] A double-sided single, 'Ticket To The Moon' and 'Here Is The News', appeared early the next year and took them to No. 24, but a fourth 45, 'That's The Way Life's Meant To Be', released in March 1982, broke ELO's six-year run of hits and failed completely.[3]

Nevertheless, the album gave them a second British No. 1. With this continued run of success, the group undertook what would be their last major world tour. Covering a period of six months from September 1981 to March 1982, it started with a thirty-nine-city American tour until November, moving to Britain for eleven shows in early December. Following a Christmas break at the end of the month and time off early in the new year of 1982, they concluded with a third leg of the tour in Europe in February and early March.

After the lack of a tour for *Discovery*, Jeff had made no secret of his intention to cut back on live work, and their schedule for concerts promoting *Time* therefore included less dates than in previous years. Some changes were inevitable, particularly as this was the first set of shows they had undertaken without any cello players. Louis Clark played additional keyboards to fill the gap they had left and to supplement Richard's work. Mik Kaminski returned on violin and also on keyboards, and it was significant that on a few numbers four keyboard players were required to reproduce the sound from the studio recordings adequately. After the criticism levelled at them for using backing tapes on the *Out Of The Blue* tour, these were dispensed with apart from in the 'Prologue' at the start of the show and the intro for 'Roll Over Beethoven'.

Another musician who had known Jeff for a good many years found himself in the group as an additional touring member for the first time. Dave Morgan, who had been a member of Birmingham band The Ugly's with Richard in the 1960s, had spent many convivial evenings with Richard and Jeff, drinking wine, strumming guitars, and seeing how many Beatles songs they could remember back in Birmingham in June 1981. Jeff also played him an acetate of the forthcoming *Time* album. One evening Dave, who was then in need of a job, rang Jeff to ask if there was anything he could do to help out on the tour, and was invited to come round to rehearsals the next day. Within a couple of days he had talked himself into playing additional guitar, keyboards, and helping out on backing vocals on tour.

After ELO had rehearsed for three weeks in August at The Boggery, Jasper Carrott's folk club in Solihull, in the first week of September they flew to America for final rehearsals at Los Angeles onstage with a new major concert prop. This time, there would be no spaceship on stage. Instead, the show would feature a robot which was never given an official name, though it was generally known as Fred. Made at a cost of around £5,000, its movement was radio-controlled by roadies backstage.

The show began every evening with a large digital clock reading down to the start, and when the clock reached 0:00, the digital readout changed to 'ELO', the robot rolled out onto the darkened stage and a tape of the 'Prologue' played, while the group walked onto the stage in darkness. As on the album, this segued into 'Twilight', while the lights came up to reveal the group performing. 'Fred' generally remained on stage throughout the show, and during the 'Roll Over Beethoven' finale, it would move its arms as if it was conducting an orchestra. Following this, a vocoder voice would announce, 'Thank you and goodnight from ELO.' But like the spaceship on the previous tour, Fred was liable to stop working or even not start, and from time to time the show would have to go on without it. At one

American show it fell off the stage, had to be removed, and was too badly damaged to use any more that night.

With an ever-growing back catalogue of hits, Jeff and the group found that compromises had to be made if they were going to include as many as possible without an excessively long show. 1981 was, in Britain at least, the year of 'Stars On 45', 'Hooked On Classics' (courtesy of Louis Clark and the Royal Philharmonic Orchestra), and a plethora of other medleys in the singles charts. To their credit, ELO never stooped to cashing in on the trend by recording a medley of their hits as a single, but they did feature one on stage, alongside a Lennon tribute which included their versions of 'Across The Universe' and 'A Day In The Life'.

Before they went on stage each night, there was what Dave Morgan referred to as 'the customary fake panic.' Though Jeff never seemed nervous, it was quite normal for him to forget the words here and there. Once or twice he went up to Dave and asked him, perhaps jokingly, what came after 'The visions dancing in my mind', that being the first line to 'Twilight', the opening number. But forgetting the words never really fazed him; he would just make up some more to fit as he went along. Dave helpfully decided that one night he would write out the lyrics for 'Across The Universe' and paste them onto Jeff's fold-back speaker so he could get them right for once. Grateful as he was, it made no difference. Group and audience were treated as usual to more meandering prose based loosely on the original.

On the American tour, the support acts on various dates were The Michael Stanley Band, Ellen Foley, for one night only The Johnny Van Zandt Band, and Hall & Oates. The presence of the last was something of an embarrassment, as the duo were then at the peak of their career, enjoying greater chart success than the headlining act. This led to problems within the audience, as most fans were there to see one or the other and not necessarily both, and there were reports that on at least one night ELO fans tried to boo Hall & Oates off the stage.

There was no such drama during the nights they played in Britain, beginning at the Empire Pool, Wembley, followed by the National Exhibition Centre, Birmingham, and one night at the Royal Highland Showground, Ingliston, Scotland (with Voyager, purveyors of one solitary top forty 1979 hit, 'Halfway Hotel', in the opening slot). Roy Wood was in the audience one night at Birmingham, where they were booked to play three shows but had to reschedule a fourth. Ice, snow, and a partial shutdown of public transport on the exceptionally bitter evening of 13 December prevented large numbers of ticket holders from reaching the venue, so another night was added forty-eight hours later.

After the Christmas holiday, Jeff worked on new material for the next album. Further rehearsals were then held in Dave Morgan's home studio in Birmingham, and at the Nomis complex, North London, prior to the European leg of the tour starting in February 1982. While they were there, Louis took delivery of a new string synthesiser. He set it up and discovered a rich string ensemble sound, which produced a perfect rendition of the first few bars of Beethoven's Fifth Symphony. When Jeff heard it, he immediately rushed over to Louis, suggesting that he ought to play it on stage for 'Roll Over Beethoven' instead of the old tape they had been using. Louis demurred on the grounds that he could play it OK at rehearsals, but after a drink and at a show he might mess it up. Jeff then suggested that he ought to record it and play it back on the sequencer. Louis accordingly spent the next three hours programming it and listening intently on his headphones while the others continued to rehearse. The final playback was pronounced perfect.

Everything went as planned on tour for several shows. Then one night they reached the encore stage and Jeff announced that they would finish with 'Roll Over Beethoven'. The audience roared their approval, the lights went down, and the place was silent. It was pitch black, and everyone was evidently holding their breath. Seconds later Jeff's whisper on stage could clearly be heard by the rest of the group; 'Lou, hurry up, will yer?' as tiny beams of pencil torches flashed around in feverish activity on Louis's rostrum. Another even more frantic whisper ensued before at last the music struck up. When questioned after the show as to what had gone wrong, Louis explained that it had been too dark to find the start button, until one of the roadies came and shone his flashlight on the panel of the keyboard. A small lamp for Louis went on the shopping list.

Just before the 25 February show in Bremen, Bev Bevan was taken ill with kidney stones and flown back to England for treatment. Pete King, drummer for After The Fire, who were the opening group for several European shows, was asked to step into the breach. He went through the set with them in their hotel room, then took a tape away with him, 'and for the next twenty-four hours I was brainwashed with ELO. We only had two rehearsals before the gig!' He took the drum stool on six dates, but Bev was well enough to play again at the final show in Munich on 5 March.[4]

8
'Secret Messages'

In August 1982 ELO began sessions for the next album. Having done several years in Munich, and with Reinhold Mack now more involved with Queen, Jeff decided it was time for a change. After trying out Polar Studios in Stockholm, as used by ABBA, and another place in Paris, they settled on Wisseloord, Hilversum, taking engineer Bill Bottrell with them. Once in Holland, Jeff again proved prolific and wrote around twenty songs in the studio.

The loosely-based concept—or rather, the title—was a tongue-in-cheek response by Jeff to allegations of hidden satanic messages in their earlier LPs from Christian fundamentalists in America. After they had accused the group of back-masking, inserting secret messages into *Eldorado*, and encouraging listeners to worship the devil, some members would actually play their albums backwards in case they might stumble upon any so-called messages. They clearly needed to get out more. As Jeff aptly remarked, 'it meant that you deliberately said something backwards but when it was played forwards, it said something completely different, like SKCOLLOB.'

The album was due for completion by December, with a single due in the first weeks of 1983. In an interview with presenter Andy Peebles on Radio 1 in January, Trevor Francis mentioned that Jeff was in Holland putting the finishing touches to a double album. This was how the project had been conceived, partly as it would complete the group's contractual obligation to Jet Records for a specified number of albums.

However, one delay after another ensued, and the release dates for single and album were scheduled and rescheduled several times. The original idea had been for a double album, with one disc consisting of new studio tracks and the other containing live material recorded on the *Time* tour. This was abandoned when Jeff succeeded in coming up with more and more new songs, so the next plan was for a double studio album with a working title of *Unexpected Moments*. Jeff's enthusiasm for the project waned when the record company asked for various changes and he objected to their interference. At last everything was finished, and the new eighteen-track double album, renamed *Secret Messages*, was due for release in May.

At this late stage CBS decided that it would have to be a single album, on the grounds that 'people just don't release double albums anymore.' Apparently, they believed that to issue a double vinyl album would no longer be cost-effective, and refused to take the risk. At the back of their mind was possibly the fear of a repetition of Warner Brothers' experience with Fleetwood Mac's double album *Tusk* four years earlier, with strong initial sales quickly followed by a decline in demand and a quick route to the bargain-basement school of disposal. Notwithstanding a general economic recession and two or three lean years for the music industry in Britain, it seemed a rather defeatist decision, particularly as ELO's two previous albums had topped the British charts and they were one of the few consistently successful global acts on the company's roster. Another likely reason was that CBS, for all their baulking at releasing a double album which would be expensive to manufacture, were aware that ELO were still a very bankable proposition. Keeping the group together for another album and perhaps two or three more hit singles from it, two or three years later, looked like a better business strategy.

Had this all happened about five years later, seventy minutes of music would have easily fitted onto a single CD. But the 5-inch digital creation was still very much in its infancy, and so Jeff had to return to the studio, select ten tracks, and remix the new intros and outros of the songs so they would fit together. After what seemed interminable delays, both single and album appeared in June 1983, a couple of weeks apart.

Some of the 'missing' songs appeared as B-sides on subsequent singles and were also included on the *Afterglow* boxed set in 1990. One making its debut on the latter was a string-laden tribute to the Birmingham of Jeff's childhood memories. 'Hello My Old Friend' was almost eight minutes long, the first time he had recorded such an epic since the sessions for the second album, and resurrected 'High-rise tower blocks with panoramic views of trains and coal, Tiehead railway tracks tread faithfully, The gas works to behold.' Another number, 'Time After Time', which appeared as a bonus track on a 12-inch single and the cassette version of the album, featured Jeff's wife Sandi on backing vocals.

One song was a tribute to Jeff's heroes, 'Beatles Forever'. Shortly after it had been finished, bass guitarist Kelly Groucutt gave an interview in which he confidently predicted that it was going to be a major hit single, 'one of those songs that you know is going to be a smash while you're working on it.' But it was never destined to be even a track on vinyl, tape, or CD, let alone a single, and there has been much speculation as to why it was kept in the can. A refrain of 'Beatles forever, Rolling Stones never' might have seemed a little derogatory to Mick Jagger's group, while the lyrics verged on being an infringement of copyright as they were taken largely from Beatles lyrics. Jeff did not know the surviving Beatles personally at this time, although that would change within a few years. But as his closest working relationship would always be with George Harrison, it might have been embarrassing for him to note that all the lyrics and titles used in 'Beatles Forever' were lifted from Lennon and McCartney compositions.

Some years later, Jeff was asked about the chances of *Secret Messages* ever being released in the form in which it was originally intended, complete with 'Beatles Forever'. Initially, he suggested that it all depended on whether the record company really wanted to release old stuff that it found lying around. Pressed further as to what he would have done if he had had the final say, he explained that some of his material had not been officially released because he had felt he could record it much better. Fans had ended up getting what he believed was the best he could do at the time. By then, what were really most important to him were the new music projects on which he was working then, not merely looking back at his old stuff. While the complete versions of Bob Dylan's *Basement Tapes* and the Beach Boys' *Smile* eventually resurfaced many years down the line, it did not look as if *Secret Messages* was likely to follow them.

'Rock'n'Roll Is King' was released as a single a couple of weeks in advance of the album. Featuring a return from Mik Kaminski on violin, the rockabilly tune—regarded by fans as rather a lightweight piece of work by their usual standards—gave the group with a final British top-twenty single, peaking at No. 13.

The album was notable for one of their most striking sleeve designs, the front presented as if it was a painting in a gallery. An imaginative montage of figures from old masters canvases juxtaposed with an industrial Midlands town landscape, and a thumbnail picture of the quartet looking out of a second floor window. Taken from the *Time* tour programme, the fact that there were no new photo sessions for the album may have indicated that the group atmosphere was not at its best. The back of the sleeve was designed like a picture frame, with the track listing on mock paper labels, accompanied by adverts for artistic frame-makers, which were anagrams of the group members, namely T. D. Ryan (R. Tandy), F. Y. J. Fennel (Jeff Lynne), C. U. Ruttock (K. Groucutt), and E. V. Nabbe (B. Bevan).

Taking the theme concept further, and unable to resist the temptation of winding people up, the group put a mock warning on the back of the sleeve about hidden messages. This backfired when American disc jockeys gave the album a wide berth for fear of offending the Bible belt brigade, resulting in a hasty and less satirical redesign by Columbia Records stateside. Some lobbies were too powerful to risk alienating.

On release, *Secret Messages* entered the British charts at No. 4, but two subsequent singles, the title track and 'Four Little Diamonds', stalled at No. 48 and No. 84 respectively later that year.[1] At around this time, major record companies were engaged in increasingly aggressive marketing to sell singles with collectable formats, bonus giveaways, and competitions, all in the name of higher chart positions and album sales. When a 7-inch picture disc of 'Secret Messages' followed the conventional black vinyl into the shops, a sticker on the bag invited purchasers to identify a line from an ELO song from four clues, for which the first prize was a personalised gold disc, two second prizes silver discs, and the twenty-five runners-up copies of the LP. The lucky winner of the gold disc reportedly sold it on eBay some years later in order to help raise funds to buy his son a drum kit.

Jeff transparently had no intention of touring to support the album—least of all an album which had been truncated against his wishes until it was no longer the record he had envisaged. The previous tour had taken him away from his family and two small daughters, with whom he would far rather have spent his time. He was having disagreements with Don Arden which would shortly see them going their separate ways, and his enthusiasm for ELO in general was waning. Although he made a few promotional appearances to promote the album and singles, gave some interviews in America and Britain, and partook in a couple of promo videos for 'Rock'n'Roll Is King' and 'Secret Messages', the album was simply sent out into the great wide world to sell on its own merits, with less help than usual from the people who had spent so long making it.

Speculation over ELO's declining activities was leading to suggestions that they had disbanded, or were about to and merely keeping quiet about it. The group was increasingly becoming a one-man band. Kelly Groucutt played bass guitar and sang backing vocals on just four tracks from the sessions for *Secret Messages*, only two of which, 'Rock'n'Roll Is King' and 'Train of Gold', made it to the album. Once again, Jeff overdubbed the remainder. In November 1983 Kelly sued the management and Jeff for unpaid royalties, claiming one quarter of the group's earnings backdated to when he originally joined in 1974. Jeff nonchalantly remarked that instead of spending his money on legal fees, Mr Groucutt would be advised to check his contract. However, Kelly and his counsel succeeded in reaching an agreement and receiving £100,000 in an out-of-court settlement. He had thus effectively resigned from the group, which in its increasingly studio-bound era had as little need of a bassist as it did a violinist and two cellists.[2]

Moreover, Bev Bevan, who had been an integral part of the line-up from the early days, was feeling increasingly dispensable, almost like the string players before him. His trademark drumming was less and less in evidence, and although he was still credited on the album sleeve, to the casual listener it was apparent that drum programming was taking over. In an interview he openly admitted that he was very frustrated with the situation and losing patience.

> Sometimes the control that Jeff exerts over everything and everyone can really stifle your creative juices. I hate it when I'm relegated to being a session drummer with the band. Hell, I've been with this group for more than ten years, and sometimes I want to say, 'hey, let me do what I want.'

In August *The Sun* reported that Bev had left the group. He put the record straight by announcing that, despite the absence of an ELO tour, he was still a member. In fact, he had joined Black Sabbath on a temporary basis to play the Reading Festival later that month and a handful of American gigs on the *Born Again* tour, filling in for their regular member Bill Ward who was absent on medical grounds. Having recently disbanded his own eponymous group which he formed soon after the demise of Deep Purple, Ian Gillan had now joined forces with Black Sabbath as their vocalist.[3] When asked in an interview whether Sabbath would be featuring any ELO songs live, Ian suggested tongue-in-cheek that they might play 'Telephone Line'.

The drummer was not the only one to demonstrate that for its members there was a musical career outside ELO, whose future was looking less and less assured. Even Jeff himself had already begun concentrating more on writing and studio production work for others. He had produced and written the 1983 minor hit 'Slipping Away' for Dave Edmunds, played on sessions with Richard Tandy for Dave Edmunds' album *Information*, and produced six tracks on his 1984 album, *Riff Raff*. In 1984, he and Richard contributed two songs, 'Video!' and 'Let It Run', to the soundtrack of the movie *Electric Dreams*, as well as a third song, 'Sooner Or Later', released as the B-side of 'Video!', a single which only just crept inside the top hundred chart. He also wrote 'The Story of Me,' recorded by the Everly Brothers on their comeback album *EB84*, and 'One Way Love', recorded by Agnetha Fältskog as the lead single from her second post-ABBA soloist album, 'Eyes Of A Woman', released in 1985.

ELO were now more a contractual obligation than anything else. Towards the end of 1984, the trio consisting of Jeff, Bev, and Richard returned to the studios. They started sessions in the sunshine at Compass Point, Nassau, and in the following year went to snow-covered Hartmann Digital, Untertrubach, near Nuremburg. Working in two climatic extremes, Jeff suggested, had something of an influence on the lyrics he was writing, which were the most spontaneous he felt he had ever got down.

> It's hard to talk about lyrics, because sometimes you don't really know where they came from, just a little idea sparks them off and you start rambling on and there's a song that you just change bits of. But I have no doubt they were a product of their surroundings.

Whereas the previous album had almost completely lacked strings, *Balance Of Power* came full circle in having none at all. At the time Jeff was not sure what sort of musical direction to go in, 'because I'd been throwing all these great big heavy thirty-piece orchestras on records at the time.' Over the previous albums he had become more and more tired of using strings, and after recording them he would pull them down lower and lower in the mix, his reasoning being that it sounded a lot better that way. Jeff and Richard were playing synthesisers as well as using more electronic percussion, and Bev's drumming was even less in evidence than usual. (It did, however, allow him more time for other ventures, such as appearing as a German stormtrooper in a video for Roy Wood's new single, 'Under Fire'). Jeff, it was reported, presented the other two with completed working versions of the songs, asked them to learn their parts, and then overdubbed them. Moreover, for the first time in the ELO catalogue, a couple of tracks featured saxophone, played by guest musician Christian Schneider.

Digital technology was a two-edged sword. Although new developments enabled musicians and producers to experiment, in Jeff's words,

> […] it's not so much fun as it was because everybody's got the same stuff. As soon as they make a new chip for software for the keyboards, all the producers have got it.

While he had the new hi-tech keyboards, 'I still use old crummy keyboards just because they sound better.'

The album was originally planned for release in the summer of 1985, but Jeff was not satisfied with the results and took the forty-eight-track tapes to Musicland Studios for further remixing. *Balance Of Power* at last saw the light of day in March 1986, and peaked in its second week of release in Britain at No. 9. To all outward appearances, this was a very different ELO. Even the packaging of the album suggested major changes. The old logo of blessed memory had disappeared, to be replaced by a rather austere, not to say unimaginative sleeve design of geometrically-shaped letters. Moreover, at just over thirty-four minutes' running time, it was the shortest album they had ever released. Four additional numbers recorded at the same sessions—'Destination Unknown', 'Caught In A Trap', 'Matter Of Fact', and 'Sorrow About To Fall'—were omitted from the running order and appeared on the B-sides of or as bonus tracks to 7- and 12-inch singles. Perhaps it was appropriate that in a decade dominated by the likes of The Human League and Erasure, ELO should have ended their fifteen-year history as an electro-pop outfit.

On the surface, it sounded in parts like an upbeat pop album, until a closer listen to the lyrics suggested otherwise. Although Jeff was keen to move on, for him it represented the end of a fifteen-year era, and on a more personal level, reflected the problems with his marriage to Sandi. For an artist to release an album on which some songs seemed based around the end of a marriage was nothing new. The examples of Bob Dylan's *Blood On The Tracks*, Phil Collins's *Face Values*, and Richard Thompson's *Hand of Kindness* spring readily to mind. The three tracks released as singles on both sides of the Atlantic certainly betrayed a sense of sadness, if not heartbreak. 'Calling America', the first and most successful—reaching No. 28 in Britain and No. 18 in America, where it would be ELO's final chart entry—told the story of someone 'out in space, trying to talk to someone,' only to find that there was nobody on the other end of the line—'there must be something going wrong, that number just rings on and on.' 'So Serious' fared poorly, rising no higher than No. 77, and also telling a tale of separation—'can it really be so serious, to be all broken up and delirious, I guess we've really been out of touch.' The final single, the ballad 'Getting To The Point'—a self-explanatory title if ever there was one—reached a derisory No. 97, due in part to industrial action at the CBS pressing plant. But it was an inglorious conclusion to what had once been such a consistent chart career in Britain.

Elsewhere on the album, 'Endless Lies' (admittedly written earlier, with a previous version having been intended for *Secret Messages*), 'Is It Alright', and 'Heaven Only Knows' certainly conveyed the impression of a less than rose-tinted view of life, just as the titles 'Baby's In Black', 'No Reply', and 'I'm A Loser' suggested grim-faced, unsmiling Beatles (as indeed they appeared on the sleeve photography) on their fourth album *Beatles For Sale*, some twenty years earlier. Jeff denied that the album was in any way a personal one, insisting that it was 'all fictional stuff.' There was, however, a little light relief in the closing track, 'Send It', a song perhaps testifying to the influence of Dave Edmunds, and was an attempt to try 'a new concept of doing a rockabilly record with brushes and synthesisers.'

Ironically, this all happened the same year as what could have been such good promotion, if not a new lease of life, for ELO. On 15 March, Heartbeat '86, a children's hospital charity fundraising venture, staged an all-star gig at Birmingham National Exhibition Centre. The line-up included not only ELO, but the cream of local acts past and present: Roy Wood and his new band assembled specially for the purpose (amid ill-founded speculation that The Move would be reforming for the evening), the Moody Blues, the Rockin' Berries, UB40, The Fortunes, The Applejacks, The Steve Gibbons Band, and Robert Plant.

ELO took the stage in a seven-piece line-up, with new member, Martin Smith, on bass guitar. As the group were in the dressing room getting ready to go on, Jeff rushed in and told the others breathlessly, 'He's here, he's just landed.' 'Who?' was the joint response.

'George'—in other words, George Harrison. Jeff briefed them to try and make him feel at home and act normally. However, acting normally was easier said than done when in the presence of a rock deity. The former Beatle ambled in casually, accompanied by Jeff, and they all lined up like toy soldiers. As he said hello to them Jeff hovered behind, glowering at the others as if to say, 'I thought I told you to act normal!'

The group played a well-received set which included 'Calling America', their then current single, among a dozen tried and trusted old favourites. 'If anybody claps, maybe we'll do a tour,' Jeff quipped on stage. Applause there was in plenty, and as the major attraction on the bill—debatably with the exception of the veteran Moody Blues—they stole the show in the opinion of many who were there. At the end of the show, an all-star finale saw George Harrison, Dave Edmunds, Noddy Holder, and Denny Laine on guitars and share vocals with everybody else on a finale of 'Johnny B. Goode'.

At the same time, Jeff was involved in another local charity initiative. Richard Tandy and Dave Morgan had combined forces in a side project, The Tandy-Morgan Band. They recorded a single comprising two songs written by Dave, 'Action' and 'Tequila Moonshot', produced by Jeff. All royalties were donated in aid of the West Midlands Children's Hospice. Although local reaction was very favourable, the single failed to make the national chart.

But the tour which Jeff had mentioned so casually was not to be. There was some live and promotional activity to support the album during the ensuing four months, amid speculation that if it sold well then they might well commit themselves to a few dates. However, disappointing sales and Jeff's increasingly evident lack of appetite for one prevented the idea from growing into something more.⁴ The group appeared on TV in a slot on the chat show *Wogan*, with former *Carry On* actor Kenneth Williams deputising that week for the vacationing eponymous host. Viewers were treated to the sight and sound of the album's second single 'So Serious', with Mik on violin plus Louis Clark and Dave Morgan on cellos—all miming, naturally, if only to make a statement on the whole farce on pretending to play live on light entertainment TV. Casual viewers either side of the Atlantic may still have remembered ELO as the group with the big fiddles, although the sound had altered considerably since the early days. The schedule was wound up with three more shows: Wembley Stadium on 5 July, Westfalenhalle, Dortmund, on 12 July, and Martin-Schleyer-Halle, Stuttgart, the next day, as support band to Rod Stewart. While there was no doubting the star status of the latter, it was a little ironic that such a globally successful group should not be topping the bill on their final gigs.

Although the writing had been on the wall for some time, few fans were fully aware that the group were not merely going on hiatus, but that to all outward appearances it was the end of the group with Jeff as the frontman. Over the years ELO had evolved and been through several changes, he mused later on. It had taken a quantum leap with *Eldorado*, their first album to go gold in America. He had been trying to track one violin and one cello for hours to make it sound like an orchestra, before he realised that it made more sense to have a proper orchestra instead. As the music was impossible to play on stage, he had had to use tapes to pretend there was a big sound. Something was needed,

[…] because it had this grandiose name, the Orchestra, and really it was just this group with a cello in it. My producer's head wouldn't let me enjoy it. I mean, it was always fun, you could have a laugh and get drunk and mess about, but I wasn't getting any pleasure out of playing. [At this point in the interview, he mimed playing guitar and looking at his watch.] Oh, only another half hour to go. It just got to be a ritual in the end, and it started driving me crackers. We had loads of success—nineteen top forty hits in America, and all that stuff—and I'm grateful to all the people that liked it, but that wasn't what I was doing it for.

9

'Handle With Care'

Having put ELO on indefinite hold, the word 'split' not yet being uttered, Jeff was free to immerse himself fully in a new role as producer for others. He had already done so on a small scale for Del Shannon and in a greater capacity for Dave Edmunds. In 1987 he produced three tracks on an eponymous album by Duane Eddy: 'Rockabilly Holiday', 'Theme For Something Really Important', and 'The Trembler', recorded during sessions which also featured Paul McCartney, George Harrison, Steve Cropper on guitar, and Jim Keltner on drums. But these were only the forerunners of much greater things. Jeff would be feted as the man behind several of the all-time greats from the music generation who had inspired him throughout his youth.

The Beatles connection had already begun before the Heartbeat '86 concert. That meeting came about through another guitarist who had shared the stage at Birmingham, and who had already benefited from Jeff's expertise …

> I [Jeff] did a song with Dave Edmunds in Holland, because I was doing an album over there—an ELO album—and he rang me up and said, 'do you fancy writing a song for me and I'll come over while you're there and I can sing it?' So he came over and we recorded this track together and he played this big six-string bass. We recorded it, finished it and a few weeks later we're having dinner, went our separate ways and he shouts down the street, 'by the way, I forgot to tell you; George Harrison asked me to ask you if you'd like to work on his new album with him!' I

said, 'what do you mean, "by the way"?' As if that shouldn't be the first thing you'd say over dinner! But that's what happened.

Jeff was accordingly invited to meet George at his house, Friar Park, Henley-on-Thames. George took him for a spin in the boat around the lake in his garden, and they discussed collaborating. They hit it off immediately, and according to George, 'drank red wine together for a year and a half.' It was the start of a close friendship which led to them working together on and off on a regular basis until George's untimely death. When asked if he wanted to come to the Grand Prix in Australia, Jeff nodded eagerly. 'Meet me in Hawaii in two weeks.' Jeff accordingly kept the rendezvous; in October 1986, they flew to Adelaide together and reached the race in a helicopter, landing in the middle of the track, getting out and meeting all the teams.

Jeff was astonished by the fact that George simply knew everybody. 'Wow, you can do anything with this guy—just go wherever you want!' As George would sometimes say with a grin, 'It's good to play the Beatle card sometimes.'

In June 1987 Jeff took part in a Prince's Trust show in London, playing alongside a formidable galaxy of stars including George, Ringo Starr, Eric Clapton, Elton John, Ben E. King, Bryan Adams, and Paul Young. The show closed with Jeff and Eric playing alongside the two former Beatles on 'While My Guitar Gently Weeps', 'Here Comes The Sun', and a grand finale of 'With A Little Help From My Friends' with the other artists taking part that evening. Ringo had been making records as a solo performer on a fairly regular basis, although with no chart success for the last twelve years or so and with probably diminished expectations of any. George, who had released several albums and singles on his own Dark Horse label distributed by Warner Brothers since the expiry of his EMI contract in 1976, had experienced a short-lived comeback of sorts in 1981 with the John Lennon tribute single 'All These Years Ago', which made the British top twenty and reached No. 2 in America, and the accompanying album, *Somewhere In England*. His only other album since then, *Gone Troppo*, released late in 1982, was poorly promoted and disappeared almost without trace on both sides of the Atlantic.

But when all three appeared together on stage, rumour went into overdrive. One or two sections of the media, either with astonishing naivety or, in the case of the tabloids, a brazen attempt to shift more copies, began running 'Beatles to reform with Jeff Lynne?' stories. Something of the kind was to come about seven years later, but not in the way that these ill-informed, over-imaginative reporters had envisaged.

What was true, however, was that Jeff had just been in the producer's chair for George's first album in five years, and it would result in one of the major comebacks of the decade. While they were in Australia they had already begun working on their first song together, 'When We Was Fab'. The entire album was recorded at FPSHOT (Friar Park Studios, Henley-on-Thames) between January and March 1987, with a team that included Ringo Starr and Jim Keltner on drums, Eric Clapton on guitar, Jim Horn on saxophone, and Gary Wright and Elton John on piano. Producing a Beatle, said Jeff, was not lost on him.

> It was great because I'd just had a year off and playing in my own studio in England and learning to be an engineer, believe it or not. I'd never really mastered engineering; I'd always been a producer and always had to tell the engineer what I wanted because I couldn't do it myself. I taught myself how to do it myself and I was much more in tune with all the knobs.

But Jeff and George were never after that huge panoramic ELO ambience. Nothing could have been further from their minds.

> I was gradually quietening that sound that ELO had done, and there were fewer strings. In ELO, it used to be a case of, 'oooh! String day tomorrow!' and then by about the tenth album it became 'oh, bloody hell! It's string day tomorrow.' I'd had enough of them. I grew tired of the strings. But that's not why they asked me. It was more the punch I was doing later on and they just liked the sound that I made, whatever it was.

George was delighted to be working with such a demanding taskmaster, who he readily admitted encouraged him to go that extra mile and was not afraid to tell a former Beatle when he was OK but could perform just a little better.

> I could have done it easier on my own, but because Jeff was there, the general standard was higher. Knowing that he was standing there and that he was such a good vocalist made me want to try harder.

For Jeff, the experience of meeting, befriending, and then working with two former Beatles was more or less like a dream come true.

> It's unbelievable really, you'd never dream of it, obviously. They'd always be on this pedestal, but to get to hang out and be pals with, and work with, and be successful with them is fantastic.

His admiration for them as musicians had always been boundless. George's skill on slide guitar, he said, was

> [...] second to none. He's my favourite slide player—he's got this touch, it's just like a velvet touch—he plays it, it's so smooth, so beautiful and soulful and yet tuneful and melodic, and I've never heard anything quite as beautiful as how he can do it. So when he asked me to work with him, it was one of the biggest thrills of my life.

He encouraged George to put more focus on his guitar in the songs, both on that peerless slide and the distinctive 12-string Rickenbacker. As for Ringo,

> He is one of the best drummers I've ever heard, probably the best, because he's just so—I dunno, he's got it! His frills are just right and his backbeat's great.

When the album's first single, 'Got My Mind Set On You', reached the shops that October, it had 'hit' written all over it. The song, written by Rudy Clark, had been a favourite of the Liverpudlian guitarist ever since he had bought it on a James Ray album on his first visit to America in 1963. Accompanied by a quaint, almost surrealist video which included a brief appearance from a Harrison doppelganger parodying a couple of dance moves by Michael Jackson—at that time the global music business's hottest property by a mile—the single immediately became a favourite on radio, television, and even on dance floors up and down the country. (Ironically, George made it evident in at least one interview around this time that he was definitely not a Michael Jackson fan!) The result was his most successful single since the heady days of 'My Sweet Lord' sixteen years before, reaching No. 2 for three weeks in Britain in November and topping the American charts after Christmas. With the release of the album *Cloud Nine*, also in November, it was evident that Jeff's production had given George's music a much-needed breath of life. The second single (and first song they had worked on together), 'When We Was Fab', had evolved into a neat send-up in which George poked fun at his Beatles past, with a cello prominent in the backing.

When it came to the third single from the album, 'This Is Love', Warner Brothers asked him for an additional track for the 12-inch single. This led to the culmination of what had been a dream project, if not a fantasy, for Jeff and George. During a wine-fuelled conversation one night while they were working together on the album, George said that they ought to put a group together. 'Who should we have in it?' was Jeff's response. 'Bob Dylan,' was George's first suggestion. Jeff laughed and said, 'Oh yeah, he'd be good. How about Roy Orbison, he can sing a bit?' Having agreed on Roy, they then both wanted Tom Petty. 'But I thought we were just joking. Anything could happen with George, everybody loved him.'

The first public mention in the media of the Traveling Wilburys was when George was interviewed by Bob Coburn on the Rockline radio station in February 1988. When the question came up as the follow-up to *Cloud Nine*, he said that what he would really like to do was an album with some of his mates. He then referred in passing to 'this new group I got' called the Traveling Wilburys. 'I'd like to do an album with them and later we can all do our own albums again.' Whether this was wishful thinking or the foundations had actually been laid must be left to conjecture, but within a few weeks it had begun to take shape. The name Wilbury was a slang term that George had used while they were recording the previous year. When they heard any little glitches resulting from faulty equipment, he jokingly remarked to Jeff, 'we'll bury 'em in the mix.' From that it was but a small step to choosing a name. George's first choice was the Trembling Wilburys, modified at Jeff's suggestion to the more favourably-received Traveling Wilburys.

Anything could happen—and for once it did. George decided it would be easy for them to knock off a new song quickly together, and he asked Jeff, who was having dinner with Roy Orbison, to come along. They did not have a studio booked, but Bob Dylan had a suitable tape machine in his garage. George needed to go and collect a guitar which he had left at Tom Petty's place, so Tom was invited along as well. Next day, all five

'Handle With Care'

were at Bob's place. George and Jeff sat on the lawn working out a tune together, while Bob as the host was preparing a barbecue. 'Give us some lyrics, you famous lyricist,' George called out to him. Someone looked behind the garage door and found a cardboard box marked 'Handle With Care'. That, they decided, was not a bad song title. Within the next few hours, they had all collaborated on the song to go with it, with Bob saying what they thought were 'some hysterical things.' George had the chorus already and Jeff wrote the verses at dinner time. Then they thought that if Roy Orbison was going to be involved, they would have to write him 'a lonely bit.' The song was sung and recorded, with appropriate overdubs added and mixing completed soon afterwards.

When Warner Brothers boss Mo Ostin heard 'Handle With Care', which had been largely George's composition, he said that it was far too good to be buried as a mere bonus track on the single. This, he declared, was 'the first track of your new group!' In May, nine more songs were duly written in as many days and recorded in Dave Stewart's home studio in Los Angeles. According to Jeff,

> Each song only took a day. We gave ourselves one day to write a song so we did ten days and ten songs. I did have to pinch myself!

There was a deadline for them in that Bob was due to go on tour after that. So each day they assembled after breakfast, sat around with acoustic guitars, and somebody would come up with a title, or a chord pattern, or both. Although every song was written mainly by one of them, the other four had a certain amount of input, and the general agreement was that giving them individual credits would look too egotistical. 'Dirty World' came about when Bob jokingly suggested that they should do something like Prince, and spontaneously began to sing 'love your sexy body,' although each member came up with ideas to fill in the closing lyric lines of 'He loves your…' Bob was also mainly responsible for 'Congratulations' and 'Tweeter And The Monkey Man'. 'Heading For The Light' and 'End Of The Line' were mainly the work of George, while 'Last Night' and 'Margarita' were largely Tom's efforts. Jeff was the main writer of the rockabilly tune 'Rattled', and of the magnificently soaring ballad 'Not Alone Any More'—a perfect showcase for Roy's unmistakable vocal. Most of the instrumental work was also done by the famous five, with

Jim Keltner augmenting them on drums, Jim Horn on saxophone, and Ian Wallace and Ray Cooper on percussion.

Working with others while creating the album was a world away from what Jeff had been used to for so long, with having been responsible for so many releases by his last group. Speaking in March 1989 to presenter Roger Scott (who had left Capital Radio to join Radio 1) shortly before his untimely death from cancer, Jeff admitted that he had learnt more during the previous year than he ever had before. Previously he had felt very insulated, just producing records by ELO which he would not play to anybody else until they were completed, delivered, and ready for release—out of insecurity as much as anything else.

> I know it's stupid, because really, you should play it to as many people as you can, and see what they think. But I never do now, all these people I work with, they hear the bits all the time, and I'm still trying to produce it, and maybe there's only one guitar and a keyboard on it, and I have to say, 'Oh, it will be fine when I've got all these other things on,' and it always is. So I've learnt that you don't have to be paranoid all the time, because it does work out fine in the end. It's given me a lot of confidence as well, because to work with all these great people, like Roy Orbison, George Harrison, Bob Dylan and Tom Petty all the time, has given me a lot more perspective, and I suddenly see that, well, I ain't so bad after all! I've had so much fun with them—with everybody I've worked with it's been great fun.

The final overdubs and mixing on the album were completed in England at FPSHOT. As the Wilburys were in effect George's group, Warner Bros had first option on release. It could easily have appeared on his Dark Horse label, but the cooperative ethic was retained with the formation of the Wilbury Records label.

Everyone in the group, formed so spontaneously almost before they had realised it, got along extremely well with each other. When an interviewer asked Jeff whether Bob Dylan was 'as strange to work with as his legend would suggest,' Jeff categorically replied that this was not so.

> Bob is Bob, and he always will be. And that's why he's Bob. He's great, he's his own person, he does his own thing, and he's amazing. He's totally himself.

As for the songs, they were intended to be an embodiment of the 'back to basics' school of thought. For Jeff, it was a world away from the grind of 'string day' during some of the ELO sessions, or indeed the soulless quick fix of programmed drum tracks. George remarked that for him, in a sense, the record was flying in the face of 1980s pop, which 'had got so computerised and so monotonous,' with the same drum sample on far too many records.

Released in October with a remarkable absence of hype, the single 'Handle With Care' and the parent album *Traveling Wilburys Vol. 1* shortly afterwards immediately attracted glowing reviews and favourable press coverage. In an era dominated by conveyor-belt pop from the Stock-Aitken-Waterman song-writing and production 'hit factory', and by the rise and rise of acid house, it all came as a breath of fresh air. The group had given themselves aliases on the record sleeves and labels throughout as the sons of Charles Truscott Wilbury, Sr, the five half-brothers, as they called themselves; Nelson Wilbury was George, Otis was Jeff, Lucky was Bob, Charlie T. was Tom, and Lefty was Roy. But the collective image on the front of the record sleeves of five well-known British and American rock icons, coupled with the unmistakable vocals, made their identities self-evident.

A short mock-biography on the inner sleeve introduced the listener to the Wilburys, 'a stationary people who, realising that their civilisation could not stand still forever, began to go for short walks,' and much more in a similar vein. These notes were credited to Hugh Jampton and E. F. Norti-Bitz, Reader in Applied Jacket, University of Krakatoa (East of Java). The writer was Michael Palin of the Monty Python's Flying Circus team, who had worked on ideas from The Beatles' former press officer Derek Taylor. Such humour was more than appropriate on a record featuring the former Beatle who had for some time been associated with the Pythons.

In Britain, the single peaked at No. 21, and the album at No. 16, staying on the album charts for almost nine months and a certified platinum with sales of 300,000. On the other side of the Atlantic the single did no better than No. 45, but the album made No. 3 and stayed on the charts for a year, selling two million copies within the first six months. It was eventually certified triple platinum for sales of three million, and won a Grammy Award for the Best Rock Performance by a Duo or Group the following year.

It all coincided with a hectic round of activity for Jeff as producer, for at the same time he was working on new albums with Tom and Roy. Everybody was buzzing with energy, and soon after the album was released there was even talk of taking the Wilburys out on tour.

Roy had been one of Jeff's idols for a very long time and Jeff was particularly keen to call him, even if it was only just to say hello. Not long previously, he had managed to obtain Roy's telephone number, called him up, and got an answer. 'I didn't know what to say then,' he admitted. After some slightly star-struck conversation on Jeff's part, Roy invited him over to his home in Tennessee, where he stayed for about four days and they began writing together. They agreed to collaborate when both were in Los Angeles and would have time to work with each other. During the Christmas 1987 season, Roy invited Jeff over to begin, and Jeff invited Tom Petty over to help out as well, and they wrote 'You Got It', based upon an idea of Roy's. Jeff worked out the song on a small Casio keyboard, while Roy and Tom added acoustic guitars. They wrote the chorus first, and the verses followed quickly after that. Over the next day or two, they also wrote the songs 'California Blue' and 'A Love So Beautiful' in the same way.

Roy, Jeff testified, was a true character, a very funny man with a sense of humour which owed much to one of the great icons of British comedy.

> And he could do all Monty Python sketches on his own! He did all the parts! When we were doing Wilburys videos, we'd be going in a van to Grand Union Station in LA to film 'Handle With Care' and he'd be doing Python sketches. And he's got this enormous and most infectious giggle you've ever heard, and we'd all be giggling like schoolgirls after a minute or two and all fall about!

Tom Petty knew that the credit for getting Roy back into the musical world after such a long absence was all Jeff's. The latter, he said, had 'made him comfortable with recording again and, really, completely revitalised his career.'

In April 1988, Jeff, Roy, and Tom were in MC Studios (Tom Petty and The Heartbreakers guitarist Mike Campbell's garage studio) to record 'You Got It'. The vocals were completed in only three takes, but Jeff told another amusing story about the first take. As they had never recorded with Roy before, they set up the microphone levels while he was practising his performance. When Roy began to record his first take, they had underestimated just how powerfully he would sing the song, and his first take maxed out the equipment. A little reduction in levels was in order, and the basic song was completed within two more takes. All three of them finished the job with backing vocals from Jeff, Tom, and Phil Jones shortly afterwards.

Tragically, Roy did not live long enough to reap the full critical acclaim or commercial success of his latest work. In December 1988, having had a heart bypass operation some years previously, he died of a massive heart attack, aged fifty-two. Partly written as well as produced by Jeff, Roy's posthumous album *Mystery Girl* was an instant hit, as was the first single, 'You Got It'. It peaked at No. 3 in Britain, where his fan base had always been strong and where a TV-advertised compilation of his classics from the 1960s had recently been No. 1. Even more gratifyingly, 'You Got It' rose to No. 9 in the US, his first top-ten entry there since the transatlantic chart-topping 'Oh Pretty Woman' almost quarter of a century earlier.

Saddened as Jeff was by Roy's unexpected death, he was thrilled to have been responsible for his hero's first hit in such a long time, calling it a 'great, marvellous feeling.' His death had been devastating for them all because it was so sudden.

> He had a heart attack and was gone. He just checked out. We'd just worked together on 'You Got It', a song I'd written with him and Tom Petty and it had been his first top five hit in 30 years. It was still in the charts when he died. He'd been so happy. If you've got to go, then I suppose you go out on a high.[1]

In tribute to Roy, a video for 'End Of The Line', the Traveling Wilburys' second single, showed his guitar rocking in a chair while the rest of the group played along. This was followed by a brief shot focusing on his framed picture. It was a modest hit in Britain, selling enough to reach No. 52.

Also in 1988, Jeff was contacted by Lenny Waronker from Warner Brothers with the offer to work on a song for Randy Newman, 'Falling In Love Again', on his forthcoming album, *Land Of Dreams*. Randy had almost decided not to include it as he was dissatisfied with the result. Randy, Jeff recalled, was another real character, always putting himself down.

> He wanted a different angle on one of his tracks, he wanted some guitar style. So I went round to his house, like this vacuum-cleaner salesman, with my guitar in my case: Hello? Mr Newman? I've come to do the drains.

Randy sat down at his piano, and Jeff took his acoustic guitar out and started strumming along; they worked out an arrangement, and took their ideas back to MC Studios—'a really good studio—none of your million-dollar equipment, and stuff, it's just regular ordinary gear.' Having laid the basic track down there, they added piano in the living room.

> So that was yet another thing—it was like learning how to be in their world for a bit—you sort of have to become part of their little world. You go to dinner with Randy, and he's really funny, and he's a fabulous songwriter.

In light of recent history, any such close partnership between Jeff and Randy might have seemed rather ironic. In 1979 the latter had recorded an album, *Born Again*, featuring the song 'The Story Of A Rock And Roll Band'. It included the following lines:

> I love their 'Mr Blue Sky'
> Almost my favourite is 'Turn To Stone'
> And how 'bout 'Telephone Line'?
> I love that ELO.

Newman had long been renowned for his acid wit, and some wrongly assumed the song was meant to be sarcastic. Jeff agreed that the press had had a field day assuming he and his group were being unmercifully slagged off,

> [...] but I got to know Randy very well and I said, 'What was that about?' He goes, 'Oh, I had a terrible trouble with that. I was going to send you a copy and see what you thought.' I said, 'Was it a nice song or what? Was

it a tribute?' He says, 'Yeah, absolutely, I really loved them records.' So there was no other side to it—he really liked it.

At the same time, Jeff was invited to work with another of his musical heroes since childhood, the arch-recluse Brian Wilson of The Beach Boys. The result would be 'Let It Shine', a song co-written and produced on Brian's eponymous 1988 solo album. For various reasons, it would not the most straightforward of his musical tasks. In fact, it was difficult,

> [...] but only because of the way it was structured, with all the doctors and that stuff, and you have to go through this chain of events before you do anything. Like you'd lay down a tape, a little rough thing of a song that I wrote with him, and suddenly someone's got a copy of it and they're playing it to the record company saying, Look at this! What's he trying to do! No foresight whatsoever. I knew what I was going to do with it, but it's like giving somebody an unfinished thing that only you know what it is. It's a cryptic sort of thing. They tried to cut it off at the pass but I finally got it finished and it was really good. I was proud of that piece of work; his singing is good and everything.

Like many others of his generation, Jeff had always revered The Beach Boys' 1966 album *Pet Sounds* as one of the seminal pop albums of all time. He thought it was 'the ultimate in production,' or at least one of them.

> I like every track; I think they're all equally as good. I couldn't even pick one out of it because the arrangements were so unusual at the time. I remember it was 1966 and in some parts it sounds like an old dance band. I'd think, 'wow'! That's so old-fashioned yet so brand new at the same time. The arrangements were weird with these big harmonicas and funny, deep saxophones and plain little paper cups and playing the drums on them. What the hell was that? Brilliant!

Next on the agenda was a new album for the youngest Traveling Wilbury, but the foundations for it had been laid some time before George brought them together. Jeff was driving by Santa Monica Boulevard one day and trying to tune into a station on the radio, when he heard somebody repeatedly sounding his horn. Looking around, he saw Tom in his (little) red Corvette, telling him to pull over. Both had met already in England when Tom and The Heartbreakers were playing one of their gigs there. Tom said he had been listening to *Cloud Nine*, and loved it. He was about to do a solo album, with Mike Campbell helping out, and how did Jeff fancy writing some songs with him? So Jeff went round to his house a few days later, they sat down together with their guitars, and between them they wrote 'Free Fallin'', recorded it and mixed it. At the time, Jeff thought that was going to be it, 'but then we started messing about, and we got this other tune going.' They carried on working in Mike's suitably sparse garage, 'full of motorbikes and oil cans and bedsteads and things like that—it was pretty amazing!' Abbey Road or De Lane Lea in London, Musicland in Munich, or Compass Point in Nassau—it was not.

Writing the songs and recording was done over a period of months, as the solo album had to go on hold when the work with Randy Newman, Roy Orbison, and above all the Traveling Wilburys all intervened. But at length all thirteen tracks were completed, all originals apart from Gene Clark's 'Feel A Whole Lot Better', which Jeff had suggested they do after they went to see The Byrds—or more accurately a partial reformation containing three of the original group, live in concert at Los Angeles one night. Of the other twelve, Jeff co-wrote seven, including the singles 'I Won't Back Down', 'Runnin' Down A Dream', and 'Free Fallin''. The latter came about very spontaneously. Both musicians were socialising one evening when a roadie bought Tom a Yamaha keyboard, and he started playing the first thing that came into his head on it. 'Wait, what was that—just play the first part over and over,' Jeff urged him. He did so, and Jeff nodded his approval, telling him to sing something. 'She's a good girl, loves her mama,' Tom sang. From there he wrote the rest of the first and second verses off the top of his head.

As well as co-producing with Tom and Mike, Jeff also contributed bass guitar, guitars, keyboards, and backing vocals, while George contributed acoustic guitar and backing vocals on one song, and Roy backing vocals with the ad hoc ensemble dubbed 'The Trembling Blenders'. The result, *Full Moon Fever*, released in May 1989, was to give Tom his greatest success on record to date. It was as if everything Jeff touched turned to gold.

One joint effort which did, however, deserve greater success than it ever achieved was another, more brief collaboration with George. 'Cheer Down', as infectious as anything else which had appeared on *Cloud

Nine, was co-written by George and Tom. It was based around a phrase attributed to George's wife Olivia, who would good-naturedly order him to 'Cheer down, big fellow,' whenever he was getting over-enthusiastic about anything. Jeff played bass guitar and keyboards, and sang backing vocals on it, while Richard Tandy played piano and Ian Paice of Deep Purple added drums. Recorded in 1989 and used in the soundtrack to *Lethal Weapon 2*, it was released as a single but failed to chart.

Around this time there was a short if less productive musical reunion with Roy Wood. He and Jeff wrote and recorded two new tracks from scratch: 'Me And You', which they called 'an out-and-out pop song', and 'If You Can't Get What You Want, You've Gotta Want What You Get', a skiffle number which would not have sounded out of place on the Wilburys' album. Roy had the basic outline for the first track, took it over to Jeff's house, played it to him,

> [...] and he added some bits of his own to it as well. We did that, and whilst I was there, we stayed up all night and played a bit of skiffle, and this is how the other one came about.

With the exception of two short throwaway tracks at the end of the third and fourth Move albums, it was the first time that they had collaborated as songwriters. Although their finished efforts were recorded and mixed, they have so far remained in the can.

Another brief reunion with some of the old Birmingham alumni ensued in September 1989, when Mike Sheridan held his fiftieth birthday party in Great Barr. Former members of The Nightriders, The Idle Race, The Move, Wizzard, and others including Steve Gibbons and Noddy Holder took their places on stage in an all-stars collective for a cheery impromptu run through various old rock'n'roll classics.

Not surprisingly, by now one of the last things on Jeff's agenda was a return to ELO. When Bev Bevan had approached him during the astonishingly productive year of 1988 to discuss making another album, Jeff's answer was a definite no. Nobody had announced that the group no longer existed yet, as they were officially on hiatus once they had fulfilled their existing contract with *Balance Of Power*.

After negotiation between their respective lawyers, 'a ton of paperwork,' and delays caused by the death of Jeff's mother Nancy, it was announced that Bev would be forming an Electric Light Orchestra Part Two, but Jeff had no intention of being involved beyond receiving a share of the reconstituted group's royalties. Richard likewise declined to take part but several past members—some of whom had played a repertoire of their new material alongside a handful of the old hits for a while on stage, and also recorded as OrKestra—were happy to take their place in the new line-up. They embarked on their first British tour in autumn 1992 with the Moscow Symphony Orchestra—an ambitious collaboration which had never been on the drawing board during Jeff's leadership. While it was a costly venture and the expense prevented any repetition, it received generous plaudits from critics. Louis Clark was once again playing keyboards and taking charge of string arrangements, while Bev, Mik Kaminski, Kelly Groucutt, and for a short time Hugh McDowell were also on board. Other vocalists and guitarists including Eric Troyer, an American former session singer with Meat Loaf and Billy Joel, plus Pete Haycock from the Climax Blues Band, Phil Bates from onetime ELO support group Trickster, and Neil Lockwood were also in the picture.

ELO Part Two continued until 1999, recording two new studio albums and selling out live gigs around the world. After that Bev sold his share of the band's name back to Jeff. Meanwhile, record buyers were still ready to snap up TV-advertised compilation albums of hits by the original ELO. A double album from Telstar, a label which concentrated most of its energies from licensing material from the majors and also issued the first ELO Part Two set in 1991, spent several weeks in the chart around Christmas 1989 with a peak of No. 23, while in 1994 a similar set from Dino Entertainment made No. 4. Although the old group was long since gone and never to return, their place in music history was secure. The new outfit could never escape from the shadow, unable to achieve more than fleeting chart success or overcome the prejudices of those who saw ELO strictly as Jeff's group.

10
'Free As A Bird'

Jeff had overseen his change of career in the music business from fronting a band with a sequence of contracted albums, each followed by a gruelling tour on two or three continents, with relief. Working in the studio on other projects with other performers now gave him much more pleasure and fulfilment. Looking back in 1990 on his fifteen years with the group, he was still glad to have seen the back of it, for the time being at least.

> It was murder, trying to get the cellos right and the violins and all that stuff. It never sounded like I wanted it to sound but people kept wanting to see it, so I just went along with it. You can have a great gig every now and again if you're in the mood but I'd rather be in the studio, making something new.

The workload involved in making a new album and then taking it out on the road was no longer part of the plan.

> I'm not planning to tour because that aspect of it was never what I wanted to do, which was just to make records. As soon as I made my first one, in 1968, I knew that was what I liked best; I couldn't wait to get in and do another one. I never get this urge to perform. In fact I used to find it a real drag because I used to spend months on the road thinking, 'Shit, I could be in a studio.'

In the spring of 1990, Jeff, George, Bob, and Tom convened again to record a second Traveling Wilburys album. Over the previous year there had been much speculation as to whether they would enter the studio again and, if so, whether it would be just the four of them or whether they would recruit a fifth member. But, as Jeff readily acknowledged, 'we thought that nobody could replace Roy Orbison.' It had been widely rumoured that Del Shannon might be the one, especially as Jeff and Tom were at the time producing, helping to write, and playing on a new album for him.

Tragically, for Del there was to be no way back from a life and career which had seen more than enough disappointments, depression, and alcohol abuse, and he took his own life on 8 February 1990. Even when taken into account that objectivity is all too often suspended on a recording artist's posthumous releases, reviews for the completed Del Shannon single 'Walk Away'—an apt title for the man remembered above all for his transatlantic No. 1 hit of 1961, 'Runaway'—and the accompanying album, *Rock On!*, were particularly good. Some critics even suggested that it was the best record he had ever made. A reviewer in one of the British broadsheets tastelessly remarked that Del's suicide suggested he did not have much confidence in his new material. Nevertheless, the demand for records and subsequent sales that had followed Roy Orbison's demise, particularly in Britain where he had generally been far more popular than in his own country, did not follow Del's. His new releases never charted in either country.

Replacing Roy had never been part of the plan, in any case. While the second Wilburys album was being recorded, Jeff said it had never even been considered.

> We'd become this unit, we were all good pals. I don't remember exactly what we thought. It was a real shock and a horrible thing to happen, but we never went 'that's it, we can't do that again.' We always knew we were going to do another one, and now it's just the four of us.

By the summer of 1990, they had recorded the basis of fourteen new tracks, and they planned to regroup in early July to complete the vocals.

> The Wilburys is not grandiose or anything, it's pretty straight guitar music, so there's not exactly a lot left to do except sing all the tunes properly. It's really quick, we write 'em quick. When you're doing your own record you sit there going, oh, I'd better change this, change

that. The Wilburys isn't like that, it's more thrashing and banging and whooping.

Once again displaying a mischievous sense of humour, the group named the new album *Traveling Wilburys Vol. 3*, as if to persuade fans that they had somehow missed *Vol. 2*. The joke was that there never was a 'Vol. 2'. According to Jeff, 'that was George's idea. He said, "Let's confuse the buggers."' Once again the group adopted aliases on the sleeve and labels. George was Spike Wilbury, Jeff was Clayton, Tom was Muddy, and Bob was Boo.

Critics had been completely bowled over by the first album, and such success would be hard if not impossible to repeat. The general view was that the follow-up, released in November 1990, was decent but fell short of its predecessor's standards. In America it stalled at No. 11 in the album charts, though it still went platinum for sales of one million, while peaking at No. 14 in Britain. None of the singles charted in America, while in Britain 'She's My Baby'—the nearest the group ever came to hard rock with additional lead guitar by 'Ken Wilbury', alias Gary Moore—stalled at No. 79. Released a few months earlier at the same time as the charity album *Nobody's Child: The Romanian Angel Appeal* organised by Olivia Harrison, was another single. 'Nobody's Child' was not the number from *Eldorado*, but an old country song from the 1940s. George had recorded it in his Hamburg days, when The Beatles were Tony Sheridan's backing group, and it had made No. 44 in the British chart. In tribute to Del Shannon, the B-side of 'She's My Baby' was a faithful cover version of 'Runaway'.

After 1990 there would never be any more new material under the same banner. Some things, particularly those which occur more or less spontaneously, can never be repeated. A few years later, Jeff admitted as much.

> You could never capture the sheer enjoyment we all got from the Wilburys, the fun of it all, the freedom from pressure. Then there was the sheer surprise in what we did. Nobody expected it. If we were to do it again, I think we'd have to do something quite different musically.

Following a tour of Japan in 1991 in which he was accompanied by a group put together for the purpose by Eric Clapton, George Harrison mused on the possibility of doing gigs with the Traveling Wilburys. He had considered the idea, perhaps with each member doing a solo set and doing 'their' songs at the end, or all going on together from start to finish 'and make everything Wilburys.' He mentioned it in a press interview at around the time of the first album. Tom was less enthusiastic. Although the subject had come up in conversation, he thought that nobody ever took it seriously; 'it would ruin it in a way' because it would make the group too formal. Jeff never publicly expressed a viewpoint, but with his unashamed preference for the studio, his views were probably closer to those of Tom. Jeff admitted that they continued to make jokes between themselves about touring, usually after a drink or two. George would suggest that they got on an aircraft carrier and follow the sunshine, playing Hawaii and the Caribbean. But joking about it was as far as it ever went.

It had long been inevitable that sooner or later a Jeff Lynne solo album would be in order. While *Cloud Nine* was being recorded, Mo Ostin (who had ironically 'lost' ELO to Don Arden's new Jet Records around fifteen years before) and Lenny Waronker from Warner Brothers came to have a listen to the work in progress, and they were so impressed that they promptly signed him up for one.

Released in June 1990 on the Warner Brothers' offshoot, the Reprise label, *Armchair Theatre* featured a much more stripped-down Jeff Lynne and friends. 'It's natural, all done by hand, no sequencing, no digital bits,' he said in an interview shortly before it was issued.

> It's made like a proper record with drums, bass, guitars, pianos, which I love to do. 'Cos I went through all that digital period, learning how to be a typist, pushing all these buttons, and it drove me mad. That's not music, it's a computer thing. I'm not interested.

The album featured eight new songs from Jeff, plus three cover versions—Jesse Stone's 'Don't Let Go', Kurt Weill and Maxwell Anderson's 'September Song', and Ted Koehler and Harold Arlen's 'Stormy Weather'. Jeff was responsible for much of the acoustic and electric guitars, keyboards, and bass, while Jim Horn contributed sax and Mette Matthiessen drums. George Harrison added guitar and backing vocals, while Tom Petty, Richard Tandy, Del Shannon, and others also chipped in. The album enjoyed modest success, as did two tracks released as singles, 'Every Little Thing' and 'Lift Me Up'.

In 1991 Jeff recorded another album with Tom Petty, *Into The Great Wide Open*. Unlike *Full Moon Fever*, this was a return for Tom to playing with The Heartbreakers. Sales-wise, it was the greatest success they ever had, entering the British charts at No. 3 on release. In the studio, things had not gone altogether smoothly. Jeff co-wrote eight of the twelve songs, and as usual played bass guitar, guitars, keyboards, and sang backing vocals. Afterwards Tom was forced to admit that it was something of a mess. Much as he and Mike Campbell had enjoyed working with Jeff, the other members of the band, who hardly knew him, were not of like opinion. In particular Stan Lynch, the drummer, was less than happy when told to play along with parts programmed on a drum machine.

One year later it was the turn of Joe Cocker to benefit from Jeff's artistry. This was in the shape of production on the title track of a new album, *Night Calls*, which he had written and on which he played every instrument. But the modern way of recording did not suit Joe. Being sent a tape for him to add his vocals to, and then return to its creator for production, Joe said, was not the way he usually worked.

Next on the list was Ringo Starr, and his new album, *Time Takes Time*. Jeff recorded four songs with him, although only two appeared on the album. Both were among the best tracks on what had been the strongest album by the famous Merseyside drummer in a long time, 'Don't Go Where The Road Don't Go', featuring Suzie Katayama on cello and Jim Horn on sax, and the rock'n'roller 'After All These Years'. A third, a cover version of Elvis Presley's 'Don't Be Cruel', appeared as a bonus track on the CD single. All three tracks were produced by Jeff, who played most of the instruments, apart from drums.

That same year Jeff was one of a team responsible for completing a posthumous album by Roy Orbison, *King Of Hearts*. After the release of *Mystery Girl*, there were inevitable questions as to the existence of any unreleased material by Roy from the previous few years. This resulted in the release of a ten-track epitaph, put together from master sessions and demos. Some of the songs still needed to be finished, even taken apart and almost completely reworked, all with the blessing of his widow Barbara. The majority of them were produced by Don Was and Robbie Robertson.

Two of the songs were not merely produced by Jeff, but completely stripped down and reconstructed by him, with the result that he played everything behind Roy's lead vocal. The better-remembered of the two,

'I Drove All Night', had been offered to Roy by its writers Billy Steinberg and Tom Kelly, and he recorded it in 1987, but it remained unreleased at the time. It was then covered by Cyndi Lauper, becoming a top-ten hit on both sides of the Atlantic two years later. Jeff's work on it sounded much more restrained than his contributions to *Mystery Girl*, as he explained:

> That's probably because I was very careful about backing vocals. I was asked to put a lot on. So I did but I kept them very quiet. There was also a kind of unspoken agreement between Don, Robbie and myself that all the tracks on the album had to respect Roy's voice, it had to be the focus of attention.

The other, 'Heartbreak Radio', co-written by Frankie Miller and first recorded on his 1980 album *Easy Money*, likewise underwent a total transformation. Roy's original vocal on the tape had been much slower, said Jeff, and it was not really happening as a result.

> But the key was spot on, so I took all the other instruments off and put Roy's voice through a sound stretching programme on the computer. That made it sound like he was singing a lot faster without altering his pitching—if I'd simply sped up the tape he'd have ended up sounding like Mickey Mouse.

He also changed some of the guitar chords, inserting a couple of minors,

> [...] to make the song jump out properly. Since Roy was originally singing along with a live drummer who was a little loose, the song speeds up and slows down in places. It was a little bit like working in jelly. It keeps slipping away from you!

The results added to Roy's tally of posthumous chart singles in Britain, with the former reaching No. 7 (as had the Cyndi Lauper version) and the latter No. 34, while neither even showed in the American Top 100.

The first few years of the last decade of the century were proving a very active time for Jeff. He provided the song 'Wild Times' to the soundtrack of the movie *Robin Hood: Prince of Thieves* in 1991. Julianna Raye, cousin of composer and arranger Michael Kamen, sang backing vocals

1. *Above left:* The Idle Race, 1967. A promotional picture for the first single, for which British release was cancelled.

2. *Above right:* The Idle Race, 1968. *L to R*: Greg Masters, Jeff Lynne, Dave Pritchard, Roger Spencer.

3. A press advertisement for 'The Skeleton And The Roundabout', The Idle Race's second British single, March 1968.

4. *Above left:* Jeff Lynne at the piano, flanked by Idle Race producers Eddie Offord and Gerald Chevin, 1967.

5. *Above right:* The Move, February 1970, at Hobbs Moat, Solihull. *L to R*: Bev Bevan, Rick Price, Jeff Lynne, Roy Wood.

6. *Below:* The Move, 1970, performing 'Brontosaurus' on BBC TV.

7. *Above:* The Move, 1971, promoting 'Tonight' on London Weekend Television's *Whitaker's World of Music*.

8. *Right:* Jeff Lynne, about 1971.

9. *Below:* ELO, early 1972. *Front, L to R:* Roy Wood, Jeff Lynne, Bev Bevan. *Centre, L to R:* Wilf Gibson, Hugh McDowell, Bill Hunt. *Back, L to R:* Richard Tandy, Trevor Smith, Brian Jones (crew), Andy Craig, Richard Battle (crew).

10. Jeff Lynne and Roy Wood on stage with ELO, 1972.

11. Jeff Lynne in tinsel wig on *Top Of The Pops*, performing 'Roll Over Beethoven', 1973.

10538 OVERTURE
Words and Music by JEFF LYNNE
Recorded on HARVEST by
The
Electric Light Orchestra
20p
ROY WOOD MUSIC LTD/CARLIN MUSIC CORP/SUGARTOWN PUBLISHING CO. LTD.
sole selling agents:
Music Sales Ltd., 78 Newman Street, London W.1.

SHOWDOWN
THE ELECTRIC LIGHT
ORCHESTRA
SHOWDOWN
The New Single by
ELECTRIC LIGHT ORCHESTRA
on Harvest Records HAR 5077

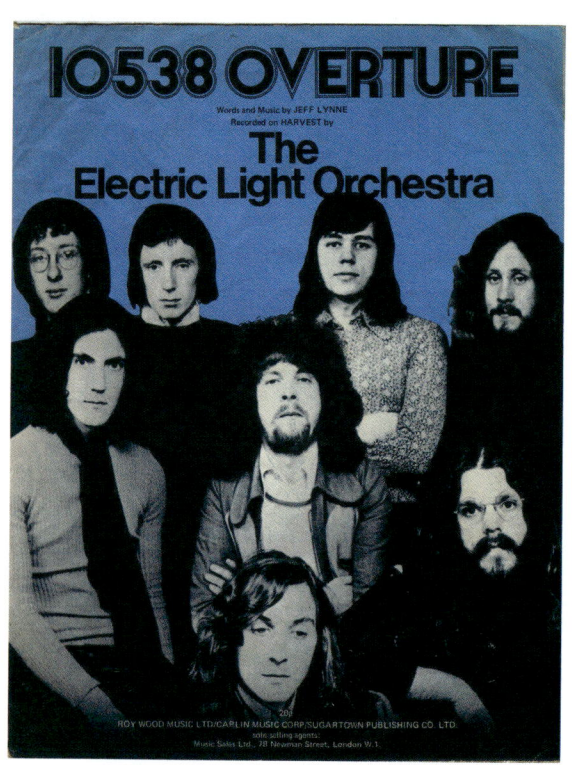

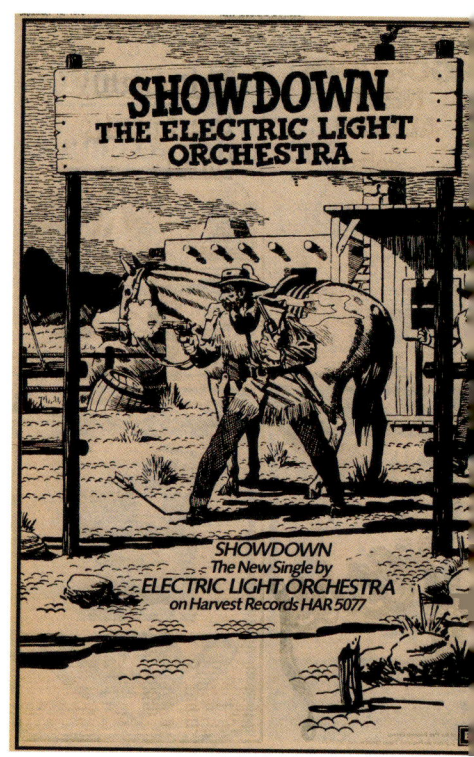

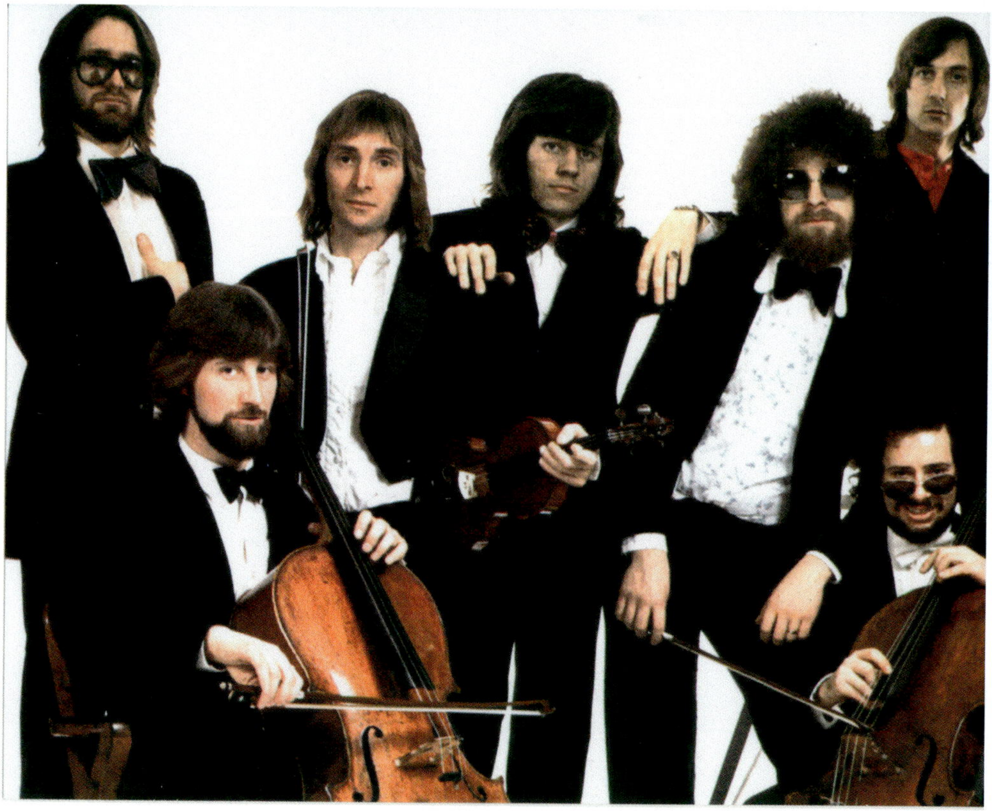

12. *Opposite left:* The sheet music for '10538 Overture', ELO, 1972.

13. *Opposite right:* A British music press advertisement for 'Showdown', ELO, 1973.

14. *Opposite below:* An unusually formally-attired ELO, 1973. *L to R*: Michael d'Albuquerque, Colin Walker, Wilf Gibson, Bev Bevan, Jeff Lynne, Mike Edwards (front), Richard Tandy.

15. *Right:* Jeff Lynne, 1974.

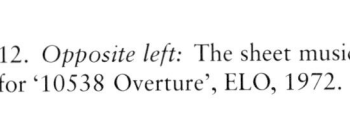

16. ELO, 1974. *L to R*: Richard Tandy, Jeff Lynne, Bev Bevan, Michael d'Albuquerque (back), Hugh McDowell, Mik Kaminski (back), Mike Edwards.

17. *Above:* ELO, 1975. *L to R:* Melvyn Gale, Hugh McDowell, Bev Bevan, Jeff Lynne, Richard Tandy, Kelly Groucutt, Mik Kaminski.

18. *Below:* ELO, 1975. The photograph used for the back of the sleeve of *Face The Music*, with Richard Tandy (bottom) alone averting his gaze from the camera.

19. A British music press advertisement for 'Doin' That Crazy Thing', Jeff Lynne's first solo single, August 1977.

20. A British music press advertisement for 'Mr Blue Sky', ELO, January 1978.

21. *Above:* ELO live on stage during the *Out Of The Blue* tour, 1978.

22. *Left:* A British music press advertisement for 'Sweet Talkin' Woman', ELO, September 1978.

23. ELO, 1979. *L to R*: Mik Kaminski, Hugh McDowell, Melvyn Gale, Jeff Lynne, Richard Tandy, Kelly Groucutt, Bev Bevan.

24. Jeff Lynne, 1979.

25. *Above:* ELO, 1981. *L to R*: Richard Tandy, Jeff Lynne, Bev Bevan, Kelly Groucutt.

26. *Below*: ELO, 1981–82, a promotional card for the *Time* tour. *L to R*: Louis Clark, Mik Kaminski, Bev Bevan, Jeff Lynne, Richard Tandy, Kelly Groucutt, Dave Morgan.

27. ELO, 1985–86. *L to R*: Richard Tandy, Jeff Lynne, Bev Bevan. The trio who recorded *Balance Of Power* were augmented by others for their last remaining live dates between March and July 1986.

28. Carl Wayne, the former Move vocalist who recorded several of Jeff Lynne's songs between 1973 and 2001.

29. *Left:* Eric Clapton and Jeff Lynne on stage at The Prince's Trust Rock Gala, Wembley Arena, 5 June 1987. (*Steve Mathieson*)

30. *Below:* The Traveling Wilburys, 1988. *L to R*: Bob Dylan, Jeff Lynne, Tom Petty, George Harrison, Roy Orbison.

31. The Traveling Wilburys, 1988.

32. Jeff Lynne honoured by the Lord Mayor, Councillor Mike Leddy, on the Broad Street Walk of Stars, Birmingham, 13 March 2014, with Jasper Carrott on the left. (*Martin Kinch*)

33. Jeff Lynne's ELO at Radio 2 Live in Hyde Park, 14 September 2014, with the BBC Concert Orchestra, musicians from Take That's touring band, and Richard Tandy at keyboards on left. (*Paul Carless*)

34. Jeff Lynne with Tom Petty and Joe Walsh at the Hollywood Walk of Fame Ceremony, 23 April 2015. (*By courtesy of Ursula David and ELO Beatles Forever*)

on it, and Jeff was so impressed that he helped to get her a record contract and worked with her on her debut album. The result, *Something Peculiar*, featured her songs with Jeff, Richard Tandy, and drummer Phil Jones playing all the instruments.

Around the same time, Jeff was also responsible for production and song-writing contributions to albums by Roger McGuinn, *Back From Rio*, songs by Aerosmith ('Lizard Love'), Bonnie Tyler ('Time Mends a Broken Heart', which he co-wrote with Kiki Dee), and Et Moi ('Drôle de Vie'). Tom Jones recorded Lift Me Up, a cover version of the song originally on *Armchair Theatre*, for his 1994 album *The Lead and How to Swing It*, with Jeff producing and playing every instrument except saxophone.

> Working with Jeff was great fun. We did the song at his studio in LA. Jeff said that I ruined one of his microphones and two of his daughters!

Another musical veteran with whom Jeff worked was Hank Marvin. He and Mark Knopfler played acoustic guitar on a new version of The Shadows' classic 'Wonderful Land' on Hank's 1993 album *Heartbeat* and the track released as the B-side of the single, 'Nivram'.

And yet, the list of those with whom Jeff would have liked to work remained inexhaustible. Of the more established performers who had been around for a while, Bob Seger remained a prime candidate, if and when there was time to do it.

> I know he'd like to work with me and I'd like to work with him because he's got a great voice and does great songs. Maybe I'll be able to help him out on his next album. But there's newer ones I'd like to work with and try and make them sound better, without mentioning any names. What I could give them is this experience which I've got now as a producer. I know what works and what doesn't. A lot of songs, you go, oh, they should have had that bit in there, or moved it there and made it twice as long, and it would have been a big hit, or a nicer song.

For the time being, the long-awaited follow-up to *Armchair Theatre* failed to materialise. Jeff had been reportedly recording a second solo album in America and Paris, but domestic issues impeded progress. Jeff moved into another house in Beverly Hills in 1993, while Sandi and their daughters stayed in their old home. Shortly afterwards Jeff's sister died and he divested himself of his Warwickshire base, selling Walsh Hall to Robin Campbell of UB40.[1]

For the man who was now becoming as well-known as a producer as he was as a performer, the ultimate prize in rock music was about to land on his plate. Thanks largely to his friendship with George Harrison, in 1994 he was invited to produce what would be the two 'final' Beatles tracks, based on recordings made on cassette by John Lennon in New York and passed to them by Yoko Ono. Paul, George, and Ringo returned to the studio together for the first time in a quarter of a century (since completing the *Let It Be* album after John had left). The Beatles' producer Sir George Martin was helping them to oversee some of their archive recordings for the *Anthology* project, helping them to choose from the large collection of previously unreleased demos, out-takes, and other material which would culminate in three double CDs and a television documentary series (subsequently released with additional material on DVD). But he declined to produce the new songs, as after a lifetime in the recording industry he was now suffering from partial hearing loss.

As the only one of the three surviving Beatles who had not yet worked with Jeff as producer, Paul McCartney had his reservations. Jeff and George had been the leading lights of the Traveling Wilburys together, and he thought that they might create a wedge between them, possibly leading to his being marginalised during or even largely excluded from the decision-making process. His initial reaction was that, since Sir George Martin had produced the material on *Anthology*, he was the obvious choice. But George Harrison insisted that if they were making a new record, they had to choose somebody with immaculate ears. Now in his late sixties, their former producer was gradually disengaging himself from the record production to which he knew he could no longer give what he had offered for so many years.

At the time, Jeff and Paul hardly knew each other. It was a condition of George's involvement that Jeff should join them as producer. Jeff later admitted that he did not know what would have happened if Paul had insisted on choosing somebody different for the job instead. As the successor to the man who had long since been regarded as pop and rock's best producer of all time, Jeff considered it one of the hardest jobs he had ever had to do. 'Because of the nature of the source material,' he said, 'it was very primitive-sounding, to say the least.' First he spent about a week at his own studio, cleaning up both tracks on his computer, assisted by Marc Mann, a fellow musician and conductor with some experience of programming and IT know-how. Together they tried out a new noise reduction system, with some success. There was a particular problem with 'Real Love', as they discovered a sixty-cycle mains hum going on throughout as well as a large amount of hiss. It had, after all, been recorded at a low level and what they had was probably a second- or third-generation copy on cassette. Once both hiss and mains hum had been purged, they found there were audible clicks all the way through. Viewing the graph of it on the computer screen, there were spikes occurring at random intervals throughout the song. They would spend a day working on it, then listen back, and still find many more problems.

> But we could magnify them, grab them and wipe them out. It didn't have any effect on John's voice, because we were just dealing with the air surrounding him, in between phrases. That took about a week to clean up before it was even usable and transferable to a DAT master. Putting fresh music to it was the easy part! 'Free As A Bird', however, wasn't a quarter as noisy as 'Real Love' and only a bit of EQ was needed to cure most problems.

Timing was one of those problems, as Lennon had never been particularly good at keeping in time with himself:

> Well, nobody is when they're just writing a song. You don't think, 'I'd better use a click while I'm putting down this idea.' You just play and enjoy yourself. So it took a lot of work to get it all in time so that the others could play to it. It's quite a complex process, but for some reason, I kind of know how to do it, through messing around on other stuff for years.

When Jeff brought the carefully-treated DATs to Paul's studio for overdub sessions, everybody made a conscious decision that analogue equipment should be used wherever possible. They were trying to create a record that was timeless, he stressed,

> [...] so we steered away from using state-of the-art gear. We didn't want to make it fashionable. It's just making the statement that they are all here playing together after all these years.

Paul did not play his Hofner violin bass on the recording, preferring instead a five-string on 'Free As A Bird', and his double bass, originally owned by Elvis Presley's bassist Bill Black, on 'Real Love'. George used two of his Stratocasters, a modern one, 'and his psychedelic Strat that's jacked up for the bottleneck stuff on "Free As A Bird".' They also both played six-string acoustic guitars, Paul a Gibson jumbo and George a Martin, and Ringo his Ludwig drum kit, 'so there are genuine Beatles drums on there.'

In February 1995, all four of them began work on a third unfinished Lennon demo, which Jeff and Geoff Emerick recalled as being either 'Now And Then', 'Grow Old With Me', or 'Miss You'. For various reasons—probably lack of enthusiasm on the part of George, who dismissed it as 'crap'—it was never completed.[2] A collaboration between Paul and George, 'All For Love', was begun but never finished. George was perceptibly losing interest, perhaps explained in part by the distraction of business problems he was experiencing at the time.

Of the time he had spent with The Beatles, Jeff admitted that being right there in the inner sanctum and hanging out with them for a few weeks was an incredible experience. Although twenty-five years had elapsed since they last recorded as a unit, they worked very well together, and for Jeff to be sitting in the control room watching and listening to them interact with each other was fascinating.

> I'd often have cause to think, 'Christ, no wonder they were the best.' But I always thought they were the greatest anyway. They're still great musicians and great singers. Paul and George would strike up the backing vocals—and all of a sudden it's The Beatles again! To be there in the middle of all this and have a degree of responsibility over the result was astonishing. It wasn't some kind of fake version, it really was the real thing. They were having fun with each other and reminding each other of the old times. I'd be waiting to record and normally I'd say, 'OK, Let's do a take,' but I was too busy laughing and smiling at everything they were talking about.

As well as directing from the control room, Jeff contributed a vocal harmony and a guitar overdub on 'Free As A Bird'.

> But I wanted to keep my hands off as much as possible. The only things I really did were the funny little bits at the end of the track. I made sure that whatever was done as a big part of the record was them.

For the man who had so long worshipped his idols from afar, it must have felt like everything he had ever achieved was leading up to the definitive experience. Was it like The Twilight Zone?

> Sometimes! I'd get up in the morning and think, 'God I'm working with The Beatles today, I can't believe it!' It was a lovely magical time. But as well as being the ultimate musical pleasure and thrill, the thought of it was very scary, because it had never been done before, and there were no points of reference. You know, what do you do on a Beatles record when the singer's not there?

The singer who had died so needlessly on the streets of New York more than a decade earlier was there, but only on tape. Reclaiming the demos on the cassette and making a record out of them was, and would remain, probably the achievement in which Jeff could take most pride in his musical career. The cost, he admitted, came in the form of 'many sleepless nights,' as he knew he had to get it absolutely right.

> When you're working on the first new Beatles singles in a quarter of a century, there aren't any half-measures. No pressure, then! But in the end we made it in a week, effectively taking John's tape, making a record and then putting John back in it. It was very emotional.

Working with their deceased colleague, the man who was no longer there, was indeed emotional. Ringo said that they pretended John had gone on holiday or out for tea, leaving them the tape to play with, as it was the only way they could really deal with such a surreal situation. Yet it was a thoroughly enjoyable experience, and Jeff got to listen to their memories of the Hamburg and Liverpool days first-hand.

As to whether he would have liked to be a member of the group, it was impossible for him to say. He knew that

> [it] wasn't all beer and skittles being a Beatle. To have been under so much pressure, to not have been able to walk down the street? I'm a very private person. I would have found that very tough, so maybe no. But to share the studio with George, Paul and Ringo, and to hear all those wonderful stories, that was very special. It was a privilege, beyond a privilege. The stuff of dreams.

Having been the frontman of ELO and a Traveling Wilbury was very fulfilling, and he was proud of the hard work he had put into making things happen. But collaborating with The Beatles was an incomparable experience.

One trick that Jeff used was cutting up Lennon's slightly out-of-time vocal to get it in proper rhythm and matching Paul's studio piano with John's piano sound—'sort of like a jigsaw puzzle, really, the way we got it to work.' Once both the songs had been completed, the inevitable discussion came up about 'The Threatles' recording a whole album of new material, but as Jeff latter put it, 'time just didn't permit it.' In retrospect, it was probably a wide decision to halt the idea in its tracks and quit while they were ahead. While fans eagerly welcomed the staggered release programme on *Anthology*—the CDs, television series, and in due course videos and DVDs—reaction to the two new songs was mixed.

'Free As A Bird' appeared on *Anthology 1* in November 1995, and 'Real Love' on its successor four months later. Both songs were also released as singles around the same time. The first took its bow to tremendous media interest and press headlines, and flew into the British charts at No. 2, at a time when it was not uncommon for well-hyped new releases to debut at No. 1 and then plunge heavily in a short chart life. But Michael Jackson's 'Earth Song' denied them the prize of what would have been an eighteenth chart-topping single in Britain, and some reviews were less than enthusiastic. While a new Beatles single after such a long interval was bound to be newsworthy, several critics were wary of being seen as too enthusiastic, and panned it as a tuneless dirge perhaps worthy of a Traveling Wilburys B-side, but no more. A few even speculated on whether John would have welcomed the attention and painstaking craftsmanship given to one of his out-takes, or whether he would have dismissed it all as rubbish. Expectations were thus somewhat lowered in spring the following year, when 'Real Love' hit the shops as the very last new Beatles single. Arguably a stronger song than its precursor, it was pointedly excluded from the Radio 1 playlist, and entered the charts at No. 4 but was gone within a few weeks.

Nevertheless, nothing could diminish the extent of Jeff's accomplishment in making it all happen, 'and it was hardly surprising that his next project would be helping to producing another Beatles solo album. In February 1995 he began working with Paul McCartney, with the intention of recording something more straightforward and without elaborate production. The sessions which resulted in the release of *Flaming Pie* in May 1997, with Paul and Sir George Martin sharing production duties with him on different tracks and Jeff on electric and acoustic guitar, harpsichord, and harmony and backing vocals, were recorded over two years. One of Jeff's productions, 'Cello in the Ruins', was planned at one stage as a single for War Child's *The Help Album* in 1995, but shelved. While the last few McCartney albums had received mixed reviews, the reaction to this last one was overwhelmingly positive, rewarding him with a No. 2 peak position on both sides of the Atlantic, and his first American top-ten album for fifteen years.

By the time it was released, Jeff had been awarded the Ivor Novello Award for Outstanding Contributions to British Music in 1996 for a second time. Three years later, a cover version of Buddy Holly's 'Maybe Baby' recorded by Jeff and Paul went on to form part of a soundtrack of a comedy film of the same name, written and directed by Ben Elton. In 2014, when the thirty-six-track tribute album *The Art Of McCartney* was released, Jeff contributed his own version of 'Junk' to sit alongside renditions of other songs by the same writer (including collaborations with John Lennon from Beatles days) from acts including Billy Joel, Heart, Brian Wilson, Bob Dylan, Steve Miller, and Corinne Bailey Rae.

Paul later recalled what a positive experience it was to work with Jeff, who went about getting his own way in his own studio, but in the best possible manner:

> You want someone who can control the situation without appearing to, and that comes from his character. He's just that kind of guy. He gets things done, but you wouldn't know he was pulling the strings. Very modest, innocent in some ways—at the same time amazingly accomplished.

George Harrison's *Cloud Nine* had been the last of a five-album deal required by Warner Brothers, and for several years he had showed no inclination to begin another. But early in 1999 he began work on recording once more. He would come round to Jeff's house, usually with a new song which he would strum on a guitar or ukulele, and Jeff admitted that these songs just knocked him out.

George talked about how he wanted the album to sound. He told Dhani (his son, then aged twenty) a lot of things he would like to have done with the songs and left us little clues.

Sadly, by this time the youngest former Beatle was not in the best of health and had been undergoing treatment for cancer. Worse still, on 30 December an intruder broke into the house at Friar Park and attacked him, but was fortunately warded off by Olivia. But he had sustained life-threatening injuries and was admitted to hospital, followed by a long period of recuperation. It left him gravely weakened, with little resistance to the cancer for which he had already been receiving treatment, and which at that stage had been in remission.

Also in 1999, a legal arrangement transferred ownership of the ELO name back to Jeff, who celebrated this and the new millennium with the release of a retrospective box set, *Flashback*. This contained three CDs of re-mastered tracks, the majority of them 'greatest hits'. Making up the number was a handful of out-takes and tracks which had been started many years earlier and only just completed, such as a short and sweet Grieg's 'Piano Concerto in A Minor', begun by Jeff and Richard as a bit of fun during the *Secret Messages* sessions at Wisseloord in 1982, with both on guitars, Richard on piano, and Jeff on drums. Also taking a bow for the first time was a re-recorded *Xanadu*, with Jeff's vocal replacing that of Olivia Newton-John. The whole affair was packaged in an attractive hardback book containing a selection of photos and a few words from Jeff offering his thoughts on each track.

It was the curtain raiser to a programme of re-issues of all studio albums from the group's back catalogue over the next few years. This had already begun in 1991 with the appearance of *Early ELO*, which included the first two albums on a double CD plus early versions of several tracks. It was also notable for the first release ever of an outtake from June 1973, 'Baby I Apologise', an uncharacteristically poppy tune recorded by Jeff with keyboards and multi-tracked vocals, but evidently never completed.

On the thirtieth anniversaries of their original release in 2001 and 2003, the two Harvest albums appeared as double CDs packaged in slipcases. Both had been expanded considerably to include outtakes, BBC sessions, and other material alongside the original tracks, among them the songs which Carl Wayne had recorded with them over thirty years earlier. Subsequent releases on single CDs also appeared on Epic/Legacy, by then part of Sony BMG Music Entertainment, which had acquired the Jet catalogue from Don and David Arden. Each one was supplemented with alternate versions, outtakes, and previously unreleased material, in addition to a new booklet or insert notes, some containing insights from Jeff. The 'new' numbers included a few tracks which had been begun at the time and were only completed many years later, after Jeff had returned to the studio for the purpose. Notable among these were the majestic 'Everyone's Born To Die', a song from 1973 without any strings, but with prominent organ reminiscent of Bob Dylan *Blonde On Blonde* era, Marc Bolan on guitar (successively on the reissues of *ELO 2* and *On The Third Day*), and a cover version of Del Shannon's 'Little Town Flirt' as a bonus cut on *Discovery*.

With the reissue of *A New World Record* came an uncharacteristically Northern soul-sounding gem, 'Surrender', which appeared briefly in the lower end of the singles chart on download sales alone in 2006. To accompany *Out Of The Blue* the following year came the newly completed 'Latitude 88 North'. Both appeared on very limited one-sided promotional singles on coloured vinyl. The few available copies were quickly snapped up and were soon available only on ebay—inevitably at a price. *Out Of The Blue*, the thirtieth anniversary edition, came in a small CD-sized hardback book, and re-entered the album chart at No. 15. Jeff was pleased with the way that the record had stood the test of time and still had enduring appeal.

> The tunes that I wrote have lived on. For thirty years they still live on and they get played and people still listen to them, which is fantastic. As a songwriter that's all you can ever ask for, that the music does reach a lot of people and it lives onto the next generation and is a part of life.

11
'A Long Time Gone'

Just when fans thought that the name of ELO had been consigned to history, in the summer of 2001 a new album, *Zoom*, hit the racks. This was in effect another more or less solo project by Jeff, but this time it came out under the group name. Like *Armchair Theatre*, it featured him playing guitars, bass guitar, and much of the keyboards and drums, as well as doing most of the vocals. On two tracks he was responsible for all voices and instruments. Also present on some of the sessions were Richard Tandy on keyboards, and two former Beatles on two numbers (although not together). George Harrison added his inimitable slide guitar on 'A Long Time Gone' and 'All She Wanted', in what turned out to be among the last sessions he ever played, while Ringo Starr contributed drums on the rock'n'roll 'Easy Money', and the more lush, dreamy 'Moment in Paradise'. Overall, the record featured a more organic feel, for it relied less on synthesisers and boasted a welcome return to strings in the form of cello from Suzie Katayama, who had played on one of Jeff's productions for Ringo nine years earlier. Backing vocals were supplied by Rosie Vela, a Texas-born performer who had enjoyed success in Britain with the single 'Magic Smile' and album *Zazu* in the mid-1980s.

Since 1986 Jeff had broadened his experience considerably, and said that his musical relationships with the other four Wilburys had influenced how he sculpted ELO's sound on *Zoom*. He thought to himself,

> What if I applied this new knowledge to a new ELO album? I'd probably see it differently and do it differently. I have learned a lot working with all those guys, all my favourite guys. It was a total pleasure. I suppose

bits of them rubbed off on me and it opened me up more. I was always locked away, working on stuff.

The thirteen songs on *Zoom* had been recorded over two-and-a-half years at his Los Angeles home recording studio and in various rooms throughout the house, utilising the built-in acoustics.

> It's interesting in that respect. You actually get different sounds than you probably would in a studio. I prefer natural-sounding wood and the echo of different rooms. Sometimes in the bathroom I've got an acoustic guitar.

Another sound he was particularly proud of using on the record was an old Wurlitzer organ which he had obtained; 'I wanted to make it really old-fashioned, almost like a fairground kind of sound, but really intimate at the same time.'

As for the songs themselves, they drew on life's ups and downs, and a number of them were quite personal:

> Some of them are about just trying to do as good as you can when things don't work out. Sometimes there are loose ends that you can never tidy up. But it's also about trying to learn to trust your instincts and do what you feel is right. [The lyrics in general] actually came to me much faster than they used to in the old days because I was basing them more on things that have happened to me. These lyrics are more heartfelt than ones in the past.

At least one was definitely autobiographical. 'Stranger On A Quiet Street' was about Jeff's original meeting with Rosie Vela. Their paths first crossed when he was working with the Traveling Wilburys, and she visited them, playing piano for them, just for fun (although she did not appear on any of their records). Some five or six years later, they met again by chance in a restaurant, and 'it reminded me of meeting somebody on a quiet street.' After this chance encounter, not only did Rosie sing backing vocals, but they also became an item for a while.

But in the fifteen years since the demise of the old band, ELO had ceased to be fashionable. Such reviews as there were for *Zoom* proved positive enough, with *All Music Guide* full of praise; 'the songwriting is melodic and memorable, the strongest Lynne has done in decades, resulting in the most consistent record released under the ELO banner since *Discovery.*' *Rolling Stone*, while remarking that it was 'pretty cheeky of Jeff Lynne to pass off his latest solo album as something from ELO,' suggested that while he could hardly claim the group was 'once again a "livin' thing",' admitted it was 'nevertheless the next-best entity.' But with the group's natural airtime constituency in Britain, Radio 2, failing to get behind the promotional single, the infectious rock'n'roll tune 'Alright', there was no airplay to speak of, and thus little promotion for the album. It sold well to the faithful and entered the British album chart at No. 34, but came and went all too quickly, while on the American Billboard chart its highest showing was a disappointing No. 94.

Nevertheless, a revitalised Jeff prepared for a North American tour, with a line-up including Richard Tandy, vocalist Rosie Vela, guitarist/keyboardist Marc Mann, the Bissonette Brothers (drummer Gregg and bass guitarist Matt), and cellists Peggy Baldwin and Sarah O'Brien. As a warm-up and for promotional purposes, they did two TV live performances, one on *VH1 Storytellers* and one on the Public Broadcasting Service network over two consecutive nights at CBS Television City, Los Angeles. The set list included several of the old favourites, alongside a selection of songs from the new album.

'Once you've rehearsed all those songs, it seems a waste not to play 'em,' Jeff said, evidently happy to take up the challenge of taking his music back on the road after a long interval. 'It's now becoming a bit more enjoyable again, and I might even look forward to it.' Twenty-five dates were scheduled on what was to have been the first set of ELO concerts in fifteen years. The opening night had been arranged for the Pepsi Arena, in Albany, New York, on 7 September, and the last at the MGM Grand, Las Vegas, on 20 October. However, advance ticket sales proved disappointing, and all the dates were scratched. 'It went off with a giant thud,' according to Chris Hansen, manager of Xcel Energy Center in St Paul, Minnesota, where the group was to appear on 17 September. 'We sold 750 seats the first day. It was a resounding stiff.' Management had intended to put on a 'grand spectacle with a massive stage and light show' as in previous years, but 'that's just not logistically or economically possible in this marketplace at this time.' For drummer Greg Bissonette, it was 'the greatest tour I never went on!' The only abiding live memory was a recording of one of the TV shows, which was released on VHS and later on DVD.

At around this time Jeff was honoured with a tribute album, when the double CD *Lynne Me Your Ears* was released. It featured thirty-two songs written by him, from The Idle Race days to the present, the majority recorded by previously unknown artists. One of the few well-known acts was former Move vocalist Carl Wayne, who had crowned a busy solo career on record and in West End musicals by replacing Allan Clarke in The Hollies a year earlier. Carl's performance of 'Steppin' Out' was acclaimed as one of the highlights of the set.

Meanwhile, work had been proceeding on George Harrison's sessions for the long-awaited follow-up to *Cloud Nine*. Rather strangely, in an interview with a German news agency in January 2001, George had said that the former ELO leader would not be producing it after all. He had stopped working with Jeff,

> [...] because I did not want him to make ELO albums out of my songs. On this album you can hear guitar, bass and drums, and no computers.

Many readers must have wondered whether this was a total leg-pull or perhaps a wry reminder to his friend that there would be no drum programming or sequencers on the record. It had after all been nearly two years since they had resumed their musical partnership.

At the same time, the possibility of another Wilburys project still remained hanging in the air. It had been eleven years since the last one and the prospect looked unlikely, but it was a case of 'never say never'. Jeff was still meeting up with Tom Petty as well as George Harrison every now and then, and the subject always came up in conversation.

> We say we should do the Wilburys again, and then we finish the night, go our separate ways, meet again and say yeah, we must do it. But who knows?

But by now, it had become evident to those who knew him that George had little time left. He and Jeff planned a return to the recording studio together in March, but the cancer had returned and spread to his lung. Despite further treatment his condition was deteriorating, and he passed away on 29 November, aged fifty-eight. Learning of his friend's death, said Jeff after receiving a call at home, was

> [...] a dreadful experience, although it wasn't really a surprise because he

had been very ill for quite a while. Even when you know someone is that ill, it still shocks you.

After a respectful interval of four months he returned to the studio in the spring of 2002 to help Dhani Harrison, who had developed into no mean guitarist himself, to finish the album. The songs themselves were basically complete, Jeff said, but basically demos and in want of tidying up. All he and Dhani did was to enhance them in places with vocal backing, and add acoustic guitars to a couple. George had asked him on the phone to help with them, stressing that 'I don't want them too posh,' but then became too ill to do any more to the recordings himself.

The album which had originally had a working title of *Portrait Of A Leg End* became *Brainwashed*. It was released in November 2002, almost twelve months after the death of its creator. The reviews were respectful and positive yet somewhat guarded, as if journalists were anxious not to let the artist's death persuade them to consign objectivity to the four winds and be too enthusiastic about a product which might sound unexceptional in the cold light of day. The record charted at a modest if not disappointing No. 52 in its first week. Sales recovered around five months later when the most radio-friendly track, the jaunty 'Any Road', was made available as a single, became a Radio 2 record of the week, and entered the charts at No. 37. This reignited demand for the parent album and resulted in a re-entry at what would be its peak position, No. 29. In America it reached No. 18 and went gold.

Jeff was also heavily involved in the memorial concert for George, held at the Royal Albert Hall on the first anniversary of his passing, 29 November 2002. The event was organised jointly by Olivia and Dhani Harrison, with Jeff and Eric Clapton as joint musical directors, and all profits went to George's charity, the Material World Charitable Foundation. A galaxy of stars who had worked with George in the past also took part—Paul McCartney, Ringo Starr, Tom Petty, Gary Brooker, Billy Preston, Jools Holland, Joe Brown and his daughter Sam, Marc Mann, and Andy Fairweather-Low, to name but a few. The show opened with a performance of Indian music by Anoushka Shankar, daughter of Ravi. This section featured Jeff's first appearance on the bill, when he sang the Indian-flavoured 'The Inner Light', the song which in 1968 had been his first Beatles B-side (coupled with 'Lady Madonna'). As a salute to George's involvement in the film world, the Monty Python team followed on stage with a comedy interlude. Most of the rest of the evening was given over to George's songs, from both Beatle and post-Beatle eras, all played in keeping with his original arrangements. Jeff sang lead vocal on 'I Want To Tell You' and 'Give Me Love (Give Me Peace On Earth)', and shared lead vocal with Tom Petty, backed by The Heartbreakers, on 'Handle With Care'. After the concert, one of his next priorities was to produce the surround-sound audio mix for the *Concert for George* DVD, released in time for the second anniversary of his death in 2003.

Around this time, the tracks which Carl Wayne had recorded with ELO were about to see release for the first time, on the re-mastered and heavily-expanded thirtieth anniversary reissue of *ELO 2* on CD. When asked about his working with the group, Carl said that Jeff probably rated him as a vocalist, but always knew full well that he could do ELO without him. Unlike Roy Wood, who after initial misgivings around the time that *Brontosaurus* was released early in 1970 had become confident in his ability to front a group, Jeff gave the impression of being less self-assured of his potential. Always extremely creative yet comparatively self-effacing, he was unashamedly happier in the studio—producing, writing, and singing—and not being put under the spotlight on stage as the lead man. Some of the other members of ELO, Carl maintained, were a diversion, but in a positive sense, detracting the focus a little from Jeff and thus contributing to the success of the group.

As for the recording which he had done with Jeff, he thought it was enjoyable but nothing serious—

[...] it was probably more to keep me quiet! Thirty years later when we listen to old recordings, there's some kind of strange validity, but did we seriously think twenty-eight years after I sang those tracks with Jeff that we'd still be talking about ELO and The Move? No—and it's great because who knows how long the future lasts? Jeff, with the revival of ELO, has proved that his music is timeless and ageless. I was pleased to sing those songs with him, but I'd be more interested in singing them again now! I've matured as a singer, become more interesting and more controlled in how I interpret a song and I'd be very interested to do an album of Jeff's material from a different perspective. Jeff showed his quality when he worked with Roy Orbison—and there was no finer singer ever than Roy Orbison. I would love to interpret a dozen of Jeff's songs from scratch, sit down with some great players and see what we could come up with. It would be interesting to see how we could translate those songs. Not that Jeff needs it—but I love it!

But Carl would never have the opportunity to work on any more material written by Jeff. Shortly after playing what would be his final gig with The Hollies, he went into hospital, was diagnosed with cancer, and died in August 2004, aged sixty-one. He had had a varied career as a solo performer in the thirty years or so between leaving The Move and joining The Hollies, making occasional guest appearances on record with the likes of Mike Oldfield on TV commercials, and also appearing in musicals on stage. A retrospective compilation of his material, re-mastered by Roy Wood, *Songs From The Wood And Beyond*, was released in 2006. Among the tracks were the 2001 recording of 'Steppin' Out' and one of Jeff's songs from *Discovery*, 'Midnight Blue', the B-side of a single from 1982.[1]

George Harrison's illness and death had ended any speculation of another Traveling Wilburys reunion. However, re-issue time was soon eagerly anticipated for the group's catalogue. After his distribution deal with Warner Brothers had expired in 1995, ownership of both albums as well as everything on his Dark Horse label reverted to him and went out of print, with second-hand and bootleg copies sometimes fetching exorbitant prices. The situation remained unresolved when he died, but not long after the Dark Horse catalogue was acquired by EMI, the Wilburys catalogue was issued in one package on the Rhino label through Warner Brothers in June 2007. It had four bonus tracks—the previously unreleased 'Maxine' and 'Like A Ship' from the 1988 sessions, and 'Nobody's Child' and 'Runaway' from 1990—plus a DVD featuring a documentary about the making of the first album. Overdubs for the 1988 tracks credited Ayrton Wilbury (in honour of Formula One racer Ayrton Senna), and in real life George's son Dhani. *The Traveling Wilburys Collection* reached No. 9 in America, and such was the built-up of demand over the years for records which had long been unavailable that nobody was surprised when it entered the British album chart at No. 1. Worldwide sales topped half a million within three weeks of release.

In July 2008 *The Washington Times* chose its five favourite knob-twiddlers (or producers) of all time. Inevitably, Sir George Martin's position at the top was unassailable, as was that of the runner-up, Phil Spector, with Quincy Jones placed third—and Jeff at No. 4. Calling him 'an inveterate wall-of-sounder from his days as the frontman of the Electric Light Orchestra,' the paper lauded his

> [...] distinctive stamp: bright guitars, sunny orchestration and ringing vocal harmonies. Using a pair of unearthed John Lennon demos, he even made The Beatles sound like Jeff Lynne.

As a producer, Jeff said his role was basically

> [...] making everything sound lovely. I don't know about how electronics work. That's my engineer's job. And I don't read music. I'm just never satisfied with what I've got and I always want to do something a little bit more, or a little bit different, to make instruments that you've never heard before by combining sounds you might never think would go together. Producers have to have ideas.

After that, for several years Jeff immersed himself in working in his home studio. Although the back catalogue had never really stopped selling over the years, the tide of critical opinion relating to ELO had ebbed and flowed. There had been a time when the group were generally held in anything but high regard. Gradually they became one of the great guilty pleasures of music. As with ABBA, another group who went briefly completely out of fashion and then rediscovered and rehabilitated in critical opinion, many people secretly liked and admired ELO but were reluctant to lose face by admitting it too freely.

> I never thought of myself as a guilty pleasure, I thought we just had a great load of pop songs—nice tunes, good words, good melodies. I'd always thought and hoped my music was good—it's been around long enough and it still has as many legs as it had to start with.

Their influence resurfaced in the sound of newer names such as Coldplay, and in the age of sampling, the group's back catalogue proved fertile ground. Daft Punk sampled 'Evil Woman' on the track 'Face to Face' in 2001. It was very flattering:

I'm delighted we're being heard by the younger generations. Every songwriter's objective is to be heard by as many people as possible. I've been sampled for the last 15 or 20 years, and I've been getting used to it. They take an obscure passage to make it into a feature of their song, which is OK as long as they pay for it.

One successful record in which an ELO influence was most obvious was Paul Weller's single 'The Changingman', released in April 1995. Co-written by Paul and his producer Brendan Lynch, his eighth solo single and the first to reach the British top ten, the song structure and instrumentation bore an uncanny resemblance to '10538 Overture'. The *NME* reviewer commented that the Bard of Woking had 'delved deeper into rock's rich past,' specifically naming the group and record. A subsequent issue of the paper printed a request from Brendan, asking them to send him and Paul 'a copy of that ELO record he was on about,' as they had never heard it. As Paul was a self-professed admirer of The Move, this sounded unlikely. A rather more faithful act of homage came a year later, when Def Leppard included their version of '10538 Overture' on *Yeah*, their album consisting entirely of cover versions of old rock classics.

In 2005, the Pussycat Dolls' 'Beep' featured an instrumental hook as good as sampled from the same song. Nine years later, Sam Smith's 'Stay With Me', it was decided, bore more than a passing resemblance to 'I Won't Back Down', the Tom Petty hit of 1989 which he had co-written with Jeff. Tom good-naturedly declared that it was 'a musical accident, no more no less,' and an out-of-court settlement resulted in Tom and Jeff both receiving an agreed share of royalties as well as a joint co-song-writing credit.

Gradually the process gathered momentum, until everyone was free to admit what a great group ELO always were. In June 2005, a twenty-track compilation of material, containing most of hits since 'Showdown', *All Over The World: The Very Best Of Electric Light Orchestra*, became the ultimate representation of their back catalogue, peaked at No. 6 in Britain, and remained on or very close to the charts for several years. There was even another brief return to the lower end of the singles chart in September 2012, when the London Olympics opening and closing ceremony some weeks later featured 'Mr Blue Sky', creating demand for the track as a download. Two years later, the youth charity Rhythmix organised a poll to find Britain's favourite feel-good tune, and 'Mr Blue Sky' came first. By this time several acts—including Joe Brown, Lily Allen, Rock Choir, and The Delgados—had recorded and released their own versions of the song, as had Jim Bob (formerly of Carter the Unstoppable Sex Machine) as a theme tune to the BBC Radio 4 sitcom by the same name. It had also been featured in several feature films, including *Eternal Sunshine Of The Spotless Mind*, *The Game Plan*, *Role Models*, *Martin Child*, and *A Smile As Big As The Moon*, television programmes such as *Doctor Who*, *CSI: Crime Scene Investigation*, and *American Dad!*, and commercials for Volkswagen and Glidden House Paint. Equally pleasing to Jeff was another airing of the song on 27 February 2011 at Wembley Stadium after the match in celebration of Birmingham City FC winning the League Cup Final, as well as at every home game, Jeff having long been a staunch Blues fan.

There was no let-up for the man who had become one of the most eagerly sought-after producers in the world. In 2005, Jeff returned to the studio with Tom Petty again. With him and Mike Campbell he co-produced his third album, *Highway Companion*, as well as playing guitar, bass guitar, keyboards, autoharp, and contributing backing vocals, released in July 2006.

Three years later he produced four tracks on *Far* for Regina Spektor. She admitted that she did not know of his work when she originally met him. For him, it was not at first sight what he would call 'an obvious pairing,' but he was asked whether he would like to work with her and was sent a couple of her albums. When he heard them, he admitted to being

> […] really blown away with them. I thought, 'this girl's superb'! She came to my studio and we talked for a while and she was a lovely girl, very sweet, and her voice is so amazing! Beautiful quality and a lovely tone. And a beautiful plumage! She was beautiful and I loved her voice, and her pitch and her sense of timing was absolutely marvellous. In fact, in her live show, sometimes her drummer is playing his bass drum to her left hand. Her hand's like a drum machine, almost. Very tight, rhythmically. We laid down four or five tracks with her on piano and sometimes she wanted to do it all at once and I'm going, 'hmmm…. Don't do that! Because I've got to separate it again and it's almost impossible to get the separation.' I wanted to have the complete control that I like; I like total separation and control over the stuff so I can make it sound good. And we did it like that, just one track, and then we did them all separate so she played the piano parts separate and did the vocals separate standing up at a vocal mic and I just really enjoyed it, you

know? I still listen back to those songs and I think they're great.

In 2012, Jeff produced an album for Joe Walsh, *Analog Man*. When Joe was discussing making a new solo album, his first for some years, his wife Marjorie (the sister of Ringo Starr's wife Barbara), gave him Jeff's contact number. The latter invited him to bring the demo tracks over to his house so that they could listen to them together, and from there they began working jointly. Jeff ended up producing and adding vocals, guitars, bass, piano, and drums to a couple of tracks. Like many before him, Joe remarked that Jeff 'really put his stamp on my music and took it in a direction I never would have gone, and I'm really grateful to him.'

At the same time, rumours were regularly filtering out about one or more forthcoming new releases from Jeff. The days of having to book studios in London, Munich, or indeed anywhere were now a thing of the past, now that he had his state-of-the-art recording complex at his Beverly Hills home. 'The studio is my place, I'm totally content, give me a bit of a tune and I'll keep on until I make it great hopefully.'

What was threatening to turn into a lifetime of waiting for some fans came to an end in October 2012 when two new releases appeared simultaneously on Frontiers, an Italian-based record label specialising in classic rock. One, *Mr Blue Sky (The Very Best of Electric Light Orchestra)*, was a set of eleven re-recordings of the old classic hits, plus one brand new song, 'Point Of No Return'. All had been newly re-recorded mostly as a one-man band, with minimal instrumental input from anyone else. The Electric Light Orchestra was now plainly Jeff Lynne and nobody else.

Ostensibly this re-recording was done because Jeff felt that he could improve the song, as well as the other ELO hits that appeared, using modern recording techniques, stating that when he heard the original recordings, he was not entirely happy with them. 'I'd like to have another go at them,' he said, 'because I don't think I did them justice.' Suggestions were made that he had recorded them again because he did not own the full rights to the original songs; they were owned by Sony, and when the songs were used in films, advertisements, and other money-making ventures, the latter reaped most, if not all of the profit. It would thus be more beneficial to Jeff if he was in a position to market his own, self-recorded versions. But he refuted the theory, reasoning that the old songs simply did not have the sound he remembered or thought he had got on them. In the old days, he maintained, they were always completed under the pressures of having an album ready before they went out on tour. Having learnt so much from producing others, he knew he could make them better, and without any deadlines he now had all the time he wanted and needed to get them exactly as he intended.

The other new record, *Long Wave*, was an eleven-track collection of covers, the songs that he had grown up with from his youth. Middle-of-the-road songs like 'Love Is a Many-Splendoured Thing' and 'She' rubbed shoulders with rock'n'roll classics like 'Mercy, Mercy'—an old Don Covay song which was once regularly part of The Idle Race's repertoire—and Chuck Berry's 'Let It Rock'.

The album got its title,

> [...] because all of the songs I sing on it are the ones heard on long-wave radio when I was a kid growing up in Birmingham. These songs take me back to that feeling of freedom in those days and summon up the feeling of first hearing those powerful waves of music coming in on my old crystal set. My dad also had the radio on all the time, so some of these songs have been stuck in my head for fifty years. You can only imagine how great it felt to finally get them out of my head after all these years.

Recording material which in some cases came from the pre-rock era presented an interesting challenge, or in his own words, rebuilding the songs 'from the ground up.' This involved getting to the basic song itself and liberating it from 'all of the flowery stuff,' or the original arrangement.

> I literally had to listen to the recordings of all of the songs on *Long Wave* and learn all of these songs. It probably took a hundred listens before I could actually understand the song, because of all of these big arrangements. When you get to where you have this tunnel hearing on, then you start listening to one instrument at a time. It is great because you can learn how all the parts go; the piano part, the bass part, the string part. You don't want to just copy them; you want to make them your own.

Like many a music lover from his generation, over the years Jeff had acquired a taste for some songs which he had not cared for in the least during his early days.

> Some of [the songs on *Long Wave*] I actually hated when I used to hear them when I was a kid and I only learnt to love them when I learnt how to play them in the last couple of years, like, for instance, 'If I Loved You from Carousel'. I never dreamed in a million years that I'd be singing that flippin' thing!—but it was actually the most marvellous thing, the most fun I ever had recording it. I just loved it, and once I'd got it right, I was frightened to death to sing it.

Not surprisingly, one of the choices he made was a tribute to his hero and good friend Roy Orbison. Tackling 'these old, beautiful songs' meant that they had to be treated with total respect;

> The fact that I knew Roy very well made that even more important. One night Roy and I were talking and he told me that 'Running Scared' was the favourite song that he ever did, of his old stuff. It was great to hear that. I know that I can't come close to his version, so, once again, I had to do my own version.

Another interesting choice was 'Bewitched, Bothered & Bewildered', from the 1957 Frank Sinatra movie *Pal Joey*. It was one of the records which his Dad owned and would play every weekend, and some nights.

> You have to listen to the chords, as it has some of the most beautiful chords, ever. You listen to it and you realize just how clever a song it really is.

The release of both albums coincided with a Jeff Lynne night on BBC 4 television on 5 October 2012. The documentary *Mr Blue Sky: The Story of Jeff Lynne and ELO* included footage of Jeff working in his studio above Los Angeles on the new re-recordings, in a portrait of his life and career, with contributions from Paul McCartney, Ringo Starr, Tom Petty, Joe Walsh, Olivia and Dhani Harrison, Barbara Orbison, and Eric Idle. It was followed by repeats of the *Rock Family Trees* documentary which had been first shown around seventeen years earlier, tracing the history of The Move, ELO, and associated Birmingham groups; of the June 1978 ELO Wembley concert, and finally of *Acoustic Live from Bungalow Palace*, an unplugged session in which Jeff reprised several of the classic ELO songs, accompanying himself on acoustic guitar and Richard on piano.

With this generous exposure, nobody was surprised the following week when the album charts placed *Long Wave* and *Mr Blue Sky* as new entries at No. 7 and No. 8 respectively, with *All Over The World* re-entering at No. 10.

Demand for Jeff's music on soundtracks continued apace, and early in 2013, he contributed three tracks to the 1970s-set Oscar-nominated movie, *American Hustle*. There were two ELO songs among them, '10538 Overture' and 'Long Black Road', and an additional solo number, 'Stream of Stars'. At around the same time appeared a third album on the Frontiers label, a live album from ELO. This featured mostly versions of the classic hits recorded in 2001 at CBS Television City as a warm-up for the *Zoom* tour that never was, although notable by their absence were many songs from that album. Also included were two previously unreleased tracks from 1992 and 2010 respectively, 'Cold Feet' and the rockabilly 'Out Of Luck'.

Another British musical icon from a more recent generation had also become part of the picture. Take That frontman Gary Barlow had been a long-term fan of ELO, as evidenced by their 2007 No. 1 hit 'Shine' with its echoes of 'Mr Blue Sky'. The group also used samples of the latter song for the live version of 'Shine' while on tour. It was a mutual admiration society, and both men immediately got on very well together. Gary asked Jeff if he would close the *Children in Need* show, and as a gesture of thanks Jeff agreed to work with him. Take That sang vocals on a couple of tracks Jeff recorded in his studio for a possible future project, and there was talk of Jeff producing the group as well.[2] But the most public evidence of this meeting of minds came when Jeff and Richard joined forces to play 'Mr Blue Sky' and 'Livin' Thing' at the *Children in Need Rocks 2013* concert at Hammersmith Eventim Apollo, backed by the BBC Concert Orchestra, and featuring Chereene Allen on violin and members of the Take That touring band.

By now, Beatles nostalgia was in full swing, and it was only natural that Jeff should be part of the celebrations. On 9 February 2014, he performed George Harrison's 'Something on The Night That Changed America', a TV special paying tribute to the fiftieth anniversary of his heroes' first appearance on the *Ed Sullivan Show*, accompanied by Dhani Harrison and Joe Walsh. Later in the same show he also backed Dave Grohl on *Hey Bulldog* from the *Yellow Submarine* soundtrack.

In March he crossed the Atlantic to return to Birmingham, where he received an honorary doctorate degree from the university.

At the ceremony, he was asked if he had any interests other than music.

> I was stumped. I can't think of anything. It's a bit weird, I suppose. But I do really love music.

As for the honour itself, he was naturally 'chuffed', and very impressed by the institution itself.

> It was a wonderful day, being among all those graduates with all their hopes and wishes. They have great music at BCU too, with all the orchestras, quintets and such. I was amazed by the musicality of it all. I told the kids at the university: 'Never give up. If you want it, and you work hard, you will get it.

That same week, Jeff was honoured on the Birmingham Broad Street Walk of Stars. This was an award reserved for residents of the city who were adjudged to have made a significant contribution to the fields of music, television, film, radio, theatre, sport, business, and literacy, and had also performed at one or more of the city's major venues. Jeff received his award from the Lord Mayor, Councillor Mike Leddy. Among those present were two others who had already received the award, Jasper Carrott and Roy Wood. It was the first time in over twenty years that Jeff had been reunited with his former musical partner, as the local press reported that the meeting began with a handshake and an awkward hug, before they eagerly caught up on each other's news. Afterwards both paid tribute to the other, and testified how good it was to meet up with Richard Tandy and other old friends from days gone by. Speculation that Jeff and Roy might work together again flourished, even if only to collaborate on another song or two.

The Hammersmith gig in November 2013 had not only resulted in a partnership of sorts with Gary Barlow, but also led to a meeting with another well-known fan, Chris Evans, presenter of the Radio 2 *Breakfast* programme. Jeff appeared on the show in March, and Chris asked him if he would do another gig in Britain.

> I said I would if anyone wanted to come—and about 10,000 people rang in in the first 10 minutes. That opened avenues and I saw this could be a reality.

Before long there was talk of offers of further one-off gigs, world tours, and even a six-night stint at London's giant O2 Arena. Jeff's reaction was mixed:

> I'm flattered when I'm told that I could sell out six nights but I can't really imagine it. It's great that people still want to hear my music, but the O2? And six nights? I don't know if I'll take the plunge and go back out on the road again, despite the offers that have been coming in. I'm still undecided. I totally prefer working in the studio to touring. But if I were to do something live again here in the UK, I'd want it to be something simple. Whether that would be ELO or just me and a few of my mates, I don't know.

But the temptation of at least one gig was impossible to resist—and what an event it would turn out to be. In the summer it was announced that 'Jeff Lynne's ELO', as it was billed, would headline Radio 2's Proms in the Parks on 14 September. This was a new one-off line-up with the ever-faithful Richard Tandy on keyboards, plus members of Take That's band, and the BBC Concert Orchestra.

Rehearsals were scheduled for the summer, and lasted a month. 'To start with, it was like wearing a pair of old boots,' Jeff said, 'but after three weeks it felt like a comfortable pair of slippers.' Having been away from the stage for such a long time, he had already started practising on his own in the studio, running through the whole set of songs twice a day just so he could get the feel again.

> You really have to get yourself back into it. Standing up playing guitar is the hardest thing, because for the last twenty years, I've been sitting down in the studio playing, so you have to learn all over again how to stand up and sing and play. Then I went to Richard's house in Wales and we practised for a week, and then we joined up with the band [the BBC Concert Orchestra]. Once we got that good, tight, we wanted to play another gig, but my manager said no. We were all fired up and it would've been a perfect time to do it.

The line-up also featured performances from Blondie, Chrissie Hynde, Billy Ocean, and Paloma Faith, but interest really centred on the headlining act. Not counting the brief *Children in Need* spot, it was Jeff's first performance on stage, or at any rate first complete show, for twenty-eight years (since Heartbeat '86 at Birmingham). Speculation in *Radio Times* that ether Roy Wood, Bev Bevan, or Mik Kaminski might appear proved unfounded. Nevertheless, anticipation was building steadily by the time the ensemble took to the stage shortly after 6.00 p.m. The seventeen-song set, lasting a little over ninety minutes, was rapturously received with a fervour that seemed to have the star of the show a little taken aback, as if unable to believe his good fortune.

Jeff bravely started with the song which, he admitted afterwards, was the most complex to play—'All Over the World'. He had never performed it on stage before, 'as it had intricate insides to it, lots of bits in there that make up the whole.' If he had chosen to compress some of the songs into a medley, as the group did on the *Time* tour, it would have been understandable. Instead, and perhaps wisely, he and the rest of the assembled company eschewed the medley principle as they gave near-perfect renditions, the main star of the show alternating between acoustic and electric guitar as they delivered a choice selection from his back catalogue of 'Evil Woman', 'Ma-Ma-Ma Belle', 'Showdown', 'Strange Magic', '10538 Overture', 'Can't Get It Out Of My Head', 'Sweet Talkin' Woman', 'Turn to Stone', 'Steppin' Out' (an album track which had grown in stature over the years), 'Handle With Care', 'Don't Bring Me Down', 'Rock'n'Roll is King', 'Mr Blue Sky' (with Richard supplying a suitably vocoderised title during the break and a 'Please turn me over' at the end, as per the original album track), and inevitably an almighty finale of 'Roll Over Beethoven', the song without which he hardly dared leave the stage.

The ecstatic 50,000 or so who made up the audience—in addition to an estimated 800,000 tuning in at home via the BBC red button and viewers of a full recording on BBC 4 TV a month later—had been treated to a veritable feast of hits. They also had the bonus of the magnificent spectacle of a full band of musicians, backing vocalists, the BBC Concert Orchestra, and a stunning sequence of back-projected images which became brighter as the mid-September daylight gradually dimmed towards dusk. Undoubtedly the most moving moment of all during this utterly joyous show was when footage of the Traveling Wilburys appeared at the back of the stage, and Jeff paid a warm tribute to the memory of George Harrison and Roy Orbison before launching into 'Handle With Care', the only non-ELO number on the set.

There was one notable absentee from the stage effects. The spaceship, which had been kept in storage for some time after the *Out Of The Blue* tour at a cost of millions and which might have graced any museum prepared to give it room, had long since been broken up in a shipyard 'somewhere in East Anglia,' to quote Jeff. Nevertheless, it had a successor: 'a digital recreation of ELO's neon jukebox flying saucer hovered above the sawing strings, driving rock, luscious chords and choral harmonies of a 60-piece band.' Fans were practically levitating with joy and the crowd sang along to one song after another. Jeff later admitted feeling a little overwhelmed;

> I was really worried before the show. I was thinking, what the hell is it gonna be like after all these years? I thought the crowd would all disperse and go their own sweet way, but they all loved it.

The positive reviews afterwards confirmed what a triumph it had been. In 1986, Jeff had been more than glad to get off the treadmill of touring:

> Back then, it was murder, trying to get the cellos right and violins and all that stuff. It never sounded like I wanted it to.

Having discovered that there was nothing to compare with being in the studio, he was always more at home in such an environment—'I'm totally content, give me a bit of a tune and I'll keep on until I make it great, hopefully.' But after this reception and the realisation that ELO were at last as hip as it was possible to be, the temptation to play live again persisted—and with advances in modern technology, it would now be much easier for him to recreate the sound properly on stage.

> With all these great string samplers and synths, it wouldn't be such a drag for me, 'cause the sound would be perfect, everything would be sweet, so never say never. But it would be nice to find a way of doing it without going anywhere.

There would be no need to take a thirty-two-piece string section out on the road, he stated, as the sound of the strings could all be done on keyboards. The orchestra itself had been mainly for the spectacle:

> It looks great to have them, but musically you don't need them. We could do it with ten people at the most.

By the end of the year, still elated by his reception, Jeff was dropping heavy hints about playing some dates in the US, which would include material from a new album on which he was currently working.

Suddenly Jeff was in demand, being written about, interviewed, and quoted all across the media. If ELO-mania had not exactly broken out, the interest was certainly at a much higher level than it had been since its late 1970s heyday. Much was affectionately made in some quarters of the man who still sported the same retro look, barely touched by the passage of time—hair, beard, and ever-present giant aviator sunglasses.

> He speaks with a warm Midlands accent, despite not having lived in England for decades, and has the slightly shambling demeanour of a subterranean creature, a man who spends most of his life in the air-conditioned, artificially lit environs of recording studios.

After all this time, the self-confessed 'studio rat' was bowled over by the acknowledgement that he was totally back in favour.

> It's amazing. It's great to be cool—I've never, ever been cool, so for people to think it's cool now is absolutely wonderful. I've thought we were cool all along, but I love it to bits to finally get the recognition from the high end of rock'n'roll—the music critics and people like that. It's a totally unexpected thing for me to be in this other league where it's good. I don't know why this is happening, but it feels great to go out there and have such warmth from an audience. I'd never known that—I'd never experienced the really deep emotional side of it, where people cry. Some of those songs have been around for forty years, and they're just going on.

Among those who joined in the general chorus of praise was James Dean Bradfield of the Manic Street Preachers, who told *New Musical Express* that *Out Of The Blue* was the first album he had ever bought. He enthused,

> Just sheer wonderment. It's an overblown, unbridled expression of every kind of sense. You just felt like Jeff Lynne was catching Venus, Mars and all their moons and putting it in music. Absolutely amazing.

Bryan Adams, who had known Jeff since the latter had come to one of his shows in the 1980s and had long been a fan, had started working with him on material to be included on a forthcoming album. He was equally generous with his praise. As a songwriter, he said that he always believed there were two levels to making records, the first being the song-writing process, where 'you get a song to a certain place and that's it.' The second was where

> [...] you need to go and take it and make it into a record and that's as much work, if not more work, than it is actually writing the song. Because making a song into a record is a huge deal.

In his view, production could 'make and break whether the song gets heard or disappears,' which was why it was so important for him to work with somebody of Jeff's calibre; 'when you get a great producer behind your song, they know what to do and they understand.'

Francis Rossi of Status Quo summed it up more concisely. When talking about Jeff and choosing 'Steppin' Out' as a track while he was a guest on Johnnie Walker's *Sounds Of The 70s* on Radio 2, he remarked, 'I hate that man—he's so wonderful!'

As speculation mounted over future live activity, Jeff remained in the spotlight. At the Classic Rock Honours in Los Angeles on 4 November 2014, he was presented with the Outstanding Contribution to Music award. In his acceptance speech, he remarked modestly that it was because he had 'done a lot of stuff.' As to the burning question on everyone's lips, he added that he had loved the gig in Hyde Park so much that he had every intention of playing more the following year. And it would be more than a reprise of greatest hits, as he was working on a new album and songs from that would definitely feature in the set list. Even so, many old songs had evolved in some way or other, taking on new meanings over the years—

> Some that I thought very straightforward aren't at all. I sing them now and I realise what they're about and it's usually about grim stuff like relationships and crap relationships.

Three months later, on 8 February 2015, the 57th Grammy Awards at the Staples Center, Los Angeles, included another performance from

Jeff Lynne's ELO. A six-piece group comprising Richard Tandy, the two guitarists, bass guitarist, and drummer from the Hyde Park gig, and backing vocalist Tyra Juliette, took to the stage for performances of 'Evil Woman' and 'Mr Blue Sky', with Ed Sheeran joining him to share vocals and play acoustic guitar on the second song. The audience included a host of celebrities including Taylor Swift, Nicole Kidman, Beyoncé, and an unashamedly enthusiastic Sir Paul McCartney, who rose to his feet as he sang and clapped along to the first song until he noticed he was being filmed. His wife Nancy gave him a gentle tug as he gave a slightly embarrassed wave to the camera and sat down again.

Yet another honour came in April 2015, when the Hollywood Chamber of Commerce announced that Jeff would later that month become the 2,548th star on the Hollywood Walk of Fame, with Tom Petty and Joe Walsh present at the unveiling in front of the Capitol Records building. The citation and press release mentioned not only his achievements with ELO and as a producer since then, but also his involvement with organisations including the St Jude Research Hospital (a pediatric treatment and research facility focused on children's diseases in Memphis), The MusiCares Foundation (established by the National Academy of Recording Arts and Sciences to benefit musicians experiencing financial, personal, or medical crisis), and HEART (Helping Ease Abuse Related Trauma, a charity providing for victimised children in Los Angeles).

Since going fully professional and first appearing on record at the age of eighteen in 1966, Jeff Lynne, 'arguably our most unassuming rock god ever,' had maintained a remarkable if not unique career in rock music. A couple of years leading one critically-acclaimed and highly-respected group who never set the charts alight were the stepping stone to becoming a driving force in a more successful unit, and ultimately the leadership of another—one which became a global name and broke one show business record after another. When that unit seemingly had nothing left to achieve, he laid it to rest and embarked on a new path as solo performer, collaborator, then producer of some of the greatest names of all time. Then it all came full circle and, almost half a century after he started, it looked as if the group which he had led to the height of its fame in the 1970s was looking at a new dawn. 'I've been in love with music since I was probably just five years old,' he once said. 'I was mad for music then—and I still am today.'

Personnel

This list includes all those who were either listed as members of the line-up on album sleeves or official members of the group for touring purposes, including the cancelled 2001 dates. Though there is often a fine line between guests and temporary members, included are all those who seem to have joined or can consider themselves as having belonged to the group at one time or another. Session singers and musicians who only made occasional guest appearances on studio recordings are excluded, as are those brought in to mime on TV, and the mythical 'Ted Blight'.

Jeff Lynne—lead vocals, guitars, bass guitar, keyboards, drums, and other instruments
Roy Wood—lead vocals, guitar, bass guitar, cello, clarinet, bassoon, oboe, drums, recorder, other instruments (1970–72)
Bev Bevan—drums, percussion, vocals (1970–86)
Bill Hunt—keyboards, French horn, hunting horn (1970–72)
Steve Woolam—violin (1970–71)
Rick Payne—cello (1971)
Richard Tandy—keyboards, synthesisers, bass guitar, guitar, backing vocals, vocoder (1972–86, 2000–01, 2012, 2014)
Mike Edwards—cello (1972-4)
Mike Atkins—cello (1972)
Trevor Smith—cello (1972)
Wilf Gibson—violin (1972–73)
Hugh McDowell—cello (1972, 1973–79)

Andy Craig—cello (1972)
Colin Walker—cello (1972–73)
Michael d'Albuquerque—bass guitar, backing vocals (1972–74)
Mik Kaminski—violin (1973–86)
Louis Clark—orchestral arranger, conductor, synthesisers, keyboards (1974–86)
Kelly Groucutt—bass guitar, backing vocals (1974–83)
Melvyn Gale—cello, piano (1975–79)
Dave Morgan—synthesisers, acoustic guitar, backing vocals (1981–86)
Pete King—temporary replacement on tour for Bev Bevan, drums (1985)
Martin Smith—bass guitar, backing vocals (1986)
Marc Mann—guitars, keyboards, backing vocals (2000–01, 2012)
Rosie Vela—backing vocals (2000–01)
Matt Bissonette—bass guitar, backing vocals (2001)
Greg Bissonette—drums, backing vocals (2001)
Peggy Baldwin—cello (2001)
Sarah O'Brien—cello (2001)

Additional line-up, 2014 concert

Milton McDonald—backing vocals, guitar
Iain Hornal—guitar, backing vocals
Mike Stevens—guitars, vocals, harmonica
Marcus Byrne—keyboards, Pro Tools
Bernie Smith—keyboards
Lee Pomeroy—bass guitar
Donavan Hepburn—drums
Mick Wilson—percussion, vocals
Chereene Allen—violin
Melanie Lewis-McDonald—backing vocals
BBC Concert Orchestra—string ensemble

Discography

Included below are the month (if known) and year of release, label, and UK catalogue number unless stated otherwise. In recent years, UK and European releases plus catalogue numbers have generally become one and the same. Bootlegs are excluded, and for reasons of space only the most important reissues and compilations are listed. All singles and albums are on vinyl up to 1990, and on CD thereafter. Most 7-inch and 12-inch singles were issued in picture sleeves from 1977 onwards. Further information and details are available on the 45cat and Discogs, websites listed in the Bibliography.

Singles and albums released on the Jet label were through Polydor 1975–76, United Artists 1976–78, and CBS/Epic and associated labels thereafter. Several of the earlier releases came out on Jet through CBS/Epic from 1978 onwards, hence the different catalogue numbers. Singles not released in the UK are excluded. A fuller worldwide discography up to 1996 can be found in Guttenbacher, Haines, and Petersdorff, *Unexpected Messages*.

Singles

THE NIGHTRIDERS
It's Only The Dog/Your Friend (11.1966) Polydor 56116

THE IDLE RACE
Here We Go Round The Lemon Tree/My Father's Son (9.1967) Liberty LBF 55997-withdrawn

Impostors Of Life's Magazine/Sitting In My Tree (10.1967) Liberty LBF 15026

The Skeleton and the Roundabout/Knocking Nails Into My House (3.1968) Liberty LBF 15054

End Of The Road/The Morning Sunshine (6.1968) Liberty LBF 15101

I Like My Toys/The Birthday (9.1968) Liberty LBF 15129—withdrawn

Days of the Broken Arrows/Warm Red Carpet (4.1969) Liberty LBF 15218

Come With Me/Reminds Me Of You (7.1969) Liberty LBF 15242

The Skeleton and the Roundabout/The Morning Sunshine (1.1976) United Artists UP 36060

THE MOVE

Brontosaurus/Lightning Never Strikes Twice (3.1970) Regal Zonophone RZ 3026

When Alice Comes Back To The Farm/What? (10.1970) Fly BUG 2

Ella James/No Time (5.1971) Harvest HAR 5036—withdrawn

Tonight/Don't Mess Me Up (6.1971) Harvest HAR 5038

Chinatown/Down On The Bay (10.1971) Harvest HAR 5043

California Man/Do Ya/Ella James (4.1972) Harvest HAR 5050

Do Ya/No Time (9.1974) Harvest HAR 5088

ELECTRIC LIGHT ORCHESTRA

10538 Overture/1st Movement (Jumping Biz) (7.1972) Harvest HAR 5053

Roll Over Beethoven/Manhattan Rumble (49th Street Massacre) (1.1973) Harvest HAR 5063—withdrawn

Roll Over Beethoven/Queen Of The Hours (1.1973) Harvest HAR 5063

Showdown/In old England Town (Boogie #2) (9.1973) Harvest HAR 5077

Ma-Ma-Ma Belle/Oh No Not Susan (3.1974) Warner Bros K 16349

Can't Get It Out Of My Head/Illusions in G Major (1.1975) Warner Bros K 16510

Evil Woman/10538 Overture (live) (11.1975) Jet JET 764

Nightrider/Daybreaker (live) (3.1976) Jet JET 769

Strange Magic/Showdown (live) (6.1976) Jet JET 779

Livin' Thing/Fire On High (11.1976) United Artists UP 36184

Rockaria!/Poker (2.1977) Jet UP 36209

Discography

Telephone Line/Poor Boy (The Greenwood)/King of the Universe (5.1977) Jet UP 36254

Showdown/Roll Over Beethoven (1977) Harvest HAR 5121, also 12-inch, Harvest HAR 12-5121

Turn To Stone/Mister Kingdom (10.1977) Jet UP 36313

Mr Blue Sky/One Summer Dream (1.1978) Jet UP 36342

Rockaria!/Poker (1978) Jet SJET 100

Telephone Line/Poor Boy (The Greenwood)/King of the Universe (1978) Jet SJET 101

Turn To Stone/Mister Kingdom (1978) Jet SJET 103

Mr Blue Sky/One Summer Dream (1.1978) Jet SJET 104, some on blue vinyl

Wild West Hero/Eldorado (5.1978) Jet SJET 109, also 12-inch, Jet SJET 12 109, yellow vinyl

Sweet Talkin' Woman/Bluebird Is Dead (9.1978) Jet SJET 121, some on mauve vinyl, also 12-inch, Jet SJET 12 121, mauve vinyl

Can't Get It Out Of My Head/Evil Woman (1.1979) Jet ELO 1 JB

Shine A Little Love/Jungle (5.1979) Jet SJET 144, also 12-inch, Jet SJET 12 144, white vinyl

The Diary Of Horace Wimp/Down Home Town (7.1979) Jet JET 150

Don't Bring Me Down/Dreaming Of 4000 (8.1979) Jet JET 153, also 12-inch, Jet JET 12 153

Confusion/Last Train To London (11.1979) Jet JET 166

I'm Alive/Drum Dreams (5.1980) Jet JET 179

All Over The World/Midnight Blue (7.1980) Jet JET 195, also 10-inch, Jet JET 10 195, blue vinyl

Don't Walk Away/Across The Border (11.1980) Jet JET 7004

Hold on Tight/When Time Stood Still (7.1981) Jet JET 7011

Twilight/Julie Don't Live Here Any More (10.1981) Jet JET 7015

Ticket To The Moon/Here Is The News (12.1981) Jet JET 7018, also 12-inch picture disc, Jet JET P12 7018

The Way Life's Meant To Be/Wishing (3.1982) Jet JET 7021

Rock'n'Roll Is King/After All (6.1983) Jet JET A 3500, also 12-inch with Time After Time, Jet JET TA 3500

Secret Messages/Buildings Have Eyes (8.1983) Jet JET A 3720, also picture disc, Jet JET WA 3720

Four Little Diamonds/Letter From Spain (10.1983) Jet JET A 3869, also 12-inch with The Bouncer, Jet JET TA 3869

10538 Overture/Roll Over Beethoven (5.1984) Harvest G45 22

Calling America/Caught In A Trap (2.1986) Epic A 6844, also 12-inch with Destination Unknown, Epic QTA 6844

So Serious/A Matter Of Fact (4.1986) Epic A 7090, also 12-inch, Epic TA 7090

Getting To The Point/Secret Lives (7.1986) Epic 7317, also 12-inch with ELO Megamix, Epic TA 7317

Alright (2001) Epic SAMPCS 9977, CD promo only

Surrender (9.2006) Epic ELOPR 1, 7-inch 1-sided promo only, blue vinyl

Latitude 88 North (2.2007) Epic 88697048787, 7-inch 1-sided promo only, orange vinyl

OLIVIA NEWTON-JOHN/ELECTRIC LIGHT ORCHESTRA

Xanadu/Fool Country (6.1980) Jet JET 185, also 10-inch, Jet JET 10 185, pink vinyl—Electric Light Orchestra A-side only

THE TRAVELING WILBURYS

Handle With Care/Margarita (10.1988) Wilbury W7732, also 10-inch, Wilbury W7732 TE, also 12-inch, W7732T

The End Of The Line/Congratulations (2.1989) Wilbury W7637, also 12-inch, Wilbury W7637T

Nobody's Child/Lumiere (6.1990) Wilbury W9773, also 12-inch, Wilbury W9773T—Traveling Wilburys A-side, Dave Stewart and the Spiritual Cowboys B-side

She's My Baby/New Blue Moon (11.1990) Wilbury W9523, also 12-inch, Wilbury W9523T

Wilbury Twist/New Blue Moon (instrumental) (3.1991) Wilbury W 0018, also 12-inch, Wilbury W 0018T

JEFF LYNNE

Doin' That Crazy Thing/Goin' Down To Rio (8.1977) Jet UP 36281

Doin' That Crazy Thing/Goin' Down To Rio, (5.1978) Jet SJET 102

Video!/Sooner Or Later (6.1984) Virgin VS 695, also picture disc, VSY 695

Video!/Sooner Or Later/Video! (instrumental) (6.1984) Virgin VS 695-12

Every Little Thing/I'm Gone (6.1990) Reprise W9799, also 12-inch containing remix and LP version of A-side, Reprise W9799T

Lift Me Up/Sirens (9.1990) Reprise W 9795, also 12-inch with Borderline, W 9795T, also CD, W9597CD

EPs

The ELO EP: Can't Get It Out Of My Head/Strange Magic/Ma-Ma-Ma Belle/Evil Woman (12.1978) Jet ELO 1, No. 34

ELO EP: Mr Blue Sky/Across The Border/Telephone Line/Don't Bring Me Down (4.1981) Jet ELO 2, release cancelled

Albums

Compilations are listed selectively

THE IDLE RACE

The Birthday Party: The Skeleton And The Roundabout/Happy Birthday/The Birthday/I Like My Toys/Morning Sunshine/Follow Me Follow/Sitting In My Tree/On With The Show/Lucky Man/Mrs Ward/Pie In The Sky/The Lady Who Said She Could Fly/End Of The Road (10.1968) Liberty LBS 83132

Idle Race: Come With Me/Sea Of Dreams/Going Home/Reminds Me Of You/Mr Crow And Sir Norman/Please No More Sad Songs/Girl At The Window/Big Chief Woolly Bosher/Someone Knocking/A Better Life (The Weatherman Knows)/Hurry Up John (11.1969) Liberty LBS 83221

Back to the Story: The Skeleton And The Roundabout/Happy Birthday/The Birthday/I Like My Toys/Morning Sunshine/Follow Me Follow/Sitting In My Tree/On With The Show/Lucky Man/Mrs Ward/Pie In The Sky/The Lady Who Said She Could Fly/End Of The Road/Come With Me/Sea Of Dreams/Going Home/Reminds Me Of You/Mr Crow And Sir Norman/Please No More Sad Songs/Girl At The Window/Big Chief Woolly Bosher/Someone Knocking/A Better Life (The Weatherman Knows)/Hurry Up John/Lucky Man/Follow Me Follow/Days Of The Broken Arrows/Here We Go Round The Lemon Tree/My Father's Son/Impostors Of Life's Magazine/Knocking Nails Into My House/Days Of The Broken Arrows/Worn Red Carpet/In The Summertime/Told You Twice/Neanderthal Man/Victim Of Circumstance/Dancing Flower/Sad O'Sad/The Clock/I

Will See You/By The Sun/Alcatraz/And The Rain/She Sang Hymns Out Of Tune/Bitter Green/We Want It All/It's Only The Dog/Your Friend (1996) EMI PRDCD2—last two tracks by The Nightriders

THE MOVE
Looking On: Looking On/Turkish Tram Conductor Blues/What?/When Alice Comes Back To The Farm/Open Up Said The World At The Door/Brontosaurus/Feel Too Good (11.1970) Fly FLY 1

Message from the Country: Message From the Country/Ella James/No Time/Don't Mess Me Up/Until Your Mama's Gone/It Wasn't My Idea To Dance/The Minister/Ben Crawley's Steel Company/Words Of Aaron/My Marge (10.1971) Harvest SHSP 4013

Message from the Country: Message From the Country/Ella James/No Time/Don't Mess Me Up/Until Your Mama's Gone/It Wasn't My Idea To Dance/The Minister/Ben Crawley's Steel Company/Words Of Aaron/My Marge/Tonight/Chinatown/Down On The Bay/Do Ya/California Man/Don't Mess Me Up/The Words Of Aaron/Do Ya (2005) Harvest 09463 30342 2 8

Looking On: Looking On/Turkish Tram Conductor Blues/What?/When Alice Comes Back To The Farm/Open Up Said The World At The Door/Brontosaurus/Feel Too Good/Lightnin' Never Strikes Twice/Looking On Part 1/Looking On Part 2/Turkish Tram Conductor Blues/Open Up Said The World At The Door/Feel Too Good/The Duke Of Edinburgh's Lettuce (2008) Salvo SALVOCD014

ELECTRIC LIGHT ORCHESTRA
Electric Light Orchestra Part II releases, which did not involve Jeff Lynne, are excluded.

Studio albums
Electric Light Orchestra: 10538 Overture/Look At Me Now/Nellie Takes Her Bow/Battle of Marston Moor (July 2nd 1644)/1st Movement (Jumping Biz)/Mr Radio/Manhattan Rumble (49th St Massacre)/Queen Of The Hours/Whisper in the Night (11.1971) Harvest SHVL 797

E.L.O. 2: In Old England Town (Boogie No. 2)/Momma/Roll Over Beethoven/From The Sun To The World (Boogie No. 1)/Kuiama (3.1973) Harvest SHVL 806

(30th anniversary re-mastered re-releases of the two above titles are listed at the end of this category.)

On The Third Day: Ocean Breakup/King Of The Universe/Bluebird Is Dead/Oh No Not Susan/New World Rising/Ocean Breakup/Daybreaker/Ma-Ma-Ma Belle/Dreaming Of 4000/In The Hall Of The Mountain King (11.1973) Warner Bros K56021. Reissued on CD with bonus tracks: Showdown/Auntie (Ma-Ma-Ma Belle) (Take 1)/Auntie (Ma-Ma-Ma Belle) (Take 2)/Mambo (Dreaming Of 4000) (Take 1)/Everyone's Born To Die/Interludes

Eldorado: Eldorado Overture/Can't Get It Out Of My Head/Boy Blue/Laredo Tornado/Poor Boy (The Greenwood)/Mister Kingdom/Nobody's Child/Illusions In G Major/Eldorado (11.1974) Warner Bros K56090. Reissued on CD with bonus tracks: Eldorado Instrumental Medley/Dark City

Face The Music: Fire On High/Waterfall/Evil Woman/Nightrider/Poker/Strange Magic/Down Home Town/One Summer Dream (11.1975) Jet JETLP11. Reissued on CD with bonus tracks: Fire On High Intro (Early Alt. mix)/Evil Woman (Stripped Down mix)/Strange Magic (US Single edit)/Waterfall (Instrumental mix)

A New World Record: Tightrope/Telephone Line/Rockaria!/Mission (A New World Record)/So Fine/Livin' Thing/Above The Clouds/Do Ya/Shangri-La (11.1976) Jet UAG 30017. Reissued on CD with bonus tracks: Telephone Line (Different vocal)/Surrender/Tightrope (Instrumental early rough mix)/So Fine (Instrumental early rough mix)/Telephone Line (Instrumental)

Out Of The Blue: Turn To Stone/It's Over/Sweet Talkin' Woman/Across The Border/Night In The City/Starlight/Jungle/Believe Me Now/Steppin' Out/Concerto For A Rainy Day: Big Wheels/Summer And Lightning/

Mr Blue Sky/Sweet Is The Night/The Whale/Birmingham Blues/Wild West Hero (10.1977) Jet UAR 100. Reissued on CD (30th anniversary edition) with bonus tracks: Wild West Hero (Alternate Bridge–Home Demo)/The Quick And The Daft/Latitude 88 North

Discovery: Shine A Little Love/Confusion/Need Her Love/The Diary Of Horace Wimp/Last Train To London/Midnight Blue/On The Run/Wishing/Don't Bring Me Down (5.1979) JETLX 500. Reissued on CD with bonus tracks: On The Run (Home Demo)/Second Time Around (Home Demo)/Little Town Flirt

Xanadu: Magic (Olivia Newton-John)/Suddenly (ON-J and Cliff Richard)/Dancin' (ON-J and The Tubes)/Suspended In Time (ON-J)/Whenever You're Away From Me (ON-J and Gene Kelly)/I'm Alive/The Fall/Don't Walk Away/All Over The World/Xanadu (last five tracks by ELO, final track ELO and ON-J) (8.1980) Jet JETLX 526

Time: Prologue/Twilight/Yours Truly, 2095/Ticket To The Moon/The Way Life's Meant To Be/Another Heart Breaks/Rain Is Falling/From The End Of The World/The Lights Go Down/Here Is The News/21st Century Man/Hold On Tight/Epilogue (7.1981) Jet JETLP 236. Reissued on CD with bonus tracks: The Bouncer/When Time Stood Still/Julie Don't Live Here

Secret Messages: Secret Messages/Loser Gone Wild/Bluebird/Take Me On And On/Four Little Diamonds/Stranger/Danger Ahead/Letter From Spain/Train Of Gold/Rock'n'Roll Is King (6.1983) Jet JETLX 527. Reissued on CD with bonus tracks: Time After Time/No Way Out/Endless Lies/After All. Time After Time had been originally included on cassette release

(*Secret Messages* was originally meant to have been a double album with the following track listing: Secret Messages/Loser Gone Wild/Bluebird/Take Me On And On/Stranger/No Way Out/Beatles Forever/Letter From Spain/Danger Ahead/Four Little Diamonds/Train Of Gold/Endless Lies/Buildings Have Eyes/Rock'n'Roll Is King/Mandalay/Time After Time/After All/Hello My Old Friend)

The Balance of Power: Heaven Only Knows/So Serious/Getting To The Point/Secret Lives/Is It Alright/Sorrow About To Fall/Without Someone/Calling America/Endless Lies/Send It (3.1986) Epic EPC 26467. Reissued on CD with bonus tracks: Opening/Heaven Only Knows (Alternate version)/In For The Kill/Secret Lives (Alternate take)/Caught In A Trap/Destination Unknown

Zoom: Alright/Moment in Paradise/State of Mind/Just for Love/Stranger on a Quiet Street/In My Own Time/Easy Money/It Really Doesn't Matter/Ordinary Dream/A Long Time Gone/Melting in the Sun/All She Wanted/Lonesome Lullaby (6.2001) Epic 5025002000. Reissued on CD with bonus tracks: One Day/Turn to Stone (live)

The Electric Light Orchestra (First Light Series): 10538 Overture/Look At Me Now/Nellie Takes Her Bow/Battle of Marston Moor (July 2nd 1644)/1st Movement (Jumping Biz)/Mr Radio/Manhattan Rumble (49th St Massacre)/Queen Of The Hours/Whisper in the Night/Battle of Marston Moor (Take 1)/10538 Overture (Take 1)/Brian Matthew introduces ELO/10538 Overture (Acetate version)/Look At Me Now (Quad mix)/Nellie Takes Her Bow (Quad mix)/Battle of Marston Moor (July 2nd 1644) (Quad mix)/Jeff's Boogie No. 2 (Live)/Whisper In The Night (Live)/Great Balls Of Fire (Live)/Queen Of The Hours (Quad mix)/Mr Radio (Take 9)/10538 Overture (BBC Session) (11.2001) EMI 724353337209

E.L.O. 2 (First Light Series): In Old England Town (Boogie No. 2)/Momma/Roll Over Beethoven/From The Sun To The World (Boogie No. 1)/Kuiama/Showdown/In Old England Town (instrumental)/Baby I Apologise/Auntie (Ma-Ma-Ma Belle Take 1)/Auntie (Ma-Ma-Ma Belle Take 2)/Mambo (Dreaming of 4000 Take 1)/Everyone's Born to Die/Roll Over Beethoven (Take 1)/Brian Matthew introduces ELO/From The Sun To The World (Boogie No. 1) (BBC Session)/Momma (BBC Session)/Roll Over Beethoven (Single Version)/Showdown (Take 1)/Your World (Take 2)/Get A Hold Of Myself (Take 2)/Mama (Take 12)/Wilf's Solo (Instrumental)/Roll Over Beethoven (BBC Session) (3.2003) EMI 724354332821

Live albums

Track listing is only provided for the first album, as it is the only one to include material not also recorded and released on studio albums, and for the last one, on which the last two tracks are previously unreleased studio cuts.

The Night The Light Went On In Long Beach: Daybreaker/Showdown/Day Tripper/10538 Overture/Mik's Solo—Orange Blossom Special/Medley: In The Hall Of The Mountain King/Great Balls Of Fire (5.1974) Warner Bros WB 56058, Germany only, Epic EPC 32700, 1985 UK

Live at Winterland '76 Eagle (3.1998) EAMCD038

Live at Wembley '78 Eagle (3.1998) EAMCD039

The BBC Sessions Eagle (3.1999) EAMCD095

Live at the BBC Eagle (3.1999) EDGCD097

Electric Light Orchestra Live: Evil Woman/Showdown/Secret Messages/Livin' Thing/Sweet Talkin' Woman/Mr Blue Sky/Can't Get It Out Of My Head/Twilight/Confusion/Don't Bring Me Down/Roll Over Beethoven/Out Of Luck/Cold Feet (4.2013) Frontiers FR CD 595 E

Compilations

There have been many compilations issued in Britain, Europe, and America. The first three listed below contain previously unreleased material and outtakes, while the fourth has proved the most durable and longest-charting in Britain, and the last contains re-recordings and one bonus track, previously unreleased.

Early ELO 1971–1973: 10538 Overture/Look At Me Now/Nellie Takes Her Bow/Battle of Marston Moor (July 2nd 1644)/1st Movement (Jumping Biz)/Mr Radio/Manhattan Rumble (49th St Massacre)/Queen Of The Hours/Whisper in the Night/1st Movement (Jumping Biz) (Quadraphonic Mix)/Mr Radio (Quadraphonic Mix)Nellie Takes Her

Discography

Bow (Quadraphonic Mix)/Whisper In The Night (Quadraphonic Mix)/Roll Over Beethoven (Single Version)/In Old England Town (Boogie No. 2)/Momma/Roll Over Beethoven/From The Sun To The World (Boogie No. 1)/Kuiama/In Old England Town (Instrumental)/Showdown Single Version)/Baby I Apologise/Auntie (Ma-Ma-Ma Belle—Early Version)/My Woman (Ma-Ma-Ma Belle—Early Version)/All Over The World (Showdown—Early Version)/Bev's Trousers (Showdown—Early Version) (1991) EMI CDS 797 4722

Afterglow: 10538 Overture/Mr Radio/Kuiama/In Old England Town (Boogie No. 2)/Mama/Roll Over Beethoven/Bluebird Is Dead/Ma-Ma-Ma Belle/Showdown/Can't Get It Out Of My Head/Boy Blue/One Summer Dream/Evil Woman/Tightrope/Strange Magic/Do Ya/Nightrider/Waterfall/Rockaria!/Telephone Line/So Fine/Livin' Thing/Mr Blue Sky/Sweet Is The Night/Turn To Stone/Sweet Talkin' Woman/Steppin' Out/Midnight Blue/Don't Bring Me Down/Prologue/Twilight/Julie Don't Live Here/Shine A Little Love/When Time Stood Still/Rain Is Falling/Bouncer/Hello My Old Friend/Hold On Tight/Four Little Diamonds/Mandalay/Buildings Have Eyes/So Serious/A Matter of Fact/No Way Out/Getting To The Point/Destination Unknown/Rock And Roll Is King Epic (6.1990) E3K 46090

Flashback: 10538 Overture/Showdown/Ma-Ma-Ma Belle/Mr Radio/Roll Over Beethoven/Mama (new edit)/One Summer Dream/Illusions In G Major/Strange Magic/Eldorado Overture/Can't Get It Out Of My Head/Eldorado/Eldorado—Finale/Do Ya (unedited alternative mix)/Mister Kingdom/Grieg's Piano Concerto In A Minor/Tightrope/Evil Woman/Livin' Thing/Mr Blue Sky/Mission (A World Record)/Turn To Stone/Telephone Line/Rockaria!/Starlight/It's Over/The Whale/Sweet Talkin' Woman/Big Wheels/Shangri-La/Nightrider/Tears In Your Life/Don't Bring Me Down/The Diary Of Horace Wimp/Twilight/Secret Messages/Take Me On And On/Shine A Little Love/Rock And Roll Is King/Last Train To London/Confusion/Getting To The Point/Hold On Tight/So Serious/Calling America/Four Little Diamonds/Great Balls Of Fire (live)/Xanadu (new version)/Indian Queen (demo)/Love Changes All/After All/Helpless/Who's That? Epic/Legacy (11.2000) 88697807792

All Over The World: The Very Best of Electric Light Orchestra: Mr Blue Sky/Evil Woman/Don't Bring Me Down/Sweet Talkin' Woman/Shine A Little Love/Turn To Stone/The Diary of Horace Wimp/Confusion/Hold On Tight/Livin' Thing/Telephone Line/All Over The World/Wild West Hero/Showdown/Ma-Ma-Ma Belle/Xanadu/Rockaria!/Strange Magic/Alright/Rock And Roll Is King (6.2005) Epic 5201292000

Mr Blue Sky: Mr Blue Sky/Evil Woman/Strange Magic/Don't Bring Me Down/Turn To Stone/Showdown/Telephone Line/Livin' Thing/Do Ya/Can't Get It Out Of My Head/10538 Overture/Point Of No Return (10.2012) Frontiers FR CD 570 E

Boxed sets

Three Light Years Jet JET BX-1 (12.1978), 3 LPs comprising *On The Third Day*, *Eldorado*, and *Face The Music*

Four Light Years Jet JET BX-2 (1980), 4 LPs comprising *A New World Record*, *Out Of The Blue*, and *Discovery*

Original Album Classics Epic/Legacy/Sony Music 88697787342 (10.2010), 5 CDs comprising *On The Third Day*, *Face The Music*, *A New World Record*, *Discovery*, and *Time*, including bonus tracks

The Classic Albums Collection Sony Music/Epic/Legacy/EMI 88697873262 (11.2011), 11 CDs comprising all studio albums from *The Electric Light Orchestra* to *Balance of Power*, excluding *Xanadu*, and including bonus tracks

THE TRAVELING WILBURYS

Traveling Wilburys Vol. 1: Handle With Care/Dirty World/Rattled/Last Night/Not Alone Any More/Congratulations/Heading For The Light/Margarita/Tweeter And The Monkey Man/End Of The Line (10.1988) Wilbury 7599-25796-2

Traveling Wilburys Vol. 3: She's My Baby/Inside Out/If You Belonged To Me/The Devil's Been Busy/7 Deadly Sins/Poor House/Where Were You Last Night?/Cool Dry Place/New Blue Moon/You Took My Breath

Discography

Away/Wilbury Twist (11.1990) Wilbury 7599-26324-1

The Traveling Wilburys Collection: Handle With Care/Dirty World/Rattled/Last Night/Not Alone Any More/Congratulations/Heading For The Light/Margarita/Tweeter And The Monkey Man/End Of The Line/Maxine/Like A Ship/The True History Of The Traveling Wilburys documentary/Handle With Care (video)/End Of The Line (video)/She's My Baby (video)/Inside Out (video)/Wilbury Twist (video)/She's My Baby/Inside Out/If You Belonged To Me/The Devil's Been Busy/7 Deadly Sins/Poor House/Where Were You Last Night?/Cool Dry Place/New Blue Moon/You Took My Breath Away/Wilbury Twist/Nobody's Child/Runaway (6.2007) Wilbury/Rhino 8122-79982-4

JEFF LYNNE

Armchair Theatre: Every Little Thing/Don't Let Go/Lift Me Up/Nobody Home/September Song/Now You're Gone/Don't Say Goodbye/What Would It Take/Stormy Weather/Blown Away/Save Me Now (6.1990) Reprise 7599-26184-1

Long Wave: She/If I Loved You/So Sad (To Watch Good Love Go Bad)/Mercy Mercy/Running Scared/Bewitched, Bothered and Bewildered/Smile/At Last/Love is a Many-Splendored Thing/Let it Rock/Beyond the Sea (10.2012) Frontiers FR CD 569 E

Armchair Theatre: Every Little Thing/Don't Let Go/Lift Me Up/Nobody Home/September Song/Now You're Gone/Don't Say Goodbye/What Would It Take/Stormy Weather/Blown Away/Save Me Now/Borderline/Forecast (4.2013) Frontiers FR CD 597 E

COMPILATION

A Message From The Country: The Jeff Lynne Years 1968–1973: Do Ya*/The Minister*/Girl At The Window**/Roll Over Beethoven***/Words Of Aaron*/Mr Radio***/The Skeleton And The Roundabout**/Message From The Country*/Come With Me**/Morning Sunshine**/10538 Overture***/Happy Birthday**/The Birthday***/No Time*/Showdown***/In Old England Town***/Big Chief Woolley Bosher**/Queen Of The Hours***/Follow Me Follow**

(1989) Harvest SHSM 2031; 7 92585 2 *The Move; **The Idle Race; ***Electric Light Orchestra

COVER VERSIONS OF JEFF LYNNE SONGS ON SINGLES

Stewpot and Save The Children Fund Choir: I Like My Toys (MGM MGM 1448, 10.1968) [Ed Stewart]
Tinkerbell's Fairydust: Follow Me Follow (Decca F 12865, 1.1969)
Helen Reddy: Poor Little Fool (Capitol CL 16007, 7.1978)
Dave Edmunds: Slipping Away (Arista ARIST 522, 3.1983)
The Everly Brothers: The Story Of Me (Mercury MER 180, 1984)
Agnetha Faltskog: One Way Love (Epic A 6351, 6.1985)
Charlie Wayne: Midnight Blue (Jet JET 7010, 1.1982), B-side of Deeper Than Love, not a Jeff Lynne song

In 1966, Norwegian group The Wizards issued a single in Sweden only, Very Last Day/I Need Your Love. The B-side was credited to writer Jeff Lynn. At the time of the *Zoom* concert in 2001, Jeff was approached by a collector with a copy of the single and picture sleeve to sign. He looked at them carefully and assured the owner it was nothing to do with him.

JEFF LYNNE TRIBUTE ALBUM, VARIOUS ARTISTS

Lynne Me Your Ears: 10538 Overture (Bobby Sutliff & Mitch Easter)/Ma Ma Ma Belle (Earl Slick)/Telephone Line (Jeffery Foskett)/Do Ya (Jason Falkner)/Sweet Is The Night (Ben Lee)/Rockaria! (Pat Buchanan)/Every Little Thing (Michael Carpenter)/No Time (Peter Holsapple)/Showdown (Richard Barone)/Handle With Care (Jamie Hoover)/Strange Magic (Mark Helm)/Evil Woman (Ross Rice)/Steppin' Out (Carl Wayne), Don't Bring Me Down (Swag), One Summer Dream (Prairie Sons and Daughters)/Can't Get It Out Of My Head (Doug Powell)/Twilight (The Shazam)/Mr Blue Sky (Tony Visconti)/You Took My Breath Away (The Heavy Blinkers)/Message from The Country (The Balls of France)/The Minister (Ferenzik)/Xanadu (Neilson Hubbard and Venus Hum)/When Time Stood Still (Bill Lloyd)/Above The Clouds (Sparkle Jets UK)/Rock And Roll Is King (Walter Clevenger & The Dairy Kings)/Morning Sunshine (Jeremy)/Boy Blue (Rick Altizer)/Livin' Thing (PFR)/On The Run (Sixpence None The Richer)/Bluebird Is Dead (Todd Rundgren)/Turn To Stone (Roger Klug)/Eldorado (Fleming and John) (2001) Not Lame NL 070

DVDs

Zoom Tour Live: CBS Television City concert 2001; interviews, 98 minutes (BMG, 2003)

Total Rock Review: Set at Six Granada TV 1972; documentary, 60 minutes (Stone Bird, 2006)

Out Of The Blue/Discovery: Wembley Arena concert 1978; 'Discovery' videos 1979, 150 minutes (Eagle Rock, 2008)

Live—The Early Years: Brunel University concert 1973; Rockpalast German TV 1974; New Victoria Theatre concert 1976, 110 minutes (Eagle Rock, 2010)

Out Of The Blue/Live at Wembley: Brunel University concert 1973; Rockpalast German TV 1974; New Victoria Theatre concert 1976; Wembley Arena concert 1978; 'Discovery' videos 1979, 205 minutes (Eagle Rock, 2015)

Jeff Lynne productions, co-productions and guest appearances

Bev Bevan: Let There Be Drums/Heavyhead (Jet JET 776, 1976)

Dave Edmunds: *Information* (Arista 205 348, 3.1983), Slipping Away (Arista ARIST 522, 3.1983); Information (Arista ARIST 532, 5.1983); *Riff Raff* (Arista 206 396, 7.1984); Something About You (Arista ARIST 564, 4.1984)

Del Shannon: Distant Ghost (B-side of Cheap Love, not produced by Jeff Lynne) (Demon D1017, 5.1983); *Rock On!* (Silvertone ZL 74929, 1991); Are You Lovin' Me Too (Silvertone ORE 26, 1991); Walk Away (Silvertone ORE 24, 3.1991)

The Everly Brothers: *The Everly Brothers* (Mercury MERH 44, 1984)

Tandy-Morgan Band: Action (FM VHF 26, 1986)

Duane Eddy: *Duane Eddy* (Capitol CDP 7468972, 1987)

George Harrison: *Cloud Nine* (Dark Horse WX 123 925 643-1, 1987); *Brainwashed* (Dark Horse/Parlophone 7243 5 41969 2 8, 2002)

Randy Newman: *Land of Dreams* (Warner Bros 925 773 1, 1988)

Brian Wilson: *Brian Wilson* (Sire/Reprise 925 669-1, 1988)

Roy Orbison: *Mystery Girl* (Virgin V 2576, 1989); *King of Hearts* (Virgin

VUSLP 58, 2002)

Tom Petty: *Full Moon Fever* (MCA MCG 6034, 1989)'; *Into The Great Wide Open* (MCA 10317, 1991); *Highway Companion* (American, 2006)

Miss B. Haven: *Nobody's Angel* (Eastwest WX 334 9031-71350-1, 1990)

Joe Cocker: *Night Calls* (Capitol CDP 7 95898 2, 1992)

Ringo Starr: *Time Takes Time* (Private 212 902, 1992); Weight Of The World (Private Music 115 392, 4.1992)

Julianne Raye: *Something Peculiar* (Reprise 9362-45081 2, 1993)

Hank Marvin: *Heartbeat* (PolyGram TV, 521 232-4, 1993)

Tom Jones: *The Lead And How To Swing It* (ZTT 6544-92498-2, 1994)

Paul McCartney: *Flaming Pie* (EMI CDPCSD 171, 1997)

Regina Spektor: *Far* (Sire 9362-49746-5, 2009)

Joe Walsh: *Analog Man* (Decca/Fantasy 0888072337718, 2012)

Take That: *III* (Polydor, Google play edition, 2014)

All This And World War II, Original Soundtrack (RIVA RIVLP 2 [double], 1976). Jeff Lynne sings With a Little Help From My Friends/Nowhere Man, with the London Symphony Orchestra

Electric Dreams, Original Soundtrack (Virgin V 2318, 1984). Jeff Lynne sings Video! and Let it Run

American Hustle, Original Soundtrack (Legacy 88843029592, 12.2013) Jeff Lynne sings Stream of Stars, in addition to the Electric Light Orchestra's 10538 Overture and Long Black Road

Endnotes

Chapter 2. 'What?'

1 In May 1972, Les Harvey, guitarist with Stone The Crows, was tragically killed in a similar accident after being electrocuted on stage at Swansea. The group replaced him, but never really recovered from the incident and disbanded about a year later.
2 The Wild Angels were a British rock'n'roll act formed in 1967, who had a good reputation as a live act but never enjoyed any chart success at home.
3 The sitar was not the Indian instrument as used by Ravi Shankar and other musicians from the same country, but a Coral electric sitar developed and manufactured in the late 1960s. It was in effect an electric guitar modified with a buzz bridge and extra strings on the body.
4 Steve Woolam left the music business, went to work on a building site, and committed suicide not long afterwards.

Chapter 3. 'Mr Radio'

1 'Dear Elaine' was released in 1973 on Roy Wood's first solo album *Boulders* and also extracted as a single, reaching No. 18.

Chapter 4. 'Roll Over, Beethoven'

1   When Michael d'Albuquerque was interviewed in 1995 by *Face The Music* and asked about the portrayal of him as this rather 'top-ho, aristo' character in Bev Bevan's *The ELO Story*, he said with a smile that there was 'a lot of licence in that book!'
2   The Beatles' version of 'Roll Over Beethoven' originally appeared on their second album, *With The Beatles*, released in November 1963. Coincidentally, the lead vocals were by George Harrison, whose career Jeff Lynne would help to rejuvenate in spectacular fashion some fifteen years later.
3   Carl Wayne released several solo singles throughout his post-Move career, although none ever made the charts. Later he turned down the Bickerton-Waddington song, 'Sugar Baby Love', dismissing it as 'rubbish'. The Rubettes picked it up and it went to No. 1.
4   According to several sources, and also a specialist round of questions on him on the BBC's *Mastermind* during the 2014–15 season, Marc Bolan played twin lead guitar with Jeff Lynne on 'Ma-Ma-Ma-Belle' and two other tracks on the album. According to the booklet notes for the 2006 re-mastered, reissued *On The Third Day* CD, Marc was present at the sessions, but his contribution was limited to the earlier out-takes of all three, plus 'Everyone's Born To Die', which did not appear on the original album but as bonus tracks thirty-three years later. A different version of 'Everyone's Born To Die' had also been included on the 2003 reissue of *ELO 2*.

Chapter 5. 'Daybreaker'

1   *On The Third Day*, *Eldorado*, and *Face The Music* failed to make the British album charts on initial release, but later did so jointly when released as a boxed set, *Three Light Years*, in January 1979.
2   Despite his exasperation with the Musicians' Union at a time when the British Labour Government under Harold Wilson and then James Callaghan was often seen as over-friendly to the trade unions, Jeff remained fairly circumspect on his political views. Bev Bevan, who had some particularly harsh words for the Union in *The ELO Story*,

never made any secret of his pro-Conservative stance, inherited in part from his father, who had died when he was eleven years old. He was, however, staunchly anti-Apartheid, and in 1987 refused to play shows with Black Sabbath in Sun City, South Africa, which had been boycotted by Artists United Against Apartheid for the previous two years. (Ironically, his place was taken by ex-Clash drummer Terry Chimes, who had been nicknamed 'Tory Crimes' on the sleeve of the first Clash album.)
3 Jet releases were initially distributed in Britain by Island, switching to Polydor in 1975 and to United Artists in 1976, prior to finding a more lasting relationship with CBS/Epic and Associated labels (UK) and Columbia (US) in 1978.
4 *Birthday Party* was reissued on vinyl in 2014 as one of a series of limited editions to celebrate Record Store Day. It appeared on the Parlophone label, using the old Liberty dark blue and turquoise colours with the Parlophone design, on gold vinyl with its original gatefold sleeve restored.

Chapter 6. 'Mr Blue Sky'

1 'Wild West Hero' reached No. 31 in its third week on the singles chart and then slid back to No. 36. Fearing a comparative flop, Jet Records quickly issued a new pressing on a 12-inch yellow vinyl. The record shot up to No. 24 the next week and climbed to its peak of No. 6 a month later. It ultimately spent fourteen weeks on the chart, a total never equalled by any ELO single before or after.
2 From the beginning of 1978 onwards, almost without exception, ELO singles and albums peaked at much higher positions in Britain than in America—a contrast to the situation of two or three years earlier. In America, 'Sweet Talkin' Woman' only made No. 17 and 'Mr Blue Sky' No. 35 (as opposed to No. 6 in Britain for both), while 'It's Over', a US-only single, stalled at No. 75.
3 According to Don Arden's memoirs, the concert was attended by the Duke and Duchess of Windsor. The Duke, formerly King Edward VIII, had in fact died six years earlier, and by 1978 the Duchess was increasingly frail and housebound at their home in Paris. Arden's book

is an interesting if not always accurate read. For example, he writes that various records by the Small Faces, Lynsey de Paul, and others reached No. 1 when they merely reached the top ten, and that *Out Of The Blue* topped the British and American album charts, when it actually peaked at No. 4 on both sides of the Atlantic.

4 Two years later, towards the end of 1980, Jet released a second boxed set, *Four Light Years*, comprising *A New World Record*, *Out Of The Blue*, and *Discovery*. All albums had sold very well on original release, and not surprisingly it failed to chart.

Chapter 7. 'Don't Bring Me Down'

1 As for the other American chart positions, *Shine A Little Love* made No. 8, 'Discovery' No. 5, and *Confusion* No. 37.
2 *Twilight* received a thumbs-down from presenter John Peel, who had championed ELO in the early days but sneered at it on Radio 1 *Round Table* when he joined a small panel reviewing the week's new singles, dismissing it as 'music for Social Democrats'. The latter were a political party formed in 1981 by several British MPs who had just resigned the Labour whip, and to the chagrin of Labour supporters like Peel were faring much better in opinion polls than their former party.
3 In America, 'Time' never rose higher than No. 16. *Hold On Tight* reached No. 10, and *Twilight* No. 38.
4 Bev made a full recovery, but Pete King's health deteriorated not long afterwards. Four years later he died of testicular cancer, aged only twenty-eight.

Chapter 8. 'Secret Messages'

1 In America, 'Rock'n'Roll Is King' reached No. 19, 'Secret Messages' No. 36, and 'Four Little Diamonds' No. 86.
2 Kelly Groucutt had already begun to pursue a solo career while with the group. In 1979 he began recording a solo album, released by RCA in 1982, playing all guitars and bass as well as handling lead vocals, and also featuring Bev Bevan, Richard Tandy, Louis Clark, and Mik

Kaminski. Later he played with the post-ELO group OrKestra and was subsequently one of the mainstays of ELO Part II. He died in February 2009.
3   As in Bev Bevan's case, Ian Gillan's role as frontman of Black Sabbath was only a short-term measure. In 1984 he joined the newly-reformed classic line-up of Deep Purple.
4   In America, *Balance Of Power* never reached higher than No. 49.

Chapter 9. 'Handle With Care'

1   The record, or rather records, still in the charts when Roy Orbison died were the Traveling Wilburys' album and single. 'You Got It' was not released for several weeks afterwards, until January 1989.

Chapter 10. 'Free As A Bird'

1   In March 2013, the local press reported that Robin Campbell had put the six-bedroom house on the market for £1.65 million.
2   In 2012 Sir Paul McCartney confirmed that the unfinished recording was still in the studios, and that one day he intended to go back and complete it with Jeff's help.

Chapter 11. 'A Long Time Gone'

1   'Midnight Blue' was the B-side of 'Deeper Than Love', one of two singles released by Carl under the name Charlie Wayne on the Jet label in 1982. Both songs were arranged by Louis Clark.
2   An eighteen-track version of Take That's album *III*, released in November 2014, was made available on Google Play, the three exclusive tracks including one produced by Jeff Lynne, 'Fall Down At Your Feet'.

Bibliography

Books

Arden, Don, and Wall, Mick, *Mr Big: Ozzy, Sharon and My Life as the Godfather of Rock* (Robson, 2004)

Bevan, Bev, *The Electric Light Orchestra Story* (Mushroom, 1980)

Frame, Pete, *The Complete Rock Family Trees* (Omnibus, 1983)

Guttenbacher, Patrik, Haines, Marc, & Petersdorff, Alexander von, *Unexpected Messages: The Story of the Electric Light Orchestra, The Move, Jeff Lynne, Roy Wood, Bev Bevan, including all members and related artists' projects with the complete world discography* (FTM Germany, 1996)

Harry, Bill, *The George Harrison Encyclopaedia* (Virgin, 2003)

Scott-Morgan, David, *Patterns in the Chaos: Reflections in Sawdust* (Lifeware, 2014)

Thomson, Graeme, *George Harrison: Behind The Locked Door* (Omnibus, 2013)

Van der Kiste, John, *Roy Wood: The Move, Wizzard, and Beyond* (A&F/CreateSpace, 2014)

Wanda, Jürgen, *Blackberry Way: Move, Electric Light Orchestra, Roy Wood, Jeff Lynne und Steve Gibbons Band* (Star Cluster, 1996)

Journals and newspapers

Bass Player
Birmingham Post
Birmingham Mail
The Daily Telegraph
Disc and Music Echo
Face The Music
The Guardian
Keep On Rockin'
Let it Rock
Melody Maker
Mojo
New Musical Express
Q Magazine
Record Collector
Record Mirror
Rolling Stone
Sound on Sound
Sounds
The Washington Times

Websites

ELO and Jeff Lynne
www.elo.biz

Jeff Lynne Song Database
www.jefflynnesongs.com

Cherry Blossom Clinic
www.cherryblossomclinic.freeserve.co.uk

Face the Music online
www.ftmusic.com

Carl Wayne
www.carlwayne.co.uk

ELOBF (Beatles Forever)
elobeatlesforever.blogspot.com

Jeff Lynne & Electric Light Orchestra, Discovery
www.elodiscovery.com

Showdown, Jeff Lynne mailing list
www.eskimo.com/~noanswer/move_archives/movearchives.html

45cat, vinyl database
www.45cat.com

Discogs, vinyl and CD database
www.discogs.com

Index

Abbreviations:
ELO—Electric Light Orchestra
JL—Jeff Lynne
RW—Roy Wood

ABBA 98, 103, 145
Acoustic Live from Bungalow Palace 150
Adams, Bryan 109, 157
Adkins, Mick 14
Aerosmith 129
After The Fire 97
All This And World War II 79
Allen, Chereene 151
Allen, Lily 146
Altham, Keith 44
Altman, Billy 80
American Dad! 147
American Hustle 151
Anderson, Ian 11
Andrews, Bernie 19
Applejacks, The 106
Arden, David 39-40, 46, 50, 64, 137
Arden, Don 29, 35, 39-40, 46-7, 50, 52, 54, 56-7, 64, 72, 85, 101, 126, 137
Arden, Sharon 62, 71
Arnold, P. P. 32
Aynsley Dunbar Retaliation, The 17

Bachman-Turner Overdrive 75
Bailey Rae, Corinne 135
Baldwin, Peggy 140
Balls 37

Barclay James Harvest 30, 73
Barlow, Gary 151-2
Bates, Phil 122
BBC Concert Orchestra 151, 153-4
Beach Boys, The 100, 119
Beatles, The 13-4, 18, 21-2, 24, 26, 30, 32, 34, 36-7, 49, 63, 69, 74, 83, 95, 100, 105, 108-12, 115, 125, 130, 132-5, 138, 142, 145, 151
Bee Gees, The 78, 89
Berry, Chuck 12, 13, 36, 43, 50, 53, 60, 149
Bevan, Bev 23, 29, 47, 67, 72, 80, 84, 93, 97, 101-2, 121-2, 154
Beyoncé 158
Bishop, Elvin 77
Bissonette, Gregg and Matt 140
Black Sabbath 32, 62, 102-3, 179, 181
Black, Bill 132
Black, Cilla 78
Blondie 89, 153
Blunstone, Colin 43
Bob, Jim 147
Bolan, Marc, and T. Rex (formerly Tyrannosaurus Rex) 11, 23, 32, 56, 59, 63, 66, 137, 178
Bonham, John 93
Bonzo Dog (Doo Dah) Band, The 17, 25
Bowie, David 11, 56
Bradfield, James Dean 156
Brandt, Brie 76
Britten, Benjamin 85
Brooker, Gary 142

Brown, Joe 142, 146
Brown, Sam 142
Buchanan, Roy 77
Burton, Trevor 23, 27, 37
Byrds, The 120

Callaghan, James 178
Campbell, Mike 116, 120, 127, 147
Campbell, Robin 130, 181
Carousel 149
Carrott, Jasper 73, 95, 152
Carter The Unstoppable Sex Machine 147
Chads, The 14
Chantelles, The 14, 27
Chevin, Gerald 17, 19
Chicken Shack 77
Chimes, Terry 179
Christie, Lou 63
Clapton, Eric 109-10, 125, 142
Clark, Dick 60
Clark, Gene 120
Clark, Louis 58, 68-9, 81, 84, 89, 95-6, 107, 122, 181
Clark, Rudy 111
Clarke, Allan 141
Clash, The 78, 179
Climax Blues Band, The 60, 122
Coburn, Bob 112
Cocker, Joe 127
Coldplay 145
Coleman, Ray 24
Collins, Phil 57, 105
Cooper, Ray 114
Cordell, Denny 26
Covay, Don 149
Coward, Noel 21
Craig, Andy 39, 40, 50
Cropper, Steve 108
CSI: Crime Scene Investigation 147

D'Albuquerque, Michael 50, 57, 63, 65, 67-8, 72-3
Daft Punk 145
Daisley, Bob 77
Dave Clark Five, The 14
Davies, Dave 11
Davies, Ray 35
Dee, Kiki 129
Deep Purple 29-30, 73-74, 103, 121, 181

Def Leppard 146
Delgados, The 147
Denny, Sandy 11
Depeche Mode 94
Doctor Who 147
Dylan, Bob 85, 100, 105, 112, 114, 135, 137

Edgar Broughton Band, The 30
Edgar Winter Group, The 60
Edmands, Bob 71
Edmunds, Dave 103, 105-6, 108
Edwards, Mike 39-40, 66, 73
Ekland, Britt 72
Electric Dreams 103
Electric Light Orchestra, original plans and name 27-9; first album 30-1, 33-6; early performances and problems with sound on stage 39-43; differences and rivalry between RW and JL 45-7 ; JL becomes leader 47-50; Reading Festival 1972 and autumn 1972 British tour 51-2; second album 52-5; joined on stage by Marc Bolan 59-60; first visit to America 60-2; and *On The Third Day* 64, 66; leave EMI for Warner Bros 64; and *Eldorado* album and tour 67-8, 70-4; and live album 69; leave Warner Bros for Jet 72; and *Face The Music* album and tour 74-6; and *A New World Record* album and tour 76-8; and *Out Of The Blue* album and tour 81-7; and *Discovery* 89-91; and *Xanadu* 91-3; and *Time* album and tour 94-7; and *Secret Messages* 98-102; and *Balance Of Power* 103-5; and Heartbeat '86 105-6; and final live shows 107; reissues on CD with bonus tracks 136-7; and *Zoom* album and cancelled tour 138-40; and 'Jeff Lynne's ELO' 153-5
Electric Light Orchestra Part Two 122
Ellis, Robert 43
Ellis, Steve, and The Love Affair 77
Elsas, Dennis 63
Elton, Ben 135
Elton, John 43-4
Emerick, Geoff 132
Emerson, Keith, and Emerson, Lake and

Palmer 12, 29, 78
Erasure 105
Et Moi 129
Eternal Sunshine Of The Spotless Mind 146
Evans, Chris 152
Everett, Kenny 20, 22
Everly Brothers, The 12, 103

Faces, The 11, 51
Fairport Convention 11
Fairweather-Low, Andy 142
Faith, Paloma 153
Fältskog, Agnetha 103
Featherstone, Roy 64
Ferry, Bryan 56, 78
Fishbaugh, Fishbaugh & Zorn 43
Fleetwood Mac 12, 99
Fleetwood, Mick 12
Focus 51
Foley, Ellen 96
Fortunes, The 106
Four Seasons, The 79
Francis, Claire 15, 16
Francis, Trevor 90, 98
Freedom City 43
Froggatt, Raymond 37, 72

Gabriel, Peter 57
Gale, Melvyn 73, 83, 84, 91
Game Plan, The 146
Gaynor, Gloria 89
Genesis 57, 78
Gibbons, Steve, and The Steve Gibbons Band 75, 106, 121
Gibson, Wilf 39, 40, 64, 66
Gillan, Ian 103, 181
Gloucester, Duke and Duchess of 85
Gorin, Kex 14
Grease 92
Grohl, Dave 151
Grosvenor, Luther 77
Groucutt, Kelly 72-4, 100-2, 122

Haley, Bill, & the Comets 12
Hall, Daryl, & Oates, John 96
Handicaps, The (later The Andicaps) 13
Hansen, Chris 140
Harris, Bob 39
Harrison, Dhani 150, 154
Harrison, George 100, 106, 108-16, 125-30, 135, 138, 141-2, 144, 151, 154
Harrison, Olivia 125, 142, 150
Harvey, Les, and Stone the Crows 177
Haycock, Pete 60, 122
Heart 77, 135
Helicopters, Roy Wood's 14
Hendrix, Jimi 33
Holder, Noddy 56, 106, 121
Holland, Jools 142
Hollies, The 141, 144
Hollingworth, Roy 35, 45, 54
Holly, Buddy 12, 135
Horn, Jim 110, 114, 126, 127
Hot Chocolate 78
Human League, The 94, 106
Hunt, Bill 35, 36, 40, 46-7, 51
Hunter, Ian 56
Hynde, Chrissie 153

Idle Race, The 16-7, 19-27, 35, 37, 59, 75, 121, 141, 149
Idle, Eric 150
Irwin, Colin 70

Jackson, Michael 111, 134
Jethro Tull 11
Joel, Billy 122, 135
John, Elton 11, 56, 78, 109, 110
Johnny Van Zandt Band, The 96
Jones, Brian (Rolling Stones) 22
Jones, Brian (ELO roadie) 65
Jones, Phil 117, 129
Jones, Quincy 145
Jones, Tom 129
Journey 75
Juliette, Tyra 158

Kamen, Michael 128
Kaminski, Mik 64, 66, 72, 84, 91, 95, 100, 122, 154
Kapelson, Sandi 91, 100, 105, 129
Katayama, Suzie 127, 138
Kefford, Ace 23
Kelly, Gene 91
Keltner, Jim 108, 110, 114
Kidman, Nicole 158
King, Ben E. 109
King, Pete 97
Kingsmen, The 16
Kinks, The 11, 18, 21, 94

Knopfler, Mark 129
Koehler, Ted and Arlen, Harold 126
Kosh, John 78, 83

Laine, Denny 106
Lake, Greg, *see* Emerson, Lake and Palmer
Lauper, Cyndi 128
Led Zeppelin 91, 93
Lennon, John 24, 63, 79, 93, 96, 100, 109, 130-2, 134-5, 145
Lethal Weapon 121
Lewis, Jerry Lee 12, 38
Lindisfarne 77
Little Feat 75
Lockwood, Neil 122
London Symphony Orchestra 79, 85
Lynch, Brendan 146
Lynch, Stan 127
Lynne, Evelyn 16
Lynne, Laura 91
Lynne, Nancy 12, 121
Lynne, Philip 12

Mack, Reinhold 98
Magnum 14, 72
Manfred Mann's Earth Band 62
Manic Street Preachers 156
Mann, Johnny 15
Mann, Marc 131, 140, 142
Marmalade, The 25
Marriott, Steve 11
Martin Child 14
Martin, Ray 37
Martin, Sir George 53, 57, 130, 135, 144
Marvin, Hank, and The Shadows 23, 129
Masters, Greg 15, 18
Matthew, Brian 19
Matthiessen, Mette 126
May, Brian 12
McCartney, Nancy 158
McCartney, Sir Paul 36, 53, 79, 100, 108, 130, 134-5, 142, 150, 158
McCracken, Hugh 16
McDowell, Hugh 39-40, 46, 49, 64, 84, 91, 122
McGuinn, Roger 129
Meat Loaf 122
Michael Stanley Band, The 96

Miller, Frankie 128
Miller, Steve, and Steve Miller Band 77, 135
Mitchell, Warren 22
Monkees, The 73
Monty Python's Flying Circus 115-6, 142
Moody Blues, The 106
Moon, Keith 62
Moore, Gary 125
Morgan, Dave (David Scott-Morgan) 14, 16, 23, 95-7, 106-7
Moscow Symphony Orchestra 122
Mott The Hoople 56
Move, The 15-7, 21-4, 26-40, 42, 44-5, 47-9, 51-2, 54-55, 59, 75-6, 106, 121, 141, 143-4, 146, 150
Mr Blue Sky: The Story of Jeff Lynne and ELO 150
Mungo Jerry 51, 77
Musicians' Union 70, 92, 178

Nagaoka, Shusei 83
Nelson, Sandy 72
Nesmith, Michael 73
Newman, Randy 117-8, 120
Newton-John, Olivia 91-3, 136
Nice, The 29
Nicholls, Paul 77
Nightriders, The *see* Tony Sheridan
Numan, Gary 94

O'Brien, Sarah 140
Ocean, Billy 153
Offord, Eddie 17, 19
Oldfield, Mike 144
Ono, Yoko 130
Orbison, Barbara 127, 150
Orbison, Roy 12, 112-4, 120, 124, 127, 143, 150, 154
OrKestra 122
Osbourne, Ozzy 32, 62
Ostin, Mo 64, 72, 113, 126

Paice, Ian 121
Pal Joey 150
Palin, Michael 115
Pannell, Rick 67
Paul, Lynsey de 72, 180
Peacock, Steve 56
Peebles, Andy 98

Index

Peel, John 19, 20, 22, 51, 180
Perkins, Carl 72
Petty, Tom and The Heartbreakers 112, 114, 116-7, 126-7, 141-3, 146-7, 150, 158
Pietsch, Rainer 94
Pink Floyd 18, 28, 35
Plant, Dick 58-9, 63, 68
Plant, Robert 106
Powell, Cozy 11
Presley, Elvis 12, 36, 37, 127, 132
Preston, Billy 142
Price, Alan 72
Price, Rick 23, 27, 29, 45
Prince (Prince Roger Nelson) 113
Prior, Maddy 12
Pritchard, Dave 15, 18, 20-2, 24
Procol Harum 60
Purcell, Henry 72
Pussycat Dolls, The 146

Quatro, Patti and Suzi 76
Queen 12, 98
Quick And The Dead, The 12

Ray, James 111
Raye, Julianna 128
Reader, Robert 13
Real Thing, The 78
Reeve, Nigel 45
Richard, Little 12
Robertson, Robbie 127
Robin Hood: Prince of Thieves 128
Rock Choir 146
Rock Family Trees 150
Rockin' Berries, The 106
Rockin' Hellcats, The 13
Role Models 146
Rolling Stones, The 11, 16, 18, 22, 66, 75, 100
Rossi, Francis 157
Roxy Music 56, 75
Royal Philharmonic Orchestra 96
Rubettes, The 178
Rundgren, Todd 78

Sayer, Leo 78
Schneider, Christian 104
Scott, Roger 81, 114
Seger, Bob 129
Senna, Ayrton 144

Sex Pistols, The 78
Shadows, The, *see* Marvin, Hank
Shankar, Anoushka 142
Shankar, Ravi 142, 177
Shannon, Del 12-3, 67, 92, 108, 124-6, 137
Sheeran, Ed 158
Sheridan, Mike, and The Nightriders (later Mike Sheridan's Lot) 15, 29, 45, 121
Sheridan, Tony 125
Silvas, Jeff and The Four Strangers 14
Sinatra, Frank 150
Slade (formerly Ambrose Slade) 20, 56
Small Faces, The 11, 180
Smile As Big As The Moon, A 146
Smith, Don 68
Smith, Martin 106
Smith, Sam 146
Spector, Phil 145
Spektor, Regina 147
Spencer, Roger 15, 18, 24
Spooky Tooth 77
Star Wars 85
Starr, Ringo 109, 110, 127, 138, 142, 148, 150
Status Quo 36, 51, 62, 157
Steeleye Span 12
Steinberg, Billy and Kelly, Tom 128
Stewart, Dave 113
Stewart, Ed ('Stewpot') 21
Stewart, Mike 52
Stewart, Rod 56, 78, 107
Stock-Aitken-Waterman 115
Stone, Jesse 126
Stranglers, The 78
Supertramp 78
Swift, Taylor 158

Take That 151, 153
Tandy, Richard 23, 37, 39, 40, 47, 50, 57, 72, 74, 81, 84, 89, 93, 101, 103, 121, 126, 129, 138, 140, 152-3, 158; Tandy-Morgan Band, The 106
Taylor, Derek 115
Tea & Symphony 30
Ten Years After 51
Thomas, Mary 76
Thompson, Richard 105
Tiomkin, Dmitri 12
Townshend, Pete 13, 86

Traveling Wilburys, The 112-5, 117, 119-20, 123-6, 130, 134, 139, 144, 154
Travolta, John 92
Trickster 72
Troggs, The 16
Troy, Doris 32
Troyer, Eric 122
Turner, Ike and Tina 32
Tyler, Bonnie 129
Tyler, Mike, *see* Mike Sheridan

UB40 106
Ugly's, The 23, 37, 95
Ultravox 94

Vela, Rosie 138-40
Village People 89
Vinegar Joe 51
Violinski 72
Visconti, Tony 26-7
Voyager 96

Walker, Colin 50, 64
Walker, Johnnie 157
Walker, Noel 24
Wallace, Ian 114
Walsh, David 13
Walsh, Joe 60, 148, 150, 151, 158
Walsh, Marjorie 148
Walsh, Peter 29
Ward, Anita 89
Ward, Bill 103

Waronker, Lenny 117, 126
Was, Don 127
Wayne, Artie 16
Wayne, Carl 27, 54, 136, 141, 143-4
Weill, Kurt, and Anderson, Maxwell 126
Weller, Paul 146
Who, The 13
Widowmaker 77
Wild Angels, The 31, 177
Williams, Kenneth 107
Williams, Mason 34
Williams, Richard 45
Wilson, Brian 119, 135
Wilson, Harold 17
Windsor, Duke of, formerly King Edward VIII 22, 179
Wings 53
Wizard of Oz, The 71
Wizzard 49, 51, 55, 64, 121
Wonder, Stevie 63
Wood, Ronnie 11
Wood, Roy 14-7, 22, 26, 32, 34-7, 43, 49, 52, 56, 58-9, 78, 96, 154
Woolam, Steve 35
Wright, Gary 110

Yellow Submarine 151
Yes 78
Young, Paul 109

Also by John Van der Kiste

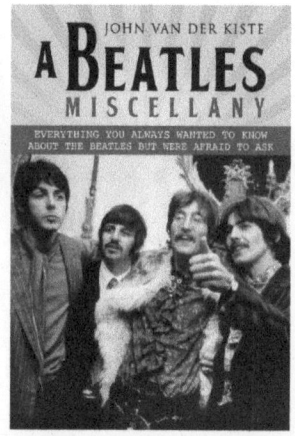

For more visit: www.fonthill.media